LIKE A WITCH'S BREW

R.P. Christman

Published by Independently Published

Printed on acid-free paper.

The characters and events in this book are fictitious. Any similarity to real persons, living or dead, is coincidental and not intended by the author.

Second Edition

Dedication

In loving memory of my youngest sister Linda who left this world way too soon. I miss you and love you very much.

Also to my wife Gretchen whose patience and support helped me realize a dream. Some say dreams are just thoughts, feelings, or visions we unrealistically imagine and aren't real. Well, I say they're wrong.

Chapter 1

My mind wandered, rendering flashbacks of that afternoon, lying on the ground, beaten and angry, on the edge of darkness, staring upon the pure evil that put me there. Nothing God created on this earth could have prepared me for that moment in time, absolutely nothing!

My name is Travis Scott. I'd like to take this opportunity to share a story of a young man I met who changed my perspective on life, of what it was, to what it is now. If you had told me a year ago I would be spending time writing a story about a perfect stranger, I would've said you're crazy. Way too busy to entertain such a thought, yet here I am. It's funny that I could be so different in my thoughts and behavior in such a short while.

I live in a fairly rural section of southwest North Carolina where the mountain views are second to none. It's a beautiful place to live, and raise a family. Somewhat of an upper-middle-class area bordered by some less affluent communities. Nevertheless, the weather is perfect most times of the year.

I'm in my early fifties, and married to a beautiful wife who blessed us with two wonderful girls. We were both young when we had children, so they are grown now, and off living their own lives.

I was fortunate to be raised by two of the best parents a guy could imagine. Not to say everything was peaches and cream, showing my age now, but we were comfortable, and I had the opportunity to go to college, and graduate with a business degree from an Ivy League college. Not too bad for a kid growing up in a modest home with two working parents.

By the way, the year is 1995, so thirty-something years ago, back in the day, completing a four-year degree was much harder than it is now. Ask a teenager today where the library is, and enjoy the silent response.

After working my way up some corporate ladders, I decided where I am today is where I want to be. It wasn't easy, but I worked my way up to become one of the top retail store managers in one of the biggest facilities on the East Coast.

My intuition tells me I shouldn't give up the actual store name, but I'm sure after I describe the environment most people will figure it out. My particular store is unique in a way only a few exist today. It's only been a short number of years since these types of stores were ever imagined, and I was fortunate enough to be part of a select few who helped develop, and design these stores we now call supercenters.

It was cool to be a part of something new that's developed into an awesome concept, thriving across many states in the country. I could have stayed with the corporate elite at the time, developing new ideas for this concept, but needed something more hands-on, and decided managing one of these supercenters was my life's ambition.

It's difficult and takes up a lot of time way outside the normal forty-hour work week most people are accustomed to. For me, it's the personal satisfaction of managing not just a facility with four walls, but the two hundred plus individuals who count on this place to make a living, so they can prosper, and maintain a happy life. That's the way it should be, right?

Like I mentioned it's not an easy task with many challenges from day to day. When I gave up the cushy elite status of the corporate hierarchy, my corner office with the plants I never had to water, I received many looks of puzzlement and disbelief. I can understand that since most people will never excel to that level, and truthfully, there have been times I told myself, wrong decision, Travis. Well, thank God those times are few.

I've always been somewhat reserved, laid back with a take-charge personality, and only want what's best for my family, along with the folks I've associated with. I consider myself a fairly intelligent person, but understand, that is only attainable by being fair and honest with the many people I've handled in my family, career, and life. I'm not perfect, and will never claim to be. I've made my share of mistakes in life, and can only pray those will be forgiven when my time comes.

I think at fifty-something I'm at the stage in my life I feel compelled to give back to others as others gave me during my journey through life to this point. My wife would say now, oh brother!

Well, enough about me. Just wanted to set the stage for the incredible six-month journey I undertook that I'm writing about today. Not sure there's even a moral to the story other than everyone should experience life outside the comforts of their own existence, and take a chance. I can guarantee your life will change when you do. I did, and somewhere along the way, I found myself. The funny thing is, I had no idea I was lost. God bless, and hope you find my life experience as rewarding as I did.

CHAPTER 2

Saying goodbye to my wife Gretchen and the parting kiss every morning is one of the most enjoyable parts of my day. Not that I want to be away from my wife, mind you. It's just a bonus that starts my day off in a positive way. My wife thinks I'm corny like that, but oh well, it works for me.

Heading out for a ten a.m. store open at six in the morning is weird. Not so if you wore my shoes. I could leave several hours earlier and still have the same amount of work to do, but I don't. It's a quality of life issue, I guess, that wasn't learned from a book, or in some classroom. I would weigh the priorities of the day in my mind, and execute the important ones. If some get pushed out that day, and are unattainable, then guess what. I can guarantee you tomorrow will come, and the opportunity to handle those starts all over again.

I usually plan the day's itinerary in my mind after I leave my garage, and start the fifteen-minute drive to my office. I don't listen to music or the radio since I get all the morning news I can handle reading the daily paper drinking my coffee with Gretchen. Don't need to hear something I already read about.

It's another beautiful day, and the skies are clear and blue. I often wonder how many people imagine, and validate where they live as the most endearing place on earth to wake up to each day. I guess I can understand that, but am confident I could convince most people where I come from is better than any other.

Now we do occasionally get some storms that come across the state that necessitates concern, but mostly the weather is perfect, and fluctuates little during the entire year. Someone try and tell me the northeast is a better place to live. I would strongly disagree after I got up off the ground from laughing so hard. Not to be so disrespectful, but sorry New Englanders you get too much snow, for anybody's blood.

Driving to work is fairly uneventful with the normal traffic congestion one might encounter in a small to midsize town. The store I manage is somewhat secluded with a smaller strip mall on one side of the supercenter. We have approximately twenty-five thousand people who live here, so it's not a tiny, or small rural town one would expect in this area. A lot of other businesses traverse up and down the main fairway as well.

The surrounding landscape boasts lots of land undeveloped I interpret as tree stands if that correctly describes what you call a parcel of land with trees on it. Don't get lost with me in the woods, folks. Your best friend is a compass, trust me.

I usually show up first to work, and partially open the store. I'll turn the alarm system off, and turn on any lights I need to get to my office safely without crashing into a display, or something of that nature. My Merchandising Manager, Winette, is usually right behind me, and takes care of the rest of the store opening to get it ready for the day.

We keep standard operating hours dictated by corporate from ten in the morning until nine p.m. We do employ a greater percentage of full-time employees than any other store of its kind in all the US states. I've got to say that makes my job far less complicated, and owe a lot of gratitude to my Human Resources Department, in particular to Mary, who manages that area tirelessly day in, and day out.

We have a great group of people who work the store, and seem to enjoy it. I try my best not to micromanage my subordinates which seems to work for the group of people I manage on a daily basis. Something not learned from that Ivy League school I attended that cost my parents a small fortune. Not to worry, Mom and Dad, I spent your money wisely, and can honestly say what I've learned has been applied to most of my career.

I'll stay focused most days after I've settled into my office, but occasionally will visit the waterhole for a cup of coffee. Just to be clear the waterhole is a break room for the associates, and not a hole in the ground in the back of the building filled with water.

Like I said before, I keep focused when I set my mind to something, but have a dry, corny sense of humor most people appreciate, I think. Ask my wife if you don't believe me. I'll crack myself up some days just thinking of a joke in my mind. I attribute this banter to the lack of sleep I got this week.

My day started off the usual with some office work, meet and greet of the employees, and a walk-through of the supercenter in all its glory. I have to tell you it's quite the sight to see folks come in to buy, let's say a rake from the garden center, and walk a short quarter mile to the grocery aisles to buy a gallon of milk. I mean, how cool is that? Come on now, ten years ago that was not even imagined. The convenience factor alone is worth its weight in gold.

I know some people are old fashioned, but let's face it, this is the nineties, and everything that will be thought of will be done so in this decade. I guess there are some areas of improvement we can expand upon, but mostly in my opinion, we have eclipsed the top of the mountain.

As a matter of fact, one meeting today is with Mary to discuss diversity workshops we need to schedule, for all our associates within the store. I can't wait for the next twenty years when all that stuff about race and religion is behind us. In my mind it was all, so stupid, but do realize some people need a reminder that we don't live in the Civil War era anymore. I mean, I'm as sorry as the next person, for the mistakes our forefathers made, but come on, when does it all stop?

I hope I live long enough to see the year 2015. It will be refreshing to see how everyone gets along, and where people can't recall why we were all fighting twenty years prior.

I noticed Mary on the main floor, and approached her.

"Hi, Mary, on my way to your office after I drop off some meeting notes to Bishop in Audio."

She acknowledged, "All right, Travis, but please don't get engaged in a long conversation with him. I have back to back meetings, and need you in my office sooner than later. See you soon, right, Travis?"

"Yes, Mary." She seemed a little stressed this morning. Oh well, who isn't, I suppose.

I worked my way over to the Audio Center where Bishop was working. "Morning, Bishop, how are you today?"

He replied, "Fine, Boss."

He likes to call me boss which at first I thought was inappropriate, but have gotten used to it. Plus, I have a first name only rule with my managers. No Mr. Scott is allowed. I guessed being called boss is somewhat the same thing. He was busy moving some audio display merchandise when I approached him to discuss some notes, for the upcoming quarterly meeting, for projected revenue.

He announced, "I worked on the numbers last night, and they look good going into the last quarter."

"Well, that's promising, we could always use a good fourth quarter, Bishop."

He added, "It looks like the holiday sales I am anticipating could put us way ahead of our counterpart's."

"That would be cool, Bishop. You do a heck of a job running this critical part of the business."

"Thanks, Boss, that means a lot."

"Well, I have a full plate today, and Mary is expecting me, so if there's nothing else, carry on."

I enjoy working with Bishop, I thought while I walked the short quarter mile to my office. He's come a long way in the four years employed at the store, and worked really hard since the time he started out as an associate. I was so proud of him when we promoted him to department manager. I would never say this to him, but he was such a geek when we first hired him.

Bishop is also my right-hand man, and assumes many roles outside of his main responsibilities. All security and CCTV system infrastructure is entrusted to him, so when I need anything technically related, he is the man. I think he knows how much I appreciate what he's brought to the staff.

On my way to Mary's office, as I approached her open door, I could see her standing at her office window with her arms folded staring at something outside.

I don't know why, but at that moment I was brought back to the days when I was a part of the team that developed these buildings. One of the cool ideas we eventually came up with was where and how the management team offices would be designed in the supercenters.

Our idea was to hide the offices from within the facility, so the open concept showing the upper support structure wasn't compromised. This idea was a challenge, but we worked it out, so even the stairs to the offices were hidden. Walking through the store, no one would notice anything, but open space and merchandise.

Now to hide the offices from the outside of the building located in the front section, we designed a floor-to-ceiling window system across the front heavily tinted, almost like a solid black facade. I can stand in front of my office window inside, see everything outside crystal clear, which is primarily the parking lot, and no one can see me from the outside. Cool concept, parking lot aside, I'll still look out my window and zone at times.

I feel fortunate because a small section of the landscape is the backdrop of mountains in the distance. Most days are clear enough to see them, and a few flying birds.

I entered her office, and said, "Knock, knock, Travis at your service." No response. After a slight pause, I repeated, "Hello, Mary!"

She turned to me, "Oh, hi Travis, I'm sorry, a little preoccupied today I guess."

We both sat to discuss the meeting topic which turned out to be the new corporate roll-out of our associate workshops on diversity. "So, Mary, why am I here to discuss this? I'm quite confident in your ability to manage these workshops without my assistance?"

She looked at me with a somewhat perturbed expression, and said convincingly, "Just deal with it, Travis."

I sighed, and thought, wonderful, diversity, my favorite subject. "So what needs my attention, Mary?"

"Look, Travis, we both knew this was coming. I know you're not a big fan of the concept, but we work for the same company, and corporate is dictating this roll-out, so we need to comply."

"Sorry, Mary, and you're right, I'm not a fan of this new program, but will try to be tolerant, of its intended purpose."

"Thank you." She explained further, "I will handle all the logistics needed to get us through the program. I've ordered all the marketing posters, training material, and booklets needed to train our associates on the subject matter. I just need you to be on board with me, and support the process."

"Fine, I promise to be your biggest advocate, and support the initiative." I continued to ask, "What else is involved in getting us compliant?"

"Well, we need to have all the associates scheduled for some workshop time to go over the material corporate will send us." She continued, "We need to have all training workshops completed within ninety days. The completed schedule will be provided to you, and the department heads in Lotus Notes email. I need to know when your schedule will allow your participation in one of the workshops."

"Seriously, Mary, I have to attend one of those?" The look on her face after I spoke made me realize, I should have never said that. I responded quickly, "Fine, schedule me in one of the later workshops, so I can solicit feedback from those who have attended." I hesitated a moment, and said, "If it were up to me you'd be the highest paid person in this building, Mary."

"Don't forget, Travis, I know how much you earn."

"I know, Mary, just saying. Are we done here, or do we need to discuss anything else?"

We both stood, and said our goodbyes. As I was leaving her office, I heard her announce, "Hey, Travis."

I did a 180 to see her once again at her office window, arms folded while she stared out her window. I replied, "Yes, Mary?"

She asked, "Did you notice anything unusual when you arrived this morning?"

I stood there, looked at her stare out the window, and responded, "Not sure what you mean. Is there something outside your window concerning you?" I walked back into her office while she spoke.

"This may sound weird," she commented, and continued to say, "I worked late last night, and we had two lot attendants call out who were scheduled to work the parking lot carriages."

I listened intently, and acknowledged, "Okay."

"It was busy last night, and there were a lot of carriages in the parking lot not in the carriage corrals, I mean, they were scattered all over the place." She added, "As I left last night, I thought I would ask Winette this morning if she had anyone available to help collect the carriages."

Again I replied, "Okay."

"Well, I know I was the last to leave since I closed, and alarmed the building. I even had to navigate around some of the carriages to get out of the parking lot."

Now a bit agitated, I asked, "Where are we going with this, Mary?"

"Travis, look out at the parking lot, and tell me what you see."

I moved closer to her window, and looked out. I scanned the area, and announced, "I see a few employee vehicles, no customers yet, and nothing else."

She looked at me, and said, "Look at the carriage corrals."

I looked again, and saw the carriage corrals filled with carriages. They looked like someone lined them up with a square ruler. "I have to say, Mary, those are the neatest stacked carriage corrals I've ever seen." I elaborated further, "I'll bet you in every one of them I could find a ninety-degree angle."

She turned to me, and declared, "Yeah, but Travis, if you were the first to arrive this morning, who put the carriages in the corrals?"

I looked at her a little perplexed, and responded, "I can't answer that, Mary. Perhaps Winette had someone collect them to the corrals after I showed up, not sure."

"Travis, you know as well as I do customers return carriages to the corrals, our people bring them inside the store."

"Mary, I have no idea what happened. My only suggestion is this. First, I would ask Winette if she had anything to do with this, or had one or two of her associates clean up the carriages this morning. Number two, if you do find out who worked the parking lot carriages, I would hire that person immediately, and pay them double. The neatest darn looking carriage corrals I've ever seen." I commented further, "Not even any trash in them, from what I can tell."

She looked at me, and blurted out, "GO!"

I thanked Mary, leaving her office, late for another meeting, and announced, "Sorry for pulling rank on you earlier." I turned to look at her as she shook her head.

Chapter 3

Ah, the end of the week I thought. I leaned back in my office chair discounting the fact I usually stop by the store on the weekends, and it's only 7:00 a.m. on this Friday morning. But still, I was thankful, for having a wife at home who tolerated my long hours during the week.

I felt good today. I got a ton of work done, and was caught up, for a change. I relished in the week's accomplishments, but it didn't last long. My thought process was interrupted by a knock on my door. I announced, "Come in."

In comes Mary with a facial expression, I'm all too familiar with, and heard her say with concern in her voice, "They're not there, Travis!"

"Sure, Mary, I'll play the guessing game with you on this fine Friday morning." The only thing that popped into my mind was, "Lost luggage!"

"No, don't be ridiculous, and stop trying to be funny, Travis."

"Fine, Mary, what are you talking about?"

"This thing with the store shopping carts has been bugging me all week." I sighed, and thought, not this again. "You know, Travis, after we spoke on Monday in my office I promised myself I would figure this out, and decided I would secretly monitor the shopping carriages each day. I made sure I was the first person here each morning, and the last person to leave at night." She continued, "At first, I thought someone was just playing a dirty trick on me, so I was determined to catch the bastard torturing me with this."

I spoke up, "Mary, slow down," and added, "When was the last time you took some time off?"

"Don't patronize me, Travis, just listen." She continued, "So for the last four nights before I left the store I would cruise around the parking lot by some of the carriage corrals, and imprinted in my mind how the carriages were stacked together." She added, "Our lot attendants do a good job of removing these to the inside of the store each day, but some get missed, and are left outside. Are you with me so far, Travis?"

"Totally," I declared.

She explained, "When I showed up Tuesday and Wednesday morning, I drove around the parking lot by some of the carriage corrals I had inspected the night before. Well, sure enough, the carriages in those corrals were moved into an almost perfect position. Like your ninety degree square obsession, for everything in your world, Travis."

"Hey now," I countered to defend the OCD like comparison.

She barked, "No, listen to me, Travis. I was like who would do that, and why would someone screw with me?"

I interrupted, and announced, "Mary, you need--" Well, I never finished my sentence, and was interrupted again by her rant.

"Travis, you need to listen to this carefully. I decided last night I would try something different, and left some carriages out on the far end of the parking lot a fair distance away from any of the carriage corrals. Travis, I physically got out of my car last night, and put three carriages randomly out in the lot. Are you still with me?"

"Yes, Mary, you have piqued my interest."

She confirmed, "Well, son of a bitch, I drove to work this morning, pulled into the lot, and the damn things are gone. I mean, who does something like that?" I tried to interject a plausible reason, but she continued to ramble on. "Seriously, Travis, if you are screwing with me, and I wasted the last four days, you and I will have a serious problem."

Finally, I got to talk. "Mary, can I speak now?"

"Yes, go ahead," but was interrupted once again. "I cannot be more pissed off right now, Travis." She continued to assert, "Like I have the time to deal with this crap." She calmed down, and I could finally speak again.

"Look, just relax. I understand your frustration. There has to be a logical reason behind all of this. Let me make some inquiries to determine what's going on?"

She proclaimed, "Travis, I swear, if this is some joke."

"Mary, I don't have the time, nor the patience for shopping cart games, trust me." I restated, "As soon as I find out what is going on, you will be the first to know. Are we all set now?"

"Travis, I don't like unexplained things. You know me. I need simple, realistic explanations, for things in my life." I agreed, and tried to make her feel better, I had hoped, with an unrelated question.

"So, Mary, how are we doing with the diversity workshops? Everything going as planned?"

"Please, don't even get me started on that! I have no issues with our regular associates." Exasperated now, she added, "As a matter of fact, most associates offered positive feedback, and are looking forward to the whole workshop concept. It's your management team that's driving me crazy, getting them onboard with it." She looked at me, and insinuated, "It's as if they all met secretly somewhere to discuss how they could get out of it. You wouldn't know anything about that, would you, Travis?"

I turned my head slightly to one side, and said, "Very funny, Mary."

After she left my office, ruining my perfectly good Friday morning, I decided to pay Bishop a visit in his office. No sense knocking on his door since he usually has one of those newfangled CD players attached to his head listening to some god awful music that sounds like a bunch of pissed off musicians just banging away at their instruments. He usually has a half dozen CD's on his desk with names like, "Toys In The Attic," "Peter Frampton Comes Alive," "Dark Side Of The Moon," blah, blah, blah. I mean, this Peter Frampton guy looked like a long-haired hippie freak. Well, I guessed, to each his own.

I walked into his office, and sure enough, there he was with his CD player on listening away. The cool thing about Bishop is he can multitask like no one I had ever met before. I mean, he could listen to music while drafting an email, and answering a page over the paging system in the store all at the same time. As for the music, I tolerate it since he does manage our audio department.

"Morning, Bishop, you realize that stuff will eventually rot your brain."

Bishop, not appreciating my dislike for his music quickly retaliated, "Well, Boss, if it weren't for me you'd still be listening to your music on eight tracks."

"What's wrong with that?" I questioned.

He smiled, and asked, "What can I do for you, Boss?"

"I need you to do me a favor."

He confidently replied, "Anything for you, Boss."

"I need you to bring up some video for me on this equipment of yours." I looked at the CCTV video surveillance system in the corner of his office with several monitors attached, and thought it looked like something from the Twilight Zone. "Mary asked me to check on something, so I need your assistance." He got up from his desk, walked over to the CCTV system, sat and turned in my direction.

"All right, Boss, what are we searching for?"

I leaned toward him, and asked, "Can you bring up the video feed for the northwest section of the front parking lot, for yesterday?"

He responded, "Sure thing," and enquired, "What are we looking for, a fender bender, or someone trying to break into a car?"

I commented, "Nothing like that, Bishop. I need the video feed, for last night at 9:30 p.m."

He turned to me, "But, Boss, the store is closed, and everyone is gone."

"I know, Bishop, just bring up the video feed please." He complied, set the controls to access the time slot, and location of the parking lot. "Stop," I announced, "Right there." He looked at the position of the video feed, and saw just a few carriages in the lot. "That's it," I confirmed, "Right there, perfect! Bishop, I need you to play the video feed, and let me know when you see those carriages move."

He looked at me all confused, and responded, "You mean like physically move, Boss, like they're ghost carriages or something?"

I turned away from the monitor towards him, and remarked, "Yes, Bishop, something like that."

"All right, Boss, I'll let you know"

I spoke up leaving his office, "Let me know when you see something. We clear?"

He responded, "Crystal clear, Boss."

After I left his office I proceeded down to the main floor of the store. My favorite time before the store opened, to do a walkthrough of the facility, and adjust anything that seemed out of place. I guessed maybe I was a little OCD like Mary stated earlier. Oh well, I'd rather be neat than messy.

I recalled a time when my grandfather used to tell me these little life snippets on occasion. I remembered once as a small child he said, "You know, Travis, finding money is easy if you don't have to look for it in a pile of crap." I always thought my grandfather was a little out there. I mean, come on, who looks for money in crap anyway. I still miss him, though. Never could apply any of those words of wisdom to everyday life. Maybe that was my grandfather's way of leaving a lasting impression on me. Look how many years have passed, and I'm still repeating what he said. Maybe he wasn't so far out there after all.

Well, our store associates did a bang-up job last night facing off the grocery aisle shelves. I only had to adjust a few items here and there. I smiled, and said to myself aloud, "Magnificent!"

I worked my way over to the Garden Center, and pulled out my notepad to jot down some notes to follow up with Steve, my department manager for this area of the business. Steve is a great guy, and is meticulous with his area of the store. Steve, however, is extremely protective of the space he manages, and knows if a display rack or a free-standing merchandise display encroached even a quarter inch into his managed area.

I have way too many visits from Steve managing border disputes between him, and some of the other department heads. Don't get me wrong, the disputes are harmless, and nothing to speak of, just a pain in my ass sometimes.

I tolerate that because he is so great with the customers. I remembered one time a person came into the store to complain about something they bought in the Garden Center, and one of his associates totally screwed it up trying to handle the matter on his own with the customer. I mean, this guy was hot-tempered, screaming and everything. I swear, after ten minutes with Steve diffusing the situation it looked like the customer was going to cry in appreciation for him taking care of his problem. We're fortunate to have someone like him on our team.

I had written down a few notes when I saw Bishop walking toward me. He looked at me writing in my notepad, and commented, "You know, Boss, most people in a position of your authority would use a PDA."

I looked at him, and questioned, "A PD what?"

"Never mind, Boss, I need you to come see this."

I smiled at him, and echoed, "Awesome, you found something. Maybe now I can get some closure for Mary." Bishop and I headed up to his office, and walked over to the CCTV system. Bishop sat down, and moved the mouse to bring the monitor out of sleep mode. I looked over his shoulder when the screen came to life, and stared at what looked like a lot attendant gathering the carriages Bishop was monitoring. I looked at him, and asked, "Is that one of our people?"

"I don't know, Boss, it could be. I mean, he's wearing a store smock. What do you think he's doing?"

I looked at him with a dumbfounded stare, and dropped my shoulders. "I can see what he's doing, Bishop. He's working the parking lot, and gathering the carriages."

He stared down at the video time stamp, looked at me, and declared, "But it's 10:30 at night, Boss."

I continued to watch the young boy gather the carriages, and push them to a corral. I also noticed the boy adjust the carriages, so they looked perfectly square. I said to myself, son of a bitch, and declared out loud, "Mary, was right."

It wasn't long before the boy finished collecting and straightening out the carriages in the corral, but we couldn't quite see the boy's face due to his distance away from the main camera. I looked at Bishop, and asked, "Is there a way to sharpen the image, or brighten the frame so we can see who that is?"

"Sorry, Boss, the boy is just too far away. If I try to adjust the frame any more, the picture will get more distorted."

"Do me a favor, Bishop. Keep watching the feed. I'll be back in a few minutes."

I left his office to find Mary or Winette. I checked their offices, but they were empty. I made my way down to the main floor where by chance I saw Mary with Winette by the front of the customer service area next to the checkout registers. I worked my way through the front of the store, and caught up with them.

Winette and Mary had been discussing business when I arrived. Winette greeted me with a smile, and said, "Good morning."

I acknowledged the greeting, "Morning, Winette."

I looked at Mary, and asked, "Can you and Winette meet me up in Bishop's office? I need to show you both something."

Mary confirmed, "Sure thing, Travis. Let me finish up with Winette, and we'll both come see you."

"Thanks, ladies. I'll meet you in his office."

I headed back to Bishop's office, and arrived with him still watching the video feed on the CCTV system. I enquired, "Bishop, anything new?"

"No, Boss, it looks like the kid is just reading a book." I was back at the monitor, leaned over closer, and saw the boy sitting under one of the lamp posts in the parking lot. Bishop explained, "He's been there the whole time just reading."

I replied, "Huh."

He looked at me, and asked, "Should we call the cops, Boss?"

I looked at him, and answered, "Seriously, Bishop, and say what? That some teenage boy had broken into our parking lot wearing one of our store smocks, and putting our carriages away?" I continued, and said, "Oh, maybe we should add he's also stealing the light from our lamp post to read a book."

Bishop, hearing all that, conceded for a moment that perhaps his suggestion to call the cops was a bit premature, and said, "I get your point, Boss."

Mary and Winette arrived, and knocked on Bishop's door. I acknowledged them both, "Hi, ladies." I turned to Bishop, and said, "Please go back to the beginning of the video feed, so Mary and Winette can have a look see." I turned to Mary, and said, "You were right, Mary." I shook my head, and repeated, "You were right all along about those damn carriages."

She looked at me with relief, and acknowledged, "You found out what was happening?"

I replied, "Have a look yourself," and motioned her toward the monitor on the CCTV system Bishop was controlling. She walked over to him to get a good look at the monitor.

Winette looked at me now, and asked, "Did I miss something?"

I answered, "Mary can fill you in on all the details. In the meantime, I'd like you to see this." Winette walked over next to Mary to get a better view of the CCTV monitor. I folded my arms, and leaned back on the edge of Bishop's desk. I stared down at my shoes while Mary and Winette watched the video feed.

I heard Mary now in a soft tone call out, "I'm going to crucify that young man."

I spoke up, and enquired, "Can either of you tell who that young boy is?"

Bishop asked Winette, "Could this be one of your associates since he has a smock on like your people wear?"

She acknowledged, "Possibly a former associate."

I stopped staring at my shoes, looked up, and asked, "You know who that might be, Winette?"

"I'm not sure, Travis, but that's not one of our vests he's wearing." I walked over to the monitor everyone was at, and looked again at the video.

"What are you talking about, Winette? I can see our logo on the vest. Well, as best as I can make out anyway."

She clarified, "No, Travis, what I meant was this boy has on an old vest we retired like six months ago." She explained, "All my associates since then have received new smocks. The old smocks were thrown out like the one this boy is wearing."

I turned my attention to Mary, and asked, "Mary, any idea who that might be?"

"No way, Travis, he's too far away, and I can't make out any facial features." She added, "I mean he looks young, right?"

I replied unsure, "I guess." I conceded, and announced, "Well, folks, let's table this for now until I can figure this all out."

Mary and Winette left Bishop's office after Mary walked past me, and blurted out, "I told you so." I ignored the comment, continued to stare at the monitor in front of me with the image of the young boy reading a book in the middle of the night under a lamp post in the parking lot. I wondered for a moment, questioning, what the heck was going on here?

I was deep in thought searching for an answer while I watched the video when the young man turned, and looked up at me. I was startled by what I saw, uncrossed my folded arms, stepped back, and almost fell over Bishop who was walking around his desk. He grabbed me, saw the frightened look on my face, and said, "Geez, Boss, you look like you just saw a ghost." He added, "You, okay, Boss?"

"He looked at me, Bishop."

"Who looked at you, Boss?"

"Who do you think, Bishop, the kid on the video?"

He looked over at the monitor on the CCTV system, and commented, "Boss, that's recorded video--," but I interrupted him before he could finish his sentence.

"I know that, Bishop!" I walked over to the monitor, and said. "I need you to rewind this, and go back a few minutes on the timeline so we can both look at this again."

Bishop looked a little concerned as he walked over to the CCTV system, had a seat, went back five minutes in time, and let the video run. I stared at the video while I leaned over his shoulder, and waited. After a short while he announced, "Boss, we're way past the time you saw the kid look up at the main camera. Maybe it was a shadow, or the angle you had that made it seem like the kid looked up at you."

I turned to him, and said, "I'm not crazy, I saw what I saw, Bishop." I stood after a moment, questioned all of this, and asked myself, could I be wrong? I wasn't sure now, but swear I saw that child look up at me. I thanked Bishop for his assistance, headed out of his office, back to my own to take this all in, and reflect on what I should do.

Chapter 4

I was plagued all day with the image of the young boy who had infiltrated my mind, and couldn't seem to focus on anything. All the while I had tried to figure out why some kid would have nothing better to do than to hang out in a parking lot of a closed store at night pushing carriages around. I mean, the kids of today aren't interested in anything that even remotely resembled physical labor. It's hard enough to hire someone to do the manual labor jobs especially when the work is outside unless they are paid well, and yet they still complain.

I remembered my girls as teenagers like it was yesterday, and boy, I don't miss those days one bit. Don't get me wrong, I love my girls, but my Lord I wish those years could have been different.

I mean, talk about lazy. I know now it was probably the result of misdirected parenting because we spoiled them so much. I guess as parents we decided at some point our way was the only way, and didn't consider alternatives to avoid those spoiled tendencies.

Gretchen and I would give our girls an allowance every single week when they were in their teens, and the only thing in return I wanted was that they were respectful to their mother, and kept their rooms neat. I didn't ask them to take out the trash, or clean the garage, or do anything that could be construed as physical labor. No, no, just two simple rules.

Now if those rules had applied to me when I was young, I would have aced them every week, but not my girls. There was an expectation every week that money was coming. Was there harmony, and church bells ringing every week when we paid them? Nope. To this day I've never heard a single church bell ring, only the sounds of two teenage girls who fought with their mother over the nothings in life every week.

Forget about the neat rooms I expected from them. I mean, that's why we paid them, right? Again, clean rooms? Nope, big fat no on that one. I can't quite remember when I resigned myself to defeat over that, but I still have vivid memories of just kicking the crap on the floor back into the girl's rooms if the crap impeded into my hallway, and closed their bedroom doors. I figured, out of sight, out of my damn hallway.

On the plus side, the girls managed to clean up their act, and are loving daughters to both Gretchen and I. I got a kick out of meeting young couples who were about to raise a child, and was occasionally asked how satisfying it was raising my own. Oh, I went on and on how wonderful it was, peaches and cream twenty-four seven, and would've change a thing. Hey, don't judge me. Nobody warned my ass about all that crap, so I wasn't reciprocating, just saying.

My mind shifted back to the image of the boy I saw on the video system, and wondered how to resolve this conflict. Think, Travis, think. There has to be a logical reason behind all of this. I decided the only logical course of action was to see if I could contact this young man, and only then could I understand what this was all about. One thing to resolve before that could happen was to try, and come up with an excuse I could give Gretchen for missing date night.

My wife and I adopted the idea many years ago, and started a ritual we both look forward to regularly. It's nothing special to speak of. We usually just order takeout food, stop by Blockbusters, and pick out a movie or two.

It started out as a casual thing getting together once or twice a month to spend quality time with one another exclusively. I'm guessing it was because we hardly saw each other with the schedule of activities we both kept, plus my ridiculous work hours.

Gretchen came up with the idea initially, and I gave it a go. At some point it became once a week on a random day we could agree on, but as of late, Friday nights seemed like the best choice. We both agreed this would be the permanent day we designated as our date night.

I decided how to break the news to Gretchen that I'd be working late tonight when Mary knocked on my door. "Hi, Travis, I'm heading home now. It's almost 6 p.m., isn't tonight date night for you, and the Mrs.?"

I replied, "Yes, it is," and added, "I'm leaving shortly, Mary." All the while I knew I'd be at the store for the rest of the night until closing, hoping the young boy would show up, so I could confront him, and find out his story.

Mary thanked me for putting up with all the extracurricular nonsense with the shopping carts the past week. Her face lit up while she said, "Hey, Travis, wouldn't it be funny if that young man came into the store, and applied for a job. We could hire him, so he could train our kids how to work the parking lot, proper like." She chuckled, looked at me, and said, "Just saying!" I thought, mocked again, for something I say regularly. "Good night, Travis."

I returned the, "Good night," to her, and picked up my office phone to call Gretchen.

She answered the phone while I said, "Hi, honey, I may have some bad news for you. I think we need to reschedule date night this week."

"Fine, what's the big emergency this time?"

"No emergency, honey. I need to finish up some important business at the store. I won't get home until well after closing I suspect."

"Fine, Travis, but don't think I'll be waiting up for you, and don't even think your supper will be waiting for you when you get home either."

I agreed, "Got it, babe. I understand, see you when I get home. Love you, honey."

"Love you back, Travis."

I wasn't worried about my supper not being there when I got home. I knew for a fact it would be. It's just how Gretchen was, and another reminder to me of how much I love her.

Well, the night ended with little ado, so I worked my way down to meet with Steve to let him know I would close the store that evening. I greeted Steve to explain this.

He replied, "Didn't know you were still here, Travis."

"Yes, I know," I acknowledged. "I've been in my office all night getting caught up on things."

"Well, I'm just about ready to start the close, so if you're all right with it, Travis, maybe I'll see you over the weekend, or on Monday."

"Thanks, Steve. Have a good night."

I don't like to give up my work schedule to my employees, managers not exclusive. Just my way of keeping my people on their toes, I guessed. I recalled how I felt when I was a subordinate in my jobs of the past. Never slacked off while not knowing when the boss would be around.

I partially closed the building, and headed back up to my office to start the night staring out at the parking lot hoping the young man would show up.

I looked at my watch to check the time, said to myself, terrific, 10:15 and a no-show. Guess the kid wasn't a big Friday night fan of hanging out in the store parking lot. I figured fifteen minutes more wouldn't kill me. Besides, the night's already screwed anyway.

After a short while, I noticed the time again, now past 10:30, and no sign of any activity in the parking lot. I told myself, well, this was a stupid idea you had, Travis. I conceded to the fact I could be here all night waiting for nothing, so I decided I'd had enough. I finished the store close, and alarmed the building while I exited the employee entrance on the side of the building.

I made my way to my car, got in, and started it. I talked to myself trying to have a conversation with my mind to justify what I had been trying to accomplish that evening. After a short bit, I realized how futile that had become, lost the argument, and determined my mind had won the battle, confirming I spent a whole lot of time, for nothing.

I put my car in reverse to give myself room to clear the Jersey barrier, looked in the rearview mirror, and saw the young boy with the store smock on. He was entering the woods behind a row of dumpsters on the backside of the supercenter where the loading docks were.

I put my car into park, and watched the young boy disappear into the dark woods behind the store. All the while I tried to rationalize where the heck he was going. There's nothing behind the supercenter but woods. I mean a lot of 'just woods.' I wondered whether or not anything existed beyond those woods. I asked myself again. So where is this boy going?

I shut the car off, opened the glove box to retrieve a flashlight, briefly paused for a moment to think about that, now somewhat conflicted, and tried to justify my actions. All the while another voice inside of me said, just drive away, Travis, this boy isn't your problem.

I decided I had to find out what the heck this was all about, so I exited my car, tested the flashlight to be sure it worked, and to see if the batteries were okay. I couldn't recall the last time I used the darn thing, and for all I knew this was the first.

I started my way down the delivery entrance road that all the semi-trailers use to deliver product to the loading docks, and stopped at the point where I saw the boy disappear into the woods. I shouted, "Hello, anyone in there?" No response, while I said to myself, of course not. Anybody walking into the woods at night is probably not looking to have a conversation, I suspect.

Understand something about me and the woods. I've always been petrified of the woods. Now you may find that hard to believe given I was born and raised in North Carolina, but trust me, this is as close to the truth as you can get.

Actually, I should rephrase, and correctly point out. It's at night that I dread the most going into the woods, alone or not makes no difference to me. I'd rather be caged with a hungry tiger than willingly go into the woods at night. It's something inherent, I guessed, or maybe it's all those horror movies I watched as a kid, and learned, no good *ever* came out of the woods at night. Plus, the fact these are North Carolina woods. I mean, the darkest woods at night you'll see anywhere.

I stood there at the tree line behind the supercenter, and tried to muster the courage to go look for the young man. I tried to justify my actions in thought. If he can walk in the woods at night with no flashlight, what's my problem? I'm bigger than he is, and I have a means to see in there.

That voice was back in my mind, counterpointing everything I had tried to convince myself, to go look for the boy. With reasonable requests like, are you freakin' crazy going in there, or are you out of your mind, or how about just walk away Travis, don't turn around, run real fast backwards to your car, and let's call it a night. I didn't back down, reluctantly decided I had to find this boy, and put some closure to all this crap. I mustered up all my nerve, and said you can do this, Travis, just look at the big picture here.

I tested my flashlight again, and started my journey into the dark woods. My nerves were frazzled as I headed into the woods away from the lights shining on the back lot of the building, and the woods were now frightfully dark. Like shark eyes, I imagined.

"Oh boy, oh boy," I kept saying to myself while I slowly walked into the woods farther. I called out again, stopped midstream of sentence, and cringed. I whispered to myself, oh great, Travis, just announce to everything in here that you're here, and where you are.

I was reminded of something someone once told me. When you're in a situation you're unsure about being in, your original decision to put yourself there, was probably wrong. I kept fighting the demons in my mind, and tried to remember what brought me here. After I walked some distance, I concluded taking on this little venture was a mistake. At that point, I couldn't come up with a reason why I shouldn't just turn around, and get the hell out of there when out of nowhere I felt a tap on my back.

Now, I had made it up in my mind earlier that all that's bad in these dark woods was a figment of my imagination, and decided if that's what it took to comfort me, so be it. However, that thought process became a useless exercise in futility when I was actually touched by something in the woods.

I remembered screaming at the point of contact, "What the hell!" while I descended back to earth after jumping about six feet in the air. I pointed the flashlight toward whatever touched me while my other hand held my chest fighting off the heart attack I surely just suffered. I again repeated the same, "What the hell!" and added, "Geez, kid, you scared the crap out of me." I stood there pointing the flashlight at the young boy trying to compose myself, and stop breathing so hard when the boy said.

"I'm sorry I scared you, Mr. Scott."

I looked back at him, and asked, "How do you know my name, kid?"

The young man responded, "It's under your picture, sir."

I tried to process those words in my head, what picture? What the heck was he talking about? It dawned on me now that my picture with my department managers hung on the wall inside the store in the customer service area. I responded, "All right, kid, you know who I am.

What's your name, and what the heck are you doing out here?"

The young man replied, "Malden."

I looked at him, and asked, "Do you have a last name, son?"

The young boy responded, "Crenshaw."

I asked him, "All right, Malden Crenshaw, what the hell are you doing out here in the woods in the middle of the night?" He just stood there, stared at me, and didn't respond. I decided to approach this from a different angle. "Malden, where do you live, so, I can get you home?" Provided we made it out of these damn woods alive, I prayed.

He reached out, and pointed to a spot in the woods behind me. I swung my arm around with the flashlight, and shined the light in the direction he had pointed. I stared at what looked to be a kind of makeshift tent with a dirty old tarp draped over two low lying tree branches. I looked back at the young boy, and said "You're kidding, right? That's where you sleep at night, Malden?"

He answered, "Yes, sir."

I was confused at that point, and didn't know what to think, or say. "All right, Malden. We need to table this conversation, preferably outside of these woods. I'll tell you what, how about I lead the way with the flashlight, and you steer me in the direction to get us back to the store. Does that sound like a plan, Malden?"

"Yes, sir," was his response.

We started our journey back to the store. Malden and I finally reached the destination point at the backside of the supercenter, and I could finally relax a bit now that I made it out of the woods.

I looked at him, and was unsure of what to make of the whole situation. I explained, "Well, Malden, you can't sleep in the woods." I looked at him, felt bad for the position I found this young man enduring, and was uncertain how to handle it.

I looked away for a moment, turned back to him, and asked if I could call anyone for him, like his mom, or dad, or a relative. He just stood there, and stared at me almost like he didn't understand the question, or maybe it was he had no family to speak of, who knows. I again asked, "Are you sure I can't call someone for you, Malden?" I added, "How old are you, son?"

He answered only one of the questions I asked him, and replied, "Sixteen, sir."

"Wow," I said. "Sixteen, huh," I thought now, sixteen, no way. I mean, everyone looks young to me, but this boy looked maybe thirteen if that. I was confused, tired, and wanted to conclude something at that point, so I offered him a place at my home for the evening with me and my wife. "Would that be okay with you, Malden?" I added, "Just, for tonight until I can figure this all out."

I thought there must be a family out there looking for a lost son, right? I tried to reason the situation, but my mind countered the rationalization, if that were the case, the child would be with his family, and not living in the damn woods, correct? I wondered for a moment, but couldn't figure out why this young man would be left all alone to fend for himself. I turned to the child again, and asked, "So are you okay with that, Malden?"

He just responded, "Yes, sir."

Malden and I started the walk up the access road to my car. I opened the passenger door for him, made my way to the driver's side, and got in. I announced, "Buckle up, Malden." I turned the car engine over, and started the drive home, to no doubt, a slew of questions Gretchen will have for me.

The ride back to my home was quiet, and unassuming, except for the fact, I had to open several windows in the car. That was due to the uncomfortable smell that no doubt emanated from young Malden's direction. Well, I thought, that made sense since I didn't notice any luxury shower facilities attached to that makeshift tent I discovered him at.

Few questions were answered by him on the way. He also wasn't amused by my humorous gestures I tried to mix into the conversation to lighten the mood as we drove to my house. I asked him at one point, "You're not sick or anything, right?"

He replied, "No, sir."

I said, "Okay, but you're pretty quiet, and I wish you would call me by my first name, Travis."

He turned his head to me, and replied, "Yes, sir."

I looked at him, chuckled slightly, and accepted the fact that no one was going to listen to me that week.

I arrived home with Malden, drove up to one of the garage doors, and opened it remotely. All the while I was just trying to get a read on the young man sitting there quietly. I pulled into the garage bay stall, and closed the door once inside with the remote. "All right, Malden, let's meet my wife, and see what she has to say about all this." We exited the vehicle while I lead young Malden to the door that entered the house. He followed me up the stairs where we walked into the kitchen area as I directed him to have a seat at the kitchen island.

I turned to walk out of the kitchen when I noticed Gretchen standing in the entrance way leaning against the frame with folded arms. I listened to her ask, "What's going on here, Travis?"

Malden sat quietly at the kitchen island reading a small book I didn't notice he had with him. I looked at her perplexed expression, and introduced Malden. "Honey, this is Malden Crenshaw. Malden, this is my wife, Gretchen." I waited a moment, and listened to dead silence.

She responded now, "Travis, could I have a word with you in the other room, please?"

I looked in Malden's direction, and said, "I'll be right back."

I no sooner got into the other room where she waited, and the barrage of questions started, not that I was surprised, mind you. It's not every day I bring a stranger home with me, much less a small child. I immediately spoke up, "I know, Gretchen, let me explain."

"You have an explanation for this? Oh, I'm sorry, Travis. I'm a little confused about what day it is. You normally only bring home strangers on *Tuesdays.*"

"I get it," I said. "I'll explain everything soon."

"Oh, I'll need you to do a lot more than that. I mean, who's this boy, and why is he in my home, Travis?"

"Please, Gretchen, can we table this for a short bit?"

"And what is that odor I smell, Travis?"

"Well, I could lie to you, and say, it's not coming from the young man sitting in our kitchen. Look, Gretchen, I'll fill you in on everything, but for now can we please get this young man cleaned up, and fed, then we can sit down and discuss all of this." I could see how perturbed she was, guessed it was not only late at night, and she was tired, but now she had to go back in time when our kids were around his age, and play mommy again.

She replied with a persistent tone in her voice, "Fine," and walked back into the kitchen where Malden sat, still reading a book at the kitchen island. She announced, "All right, Malden, why don't you come with me, so we can get cleaned up, and if you're up for a late night snack I'll put something together for you."

He acknowledged the request, followed her out of the kitchen, and upstairs where the guest bed and bath were. She found an old bathrobe, and some old clothes of mine, for him to wear until she could wash and dry the filthy ones he had on. She spoke to him as she handed him the bathrobe, the clothes she found, and said, "These will be big on you, Malden, but will have to do until I can get the clothes you're wearing washed."

He stared at her, and replied, "Thank you, Mrs. Scott."

She paused, for a moment, while she stared back at him not knowing this person who stood in front of her. I guessed this may have been the moment in time my wife found a soft spot in her heart for this young man, and his situation. She replied with a nod, collected the discarded clothes he had on, and hurried to the basement to get them in the wash never saying a word to me as she passed me on the staircase.

Gretchen and I eventually had a sit down after we attended to Malden, and got him fed and bunked into the guest bedroom. I begged her to hold off on any questions until I could explain the events of the last week up to this evening pertaining to Malden. Eventually, the conversation ended with me, and the questions came to life from her. "Travis, don't you think we should call someone like the police, or whoever you call to report an abandoned child?"

I responded unsure, "I guess so under normal circumstances, but do you see this as normal, Gretchen?" I continued, "I mean, the kid said he was sixteen when I asked him how old he was, and what if we do find the parents, or the guardian of this boy, and discover they left the child to fend for himself? You should have seen where he was living, Gretchen. No one deserves to live like that, especially a child."

With a surprised look, she exclaimed, "You bought that sixteen-year-old crap, Travis! That child is no way sixteen years old. I don't care what he said."

"Look, Gretchen, regardless of how old he is, don't you think we should help the boy out until we can determine where he does belong?"

"Terrific," She responded. "Well, I'm going to bed since it's late. We'll continue this conversation in the morning." She paused, and said, "After the boy leaves." I realized the stress and strain of bringing Malden home, but decided this was the right thing to do.

CHAPTER 5

Gretchen and I woke the next morning, and little was said initially while we both walked downstairs to start our morning, knowing a child was sleeping in our guest room we knew nothing about. I could tell she was still annoyed by the whole situation, but was trying to deal with it.

She announced while we walked downstairs to the kitchen, "We should let Malden sleep for now, and discuss what we should do." She added, "We'll just ask Malden where he lives, and find out why he ended up here, and not with his family, simple, right?"

I turned to her, and said, "Good luck with that." I further explained, "I asked those same questions last night, and got squat from him."

She started to respond, but stopped when we both hit the bottom landing of the staircase, and noticed Malden in the sitting area by the front door in the great room. He was reading his book, already dressed in the clothes Gretchen washed, and dried last night, including the old store smock vest. I looked in his direction, and asked, "Malden, everything okay?"

He acknowledged, "Yes, sir."

Gretchen added, "I guess you found your clothes in the laundry room."

He replied, "Yes, ma'am."

I looked at her, and said in a soft voice, "If nothing else, this kid is the most courteous, and respectful teenager I've ever met."

She looked at me a bit annoyed over my comment, and said, "Not funny, Travis."

I looked back at her, and said, "What? I'm being serious."

I looked over to Malden, still engrossed in the book he was reading, and said, "Malden, let's have breakfast." He acknowledged me while Gretchen made her way into the kitchen to start the morning coffee. Breakfast was normal for the Scott family that day if we don't consider there's a perfect stranger in our home. I guess that canceled out the normal part.

Gretchen and I tried our best to question young Malden about his life, and why he ended up living in the woods in the back of a supercenter, but he wouldn't budge, and either didn't want to answer the questions, or just didn't understand them.

Gretchen and I realized this boy had some serious baggage he'd carried around with him. I felt bad for the young man who kept things so bottled up, and didn't want to talk to anyone about it. Eventually, I guessed, Gretchen felt the same way, so we decided the best course of action was to let Malden tell us when he was ready. In reality though, it was just me who decided that. Gretchen, however, was looking for the answer to the million dollar question which was, what are we going to do with this young child?

I decided I needed to get to the office to do some work, and see if I could shed some light on this young man's origin, so to speak. I showered, and explained to Gretchen what my plan was when Malden approached me to ask if he could come to the store.

I looked at him with those innocent eyes, and tried to come up with an excuse to avoid the question, but didn't want to disappoint the child. I said, "You know, Malden, I wanted you to spend some time with my wife today, and maybe take a drive with her to go shopping for some new clothes." Gretchen listened to me while I spoke to him. I looked over at her, and could see her dismay with having to go shopping, for clothes for young Malden. I looked back at him, and said, "Plus, those sneakers you have on Malden, look like they're about a step away from disintegrating into a dust bowl. Would that be okay, Malden, for today, to hang out with Gretchen?"

He looked at me, and said, "Yes, sir."

"All right, then, I will see you both later."

Gretchen walked with me out the front door, stopped briefly, and asked, "Where are we going with this, Travis?"

I just looked at her, and said, "I'll be back later this afternoon. Maybe we can all sit down, relax, and watch a movie or something."

She stared at me, and responded, "You owe me big time, Travis."

I mulled over everything while I drove to the store about what might have led this young boy to be abandoned, and left to fend for himself. I kept thinking, how was it possible no one had discovered this boy's demise. I couldn't seem to rationalize a reason. It's not like we live in some remote place in the world where something like this could happen. How is it that this child could survive on his own, unnoticed by anyone? And why is it I'm the only person who cared enough to step up to the plate to help the young man?

I tried to find the answers to those questions while I drove. Well, I was no less conflicted at that point, and hoped I could shed some light on the whole situation at the office. I tried to stay positive, and decided I can make this right for the young boy. After all, the child is what mattered here, while I thought about the situation I found myself in.

I arrived at the store, and made my way to my office after a few brief stops from store personnel who greeted me. I stayed focused, even with all the added stress of not knowing how to deal with the young man I found. I managed to multitask some items left on my desk that required my attention. I finished the important paperwork I considered dealing with later. I could finally focus on finding out where Malden came from, or at the very least, try to find some information related to the young man's life.

I fired up my Internet browser, and searched for Malden's last name to see how many hits I got for the State of North Carolina. As I searched the last name Crenshaw, I was surprised by the number of people in my state with that last name. I was shocked, wow. I would have guessed little to none with the last name Crenshaw.

Well, this was going to be a chore, I surmised, and searched now for the full name hoping to find some article about the boy if one existed. Malden Crenshaw came back with nothing, not even a hit on his first name. I sat back in my chair, chilled for a moment, and decided I would need to get creative in my search for any information about the young boy.

I continued my search for many hours, and took a short pause after coming up with literally nothing in my attempts to find out who Malden was. I decided, well, I could try printing out people with the same last name, and call them to see if anyone knew a Malden Crenshaw, but wouldn't that come across a little strange. I mean, a grown man calling to find out information about a little boy, and asking where he might be from, or even live. That would definitely make me out to look like some kind of pervert. I decided this would not be the most appropriate route to take.

I decided I needed a break from trying to find Malden's family, and left my office to walk around the store. I ran into Winette, and greeted her.

"How are you today, Travis?"

"Fine, Winette." I asked her now, "I may need a favor next week." I continued, and said, "I have a young man who would like to spend some time here at the store for a few days, maybe working the parking lot shopping carts, or doing some merchandising work stocking shelves, or some other simple jobs."

"Sure, Travis, is this person a new hire coming from Mary's office?"

I looked at her, and answered, "Not exactly." I tried to justify my request knowing full well I would be asking too much of my wife to take care of Malden all week if we couldn't find his family. Plus, I figured it best if I kept close, and around the young man, that might help me determine where he came from.

I turned my attention back to Winette, and said, "No, this is just someone staying with Gretchen and me with a few days of downtime, and asked if he could spend some time at the store." In my mind I said forgive me, Lord, I'm not lying here. Malden did ask if he could spend time at the store, just saying.

She stared at me with a perplexed look, and responded, "I guess, Travis. Seems a little out of the ordinary, but yes, just let me know, I'll set him up with a store smock, and put him to work." I could see the reluctance in her demeanor over the unusual request, but not at all surprised by her compliance. After all, who says no to their boss?

I responded, "Super, and thanks, Winette. I'll introduce you to the young man on Monday morning."

I looked at my watch, saw the time gone since I've been at the store, and called it a day. I made my way back to my office to grab my briefcase before I went home to see how Gretchen's day went with young Malden.

***

I arrived home to see Malden in the same place I left him that morning sitting by the front door reading. I noticed him wearing new duds, and announced, "You look sharp there, Malden."

He acknowledged the compliment, and said, "Yes, sir."

"Did you have fun shopping with Gretchen?"

Again, He looked at me, and replied, "Yes, sir."

As I turned to walk away I said to myself, it's like being in boot camp around this child.

I made my way to the kitchen where I heard Gretchen, and announced myself. "Hi honey, how was your day?"

She responded, "Fine, Travis, and yours?" while she spoke with a slightly sarcastic undertone in her voice.

"It was okay. I had no luck finding anything out about Malden however." I announced, "It's like he dropped out of the sky, or something." I asked now, "How was shopping with him? Everything go okay?"

She stopped what she was doing, and said, "It was like shopping with a mannequin, Travis. The boy said nothing the entire time we were out. I shopped for him the entire time with no input on anything."

I looked at her, and said, "Why am I not surprised by that?"

She continued, and added, "Plus the fact I felt like everyone had stared at us the whole time we were out today. People are so judgmental."

"What do you mean?"

"Seriously, Travis, you have to ask that?"

"What?" I guessed, "It's because he's black, right?"

With a surprised look, she said, "Very good, Travis. You got it on the first try." I concluded now, maybe my company's diversity program should be expanded to the entire State of North Carolina.

She continued prepping dinner, and commented, "It wasn't all bad, and at least the child has some proper clothes to wear now."

I had sat at the kitchen island at that point while I listened to her, and thanked her for spending the day helping the young man out.

She looked at me, and simply said, "You're welcome, dear."

The rest of the weekend was pretty much the same while I continued my search for any information I could find to locate the family of young Malden. Gretchen and I tried our best to get any further information from him, but he didn't give up anything at all. I wondered why and how a small child could be so reclusive. Young boys are full of life, and energy, especially teenage boys, uncontainable in every way. I figured maybe some time with me at the store would bring out something in the boy that resembled something normal, maybe.

Monday morning came quickly. I made my way down to the kitchen where Gretchen sat, drinking her coffee. I explained to her that I wanted Malden to work with me the next few days at the store. I had hoped I'd have a better chance to figure out some things about him, and this way, she could relax, and carry on her normal routine. I enquired where Malden was, and said, "Wait, don't tell me." I guessed, "Reading in the great room!"

She looked at me, and nodded in agreement. I exclaimed, "*YES*, got that right on the first try." She sipped her coffee, shook her head, and listened to me relish in my accomplishment. I asked, "I assume Malden had breakfast?"

"Yes, he did." I finished my coffee, and tabled the newspaper. I kissed her goodbye, and headed out of the kitchen to see if Malden would like to come to the store with me that day.

I walked into the great room toward him, and announced, "Hey, Malden, I'm leaving for work now. I was wondering if you would like to tag along, and spend time at the store with me today."

He got up, put his book in his back pocket, and answered, "Yes, sir."

"All right, Malden, one thing we need to do is get rid of that smock you have on."

He looked up at me, and said, "Did I do something wrong, Mr. Scott?"

"No, no, Malden it's just--."

He interrupted me, and explained, "I found this, sir."

"That's okay, Malden. I didn't say you took it from anywhere." I saw the disappointment in his eyes, and tried to assure him everything was all right. I leaned down closer to him, and explained, "We have new smocks at the store, Malden, and this one you have on is old. We have different ones now. That's all."

He stared back at me, removed the smock, and said, "Yes, sir." I turned to see Gretchen at the kitchen entrance observing us, while she held her cup of coffee.

She spoke up, and announced, "Just leave the smock there, Malden. It will be up in the spare room for you when you get back."

I listened, and said, "Thanks, Gretchen. I'll talk with you later, honey."

She smiled, and said, "Bye, guys. Have a nice day," while she turned to walk back into the kitchen.

I was conflicted while I drove to work that morning trying to figure out how on earth to explain Malden being there to my store staff. I decided, oh well, playing this one by ear I guess. What else do I have? I paused for a moment, and thanked God, I'm the boss. Otherwise, this conversation in my mind would be pointless. On the other hand, I haven't had to explain this to Mary yet. Well, this will be one for the books.

Malden and I arrived at the store, parked on the side of the building, and made our way in through the employee entrance. Malden walked behind me as we entered when I saw Winette in the distance making her way toward the receiving docks. I caught up with her, and said, "Good morning," and introduced Malden. "I appreciate you doing this last minute," I announced.

Winette had been staring at Malden the whole time when she turned to me, and asked, "Can I have a quick word with you, Travis?" She walked a few feet away, so she could place some distance between herself, and Malden. She looked at me while fumbling her words, and said. "Umm, Malden looks pretty young, Travis. Is he old enough to be working here?"

I looked at her, and explained, "Malden is sixteen, so that shouldn't be a problem, right?"

She stared at me with a surprised look, and said, "Really! Sixteen!" paused a moment, and looked over at Malden again. She hesitated again for a second, and said, "Well, okay then," looked back at me, and simply stated, "I'll get him a smock, and give him some work to do."

"Thanks, Winette."

I walked over to him, and said, "I should be in my office, Malden, if you need anything, but for now Winette will set you up with some work. Sound like a plan?"

He replied, "Yes, sir."

"Great, go with Winette, and I'll check with you later on."

He acknowledged me, and turned to walk toward Winette while she stood there waiting for him. I turned around to walk away, but couldn't. My mind was reminding me of that morning again, watching Malden on the video system in

Bishop's office. I couldn't stop thinking about it, and attributed that to my OCD type nature. While I regressed, even at the risk of complicating an already complicated situation, I decided I needed at that moment in time to address my obsession.

I turned around, and said, "Wait a second, Malden." He stopped, and turned to look at me. I walked over to him, and crouched while I said, "I need to know something, Malden, and have to ask you a question. Is that, okay?

He stared at me, and said, "Yes, sir."

"Last week Malden, you were in the parking lot reading under one of the lamp posts the night before I found you. You had just finished putting some shopping carts in one of the carriage corrals. Do you remember that night, Malden?"

He acknowledged, "Yes, sir."

I continued to question him, "Do you remember if you looked up, and over at the main store at any point during that time?

He continued to stare at me, and answered, "Yes, sir"

I was uncertain for a moment after he answered me. My mind posed the question, are you sure you want to go down this road, Travis? I couldn't wait any longer, and asked now, "Why, Malden? What were you looking at?"

He paused a moment, and said, "You, sir."

I stood after I heard Malden's response, and stared at the young man in front of me while a slight chill ran through my entire body. He just confirmed what I already knew, but couldn't prove, and more importantly, can't possibly be true. I was speechless, and tried to understand how that was possible. After a moment I felt a hand on my arm, and turned to see Winette next to me with a concerned look. She stared at me, and said, "Are you all right, Travis?"

I stood there for another moment or two unable to break free from my confused state of mind when I turned back to Malden, and saw him just stare back at me. I looked back to Winette, and said, "Yes, Winette, I'm fine. I'll be in my office if you need anything."

I looked back down now to Malden, and said, "Okay, Malden, thanks, I'll hook up with you later, all right?" He acknowledged me, and turned now to walk with Winette. I continued to watch the young man while he walked away.

I made it up to my office, and started to set up for the day, but couldn't stop thinking about Malden. I leaned back in my chair, and reviewed what had just happened. My whole life to that moment in time had been predicated on a simple set of rules I was raised on. Rules of logic! Everything I had ever experienced in my life was explainable. So why would anything have to be different now? I shook my head, and decided I needed a new set of rules!

I turned my computer monitor on, looked at all the email I had to handle, and whispered to myself, "Holy crap." I shook my head, and whispered some more, "Doesn't anyone have anything better to do, than email me? My, Lord!" I had addressed a slew of emails I received when I saw Mary walk up to my office. She knocked while she entered, and shut the door behind her. I stopped typing, leaned back in my office chair, and simply said, "Morning, Mary, I've been expecting you."

She stood with her hands on her hips, with a surprised look while she replied, "Well, have you now, Travis. Let's just skip the formalities of this conversation, and let me get right to it, and say, are you out of your freakin' mind, Travis?"

I sighed, looked at her, and said, "Have a seat, Mary, so I can explain what has happened."

She looked at me, and concluded, "He's the boy we all saw on the video system, isn't he?"

"Yes, Mary, and please, take a seat so I don't have to look up to you while we talk. Thank you."

She sat, and continued to question me. "How old is this child, Travis? He looks nowhere near the legal age."

I looked at her, and said, "Sixteen is what he told me, Mary."

She responded with an expression of disbelief, "Oh, so you have proof of this? *Sixteen*, Travis, he showed you some ID that can prove that?"

"No, he didn't, I'm just telling you what he told me. Look, Mary, let's go back to the beginning here, let me explain everything to this point, and then you can ask your questions. Can we agree to that?"

She leaned back in her seat now, and said, "Fine, I'm listening, Travis."

I brought her up to speed on everything that had transpired since last Friday night when I found Malden living outside in the woods behind the store. I continued to explain everything through the weekend up to this morning, and said to her, "Now you can ask your questions."

She looked at me, and asked, "So, Gretchen is okay with all of this?"

"Well, not at first, and maybe not even now, but she will come around I guess."

I could see how perplexed Mary was over everything I had just said when she spoke, and asked, "So, when was it decided this child, Malden, was your responsibility?" She continued to question. "I mean, when you called the police, they just said, here, you take care of the boy. I'm totally lost here, Travis."

I explained to her why I didn't call the police, and my reasons for not calling.

She looked at me with a concerned stare, and said, "Oh, Travis," with even more concern in her voice. "Are you sure you've done the right thing here? I mean, I know you may think you've done the right thing, but seriously."

"I know, Mary, but I went with my gut on this, and I think I know what was right here."

"All right, Travis, we got that out of the way, so let's discuss why this young man is in our store parking lot with a garbage bag picking up trash."

"Look, Mary, I need the boy around so I can try, and figure out what's going on with him. It should only take a day, or two, max, and I'm sure by then I'll have found where the boy's parents and family are."

She looked at me with a not so optimistic expression, got up, shook her head, and declared, "Well, Travis, I can't acknowledge this young man being here. I mean, what do we say to our staff, and what if something should happen. Aren't we responsible for this young boy on our property?"

I stood, and stated, "Look, Mary, anybody questions why Malden is here you just say Malden who, what, and direct them my way. I take full responsibility for him, and as far as I'm concerned, this conversation never even took place." I realized how this is something that could be potentially career-threatening if word got out to corporate. I couldn't, and would not compromise her position in any way. "Are we okay now, Mary?"

"Not really, Travis, but I know you, and I'll have to be okay with it, for now, I guess."

"Fine, how about we meet for lunch later, and I'll fill you in on some ideas I have for the upcoming Fourth of July pre-holiday sales announcement?"

She looked at me, and said, "All right, but remember this. That line you're not supposed to cross in life, Travis," She paused a moment, and continued to say, "Well, you're closer to it than you think."

I reasoned that for a moment, and said, "You got it, Mary, and thanks."

She left my office while I evaluated the conversation I just had with her. Maybe she's right about a few things that are out of the ordinary. I moved closer to my window, stared out at the parking lot, observed young Malden working, and picking out some trash from the carriages. I wondered again, what the heck is wrong with this picture.

I thought for a moment, and came up with an idea. With that, I left my office, and started my way down to the main floor to have a discussion with Marshall. He is one of our seasoned associates who worked for Winette in Merchandising. He is in his fourth year with the company, worked part-time for us while he was in high school, but graduated last year, and was full-time now.

I guess Marshall never figured out what he wanted to do in life to that point, but has been a good kid, and worked hard most of the time. He'd only slack off occasionally, about what you'd expect from an 18-year-old. I located him at the front of the store, and caught up with him by the front entrance while he loaded some carriages from the parking lot. "How are you today, Marshall?"

He looked over at me, and replied, "Fine, Mr. Scott. Can I help you with something?"

I walked over to him, put my hand on his shoulder, steered him off to the side, out of the way of customers entering the storefront, and said, "Yes, you can."

He stood there with his hands on his hips, and said, "Sure, Mr. Scott, what can I do for you?"

"Have you met Malden, yet?"

"Yes, I did. Winette introduced him to me earlier."

"Well, Marshall, I need you to do me a favor, and keep an eye on Malden for the next couple of days. Just mentor him if you would, and be a friend if you don't mind."

He looked to me, and said, "Sure, Mr. Scott, not a problem."

I smiled back, and nodded. "Great, Marshall, I appreciate you taking him under your wing for a few days, and just let me know if you need anything."

He confirmed, "Will do, sir." I walked away, and hoped a bond between the two would open Malden up. Maybe, I thought, while I made my way back to my office.

I tried to focus on the tasks at hand for the rest of the day. Mary had to reschedule our luncheon due to another meeting she'd previously scheduled, and needed a rain check. I took that opportunity to manage the store work, around my thoughts of Malden, and occasionally would come up with another idea on the computer to find out any information about him. I landed a big fat zero on everything I tried, but was glad the young man was here apparently enjoying what he was doing. Well, at least from my perspective anyway.

The day wound down with a call from Gretchen who enquired what time she should expect Malden and I. I talked with her for a bit in my office looking out over the parking lot while I watched Malden and Marshall teamed up collecting, and pushing carts through the lot. "I should try to be home around 5:30," I explained to her.

She surprisingly said, "Wow. That would be a first, Travis. What's the occasion? I know it's not our anniversary."

I replied frankly, "Very funny, Gretchen." I guessed, and thought since Malden had been here all day, I should give the kid a break. I repeated, "So, around 5:30."

"All right Travis, you can tell me how it went with Mary today when you get home. That must have been a fun time for you," while she chuckled slightly.

"Yeah, yeah," I responded, "I'll see you in about an hour. Love you."

"Love you back, Travis."

I had left my office now for the day, and walked past Mary's open office, and said, "Good night."

She responded, "Have a good evening, Travis," with an underlying tone in her voice that told me she was still not happy with the day's events. I made my way down to the front of the store where I found Marshall, and briefly had a conversation. I could see Malden off in the distance in the parking lot retrieving some shopping carts.

"So, Marshall, how did Malden do today?"

"He did just fine, Mr. Scott. Quiet kid, but he worked really hard."

"So, did you two talk about anything interesting today, or was everything just shop talk?"

"Well, sir, like I said, he was pretty quiet. I took him over to the sub shop next door for lunch, but he had little to say. Maybe he's just shy, or something."

"Well, Marshall, I appreciate you spending time with him. Oh, and by the way." I reached into my pocket to pull out my wallet, gave him a twenty dollar bill, and said, "Thank you for taking Malden out to lunch."

He tried to avoid taking the money, and said, "That's okay, Mr. Scott. It was my treat."

I looked at him, and said, "No, it was my treat, son," as I forced him to take the money.

"Well, thanks."

"All right then, Marshall, you have a good evening, and will see you tomorrow."

He smiled, "You too, Mr. Scott," as he turned to walk away.

I met up with Malden, and asked if he was all set to go home now. He replied, "Yes, sir," as we walked from the front lot to the side of the building to my car. While we drove home, I enquired how his day went. He just replied,

"Fine, sir." I asked if he was tired from working all day which he responded, "Not really, sir." I chuckled, and wondered how great it would be, to be sixteen again.

Malden and I arrived at the house, parked in the garage, and made our way upstairs. I greeted Gretchen in the kitchen, "How are you, honey?"

She replied, "Fine, Travis," while she stared at Malden, who sat at the kitchen island.

She addressed him, and asked if he had a nice day at the store with me.

He answered, "Yes, ma'am, I did."

She turned to me, and said, "I can't believe this!"

I looked back at her. "You can't believe what?"

She jokingly replied, "Eating dinner before 5:30 at night. I mean, it's still light out, Travis." I stared back at her, said nothing, and just smirked at my wife trying to be funny.

Dinner was a blast as usual with the same awkward moments of silence from Malden with more questions unanswered than acknowledged. Gretchen and I discussed the day's events after dinner which included the awkward conversation I had with Mary in my office that morning.

Gretchen was still asking the same questions we both didn't have the answers for, which made me feel a little uncomfortable. I was frustrated to some extent, but still felt in my heart there was a reason Malden was here, and at the very least was being taken care of.

I pictured the place where I found this boy, the living conditions he endured, and felt justified in everything I had done. What kind of circumstances would abandon a small child to this world, or create a situation that would exclude the child from being with his family? Oh well, I thought, this is all I can do for today. The child has a roof over his head with two loving people who could tolerate this situation until it could be resolved.

CHAPTER 6

The days rolled past while I tried my best to manage the work at the store while I observed Malden, plus steering clear of Mary as much as I could under the circumstances. I met with Bishop in his office for an unrelated matter, and asked him, for a favor. I explained to him how I wanted Malden to interact with other people in the hopes of finding out something more about the young man. Bishop agreed, "Sure, Boss, I can have him work in my department for a couple of days, not a problem."

I headed downstairs for a meeting with some of my staff in the receiving area, and diverted briefly to hook up with Malden. I saw him with Marshall, and a new hire, I assumed, at the front of the store.

I acknowledged Marshall, and the new hire as I approached them. I looked at Malden, and said, "Need a moment with you," while I guided him away from Marshall and the new hire a few feet away to talk in private. "So, Malden, I had an idea, and thought you might like to work in the store today in the Audio Department. Does that sound like something you might like to do?"

He looked up at me, and replied, "Yes, sir."

"Okay then, let me take you to see Bishop in his office, so he can set you up."

He replied, "I know where his office is, sir."

I looked down at him as we were about to walk away, and responded, "All right, Malden, I have a meeting in the receiving area. I'll check in on you later."

He acknowledged me, and walked toward the main offices. I walked in the opposite direction to the receiving area for my meeting, and glanced over at him walking away. All the while wondering how he knew where Bishop's office was.

After Malden and I had departed, the new hire, Bill, looked at Marshall, and said, "Who was that with the spook?"

He turned to stare at Bill with a somewhat surprised expression, and said, "That was the store manager," and added, "I wouldn't let him hear you talk like that, especially about Malden."

Bill proclaimed, "What's so special about him? Is it his kid or something?"

He replied, "I don't think so, but I heard he lives with his family."

Bill looked at him, and grumbled, "That's just not right," with a disgusted look. "I mean, why does he get to work inside, and we have to push carriages?" Marshall ignored the comment, and walked past Bill just shaking his head.

Malden arrived at Bishop's office, and knocked on his door. Bishop was at his desk listening to music on his CD player, and working on his PC at the same time. He looked up, saw Malden standing in the doorway, and said, "Hi, Malden, come on in." He added, "Come over here for a moment, Malden. I want you to listen to this, and tell me what you think."

Malden walked into the office toward Bishop as he took off the earplugs to his CD player, and placed one next to Malden's ear. Bishop smiled, and said, "Have a listen to this, Malden." He listened for all of a millisecond, and stepped back from the earplug next to his ear with disapproval.

Bishop looked at him, and said, "Not a big fan of the Ozz man, are you, Malden?" as he chuckled. Bishop wondered for a moment, and said to himself, who doesn't like Ozzy Osborne. Oh well, looked at Malden, and said, "Let's take a walk down to the main floor, I have some work I need taken care of today." He acknowledged Bishop's request while they walked out of his office.

Malden worked the rest of the day setting up some promotional display racks in Bishop's department, and stocking them. Bishop followed up occasionally with Malden to check in on the young man, and was pleasantly surprised by the progress he made of everything he'd accomplished. Bishop was back in his office, mulling over all this when I walked in, and asked, "Hey, Bishop, how did Malden do today?"

He looked at me, and said, "Boss, he completed everything I asked him to do amazingly. I mean, where did this kid come from? I would have thought at the very least I would've needed to explain a few things to him, but nothing." He also noted, "I checked with some of my associates, and they said he just worked away, and didn't ask for any help on anything. Don't get me wrong, Boss. I mean, he somehow knew what to do, which was great, but even I have had trouble understanding the setup of some of those merchandise displays. The kid just put them together like it was nothing."

I smiled at him, and said, "Don't worry, Bishop, we're not grooming Malden to replace you."

He looked back at me, and stated, "Yeah, well, that thought will still be kept in the back of my mind."

I laughed, and thanked him, for placing Malden in his department for the day as I left his office.

I walked past Mary's office when she called out to me, and asked if I had a moment. I walked into her office, sat down while she enquired about any new information I might have on locating Malden's family.

I responded, "Not a thing Mary. I can hardly believe it myself. How does a human being appear out of nowhere these days? Can you explain that, Mary?"

She looked at me, and agreed, "Well, I can't figure that out either, Travis. I'm just as confused as you are." She added, "Maybe it would help if you brought the young man to someone who had experience with this type of situation."

I looked at her, and said, "And who might that be, Mary? I mean, come on."

"I don't know, Travis. I was just trying to come up with a suggestion that might help expedite the process of finding his family."

"I know, Mary, and I appreciate your input. I had hoped we could've resolved this sooner than later. Well, I'm done for the day, and need to find Malden, so we can head home."

Mary and I stood when she looked at me, and repeated my words, "Your home, Travis?"

I confirmed, "Yes, Mary, my home. Have a nice evening."

She acknowledged, "You as well."

Malden and I were driving home that day when I announced, "So, Malden, you did well today from what I was told. Bishop was a little intimidated by the work you accomplished. That's a good thing, Malden, don't you think?"

He replied, "Yes, sir."

"Well, Malden, I think so." The remainder of the drive home was the same as past days with no output from the young man who sat content beside me.

After dinner that evening Gretchen looked at Malden, and asked if he would like to watch TV in the den, so she could speak with me. No response from him, so she rephrased, "Or you could go into the great room, and read your book if you'd like."

He got up from the dining room table, said, "Yes, ma'am," and walked out of the room.

I looked across the table at her, and asked, "What's up?"

"Travis, I've become as smitten as you over this young man, but seriously, it's getting to the point that we're no closer to understanding where this child came from. I mean, it's been a week, and nothing has been resolved."

I looked at her, and said, "Gretchen, I agree with everything you said, but I'm just not sure what to do. I keep thinking each day that goes by something will come up, or happen that helps us understand what is going on with this child." As frustrated as I had become, I looked to her, and said, "Look, give me a few more days, and if we can't locate his family, or find out anything new, I'll contact the authorities to get them involved in the search."

"All right, Travis, and please don't misunderstand me. I want what's best for Malden just as much as you do."

I got up from the dinner table, and said, "I know you do, Gretchen."

The following day Malden and I arrived at the store, and were approached by Winette looking to speak with me. "How are you this morning, Travis?"

I responded, "Fine, Winette, and yourself?"

"I'm good, but need a favor." She asked now, "If it's not too much trouble, I was wondering if Malden could work with Marshall today since one of my associates called out sick. I know Malden worked in Bishop's department yesterday, but it would be huge if you could divert him to my area just for today."

I looked down at him, and asked, "So what do you think, Malden? Are you okay working with Marshall, for the day?"

He looked up at me, and said, "Yes, sir."

"All right, Winette, he's all yours." I looked at Malden, and said, "I'll catch up with you later for lunch, all right." He acknowledged me, walked past Winette to get a store smock from the front registers, and headed out to the parking lot to start work. Winette thanked me, and went about her business.

I made my way to my office, and stopped by Bishop's office to let him know Malden was diverted to work in Winette's department for that day. He greeted me, and said, "Good morning, Boss," and added "Fine, I'll manage somehow today." I smiled at him as I turned to walk toward my own office.

I sat back in my office chair, stared out my office window, and observed Malden and Marshall working the parking lot carriages. I recalled the conversation I had with my wife last night, and questioned for a moment if I could be wrong, and not doing the right thing for him. I realized, perhaps the longer my association is with this young man, the harder it would be to face the truth about where he truly belonged, wherever that might be. I made up my mind, and decided dealing with this later is better.

I received a phone call from Steve a short while later requesting my presence in the outdoor garden center, and responded, "Will head over there in a few minutes, Steve." I finished up an email I was working on, and exited my office to start the short quarter mile walk to Steve's area.

I cut through the Audio Department when I saw Bishop while he worked on a new merchandise display, and appeared to be struggling with it. I walked over to him, and jokingly said, "If you can wait until Monday, I can have Malden stop by, and take care of that for you." I could see how perturbed he was after I said that.

He stopped what he was doing, turned to me, exasperated now, and said, "Eight-track-player, Boss."

I laughed, and said, "Carry on, son," and repeated one more time, "Carry on."

I made my way to the Garden Center near the receiving docks where I saw Steve arguing with a man who looked like a truck driver. I approached both men, and said, "Whoa, guys, what's the problem here?"

Steve turned to me, and uttered, "Travis, this guy just tried to deliver a semi full of ornamental shrubs that are close to, if not already, dead." I worked my way to the loading dock where the semi was docked, and walked into the truck to look at what he had talked about. I inspected the shrubs, and was oblivious to what Steve referred to.

I walked back out of the truck, over to the men, and announced to Steve, "They seem fine to me."

The truck driver spoke up now, and said, "That's what I tried to tell him," while he looked at Steve.

Steve turned to me, and objected. "What are you talking about, Travis? Look at this shrub we pulled out of the truck." He pointed to it, and said, "See all these buds! Every single one of them, are dried out. Even if we water these now, Travis, there is no way in hell they'd come back to life." I now examined the shrub Steve had shown me.

Meanwhile, back out in the front of the store, Marshall was working the carriages with Malden on opposite sides of the lot. Marshall had gathered some carts from a few corrals when he heard some commotion coming from the area where Malden was. He looked up over the lot, could see in the distance a bunch of people huddled around one of the corrals, and saw some kids running away from the group of people gathered there. He scanned the area, but couldn't see Malden anywhere.

Marshall made his way to where the people had gathered, and when he finally got there, everyone was staring at something on the ground. He looked down to see Malden all beat up, bleeding from his head and mouth, and gasped at the sight of the young boy lying there.

He did the first thing that came to mind, and ran toward the front of the store to get help for him.

He rushed into the store, and scanned the area for a manager or someone who could call for help. He saw Bishop in the distance in the Audio Department, and hurried over to him. Bishop noticed Marshall running toward him with a concerned look about him, and asked, "What's the matter, Marshall?"

He blurted out, "Malden is hurt in the parking lot, and someone needs to call 911!"

Bishop rushed over to the main customer counter in his department, and shouted at Marshall, "Find Travis, and let him know what happened!" Marshall quickly turned, and ran through the department towards the main office while Bishop dialed for help.

Marshall ran past one of the associates, Catie, and briefly stopped to ask, "Have you seen Mr. Scott?"

Catie replied, "I think I saw him out by the receiving docks. What's the matter, Marshall?" By the time Catie could finish her sentence he had already rushed through her department.

I was still at the receiving dock with Steve, and the truck driver trying to resolve the delivery of some shrubs when I noticed Marshall running through the store in my direction. I interrupted my conversation with Steve to shout at him, and remind him of the safety policy in the store, that was no running.

He stopped, and explained, "I'm sorry, Mr. Scott, but Malden got hurt out in the parking lot."

My face turned to stone when he said that, and blurted out, "What do you mean, Malden got hurt?" I didn't wait for an answer since my immediate reaction was to get to Malden to find out what had happened.

Marshall and I ran through the store, and made it out to the front parking lot where some people were gathered around a carriage corral in the distance. I didn't see Malden among the people, and wondered if Malden got hit by a car, or worse, did he get run over by one. I speculated all kinds of horrible scenarios while I ran through the parking lot trying to get to where the people were gathered.

I finally arrived with Marshall behind me. I saw Malden lying on the ground all bloody from cuts on his face, and blood coming out of his mouth. I knelt down next to him, sighed, and said, "Ah, geez, Malden, what happened?" I was emotional while I tried to comfort the young man lying on the ground.

He tried to get up, looked at me, and said, "I'm sorry, Mr. Scott."

I had my hand on his chest to stop him, and said softly, "Shhh, don't get up, Malden, just relax." I looked up while several customers, along with Marshall, stood there just looking down at me when I shouted, "Did anyone call 911?" with anger in my voice.

I looked to Marshall with determination while he confirmed, "They're on their way, sir."

I no sooner looked back down to Malden when I heard the sirens of police, and ambulance vehicles entering the parking lot. I stayed with him the entire time until I was motioned away by the EMT's. I stood while police officers asked people to move back to give space for Malden, and the ambulance crew. One officer approached me while I noticed Bishop among the people who had gathered to see what was going on. I turned to the police officer, and declared, "I'm Travis Scott, the store manager here."

The police officer asked, "Do you know what happened, Mr. Scott?"

I responded, "I don't," and explained I was called out of the store by one of my associates who told me Malden was hurt in the parking lot. I looked at Marshall now, and asked, "Do you know what happened here, Marshall?"

He answered, "No, sir. I was on the other side of the parking lot when I noticed a bunch of people gathered here, and that's when I found Malden all laid out. I'm sorry, Mr. Scott."

I reassured him, "That's all right, Marshall."

The officer looked back at me, and said, "Well, Mr. Scott, I'll need the young man's name, age, and address for now. Do you need a moment to get this?"

I looked back at the police officer, and said, "His name is Malden Crenshaw," then paused.

The officer enquired further, "Do you have his home address, Mr. Scott?" I thought real fast, and wondered if this was the moment in time I needed to tell someone I had no idea where Malden lived, or anything else for that matter.

I decided what was best for him right now, gave the officer my home address, and said, "Sixteen, Malden's age, officer"

The officer wrote down the information, and walked over to the EMT's where they had Malden on a gurney placing him into the back of the ambulance. I made my way over to the ambulance, looked at Malden, and smiled while I said, "Look, buddy, I'll be right behind you, okay? These people are going to make sure you're not hurt." I reached into the ambulance, and squeezed his hand. I stared into his eyes to assure him what I said was true. He stared back at me with a scared look, so I repeated, "I'm right behind you, Malden."

I stepped back to allow the EMT's to finish their work to transport him to the urgent care center not far from the supercenter. I made my way back to the police officers, and motioned Bishop over to where we stood.

I addressed him, and asked if he could get the video feed for this part of the parking lot, so we could look to see what the hell happened here.

Bishop looked back to the main store, scoped out the area, and stated, "I should be able to get this for you, Boss. It's a bit far from the main camera, but I think we should be able to see what happened at least."

I looked at the police officers, and asked, "Would that work for you guys?"

Both officers agreed while one said, "Yes, that would be huge if you can provide a video of the incident."

I looked at Bishop, and told him, "Please take these officers up to your office, and get them whatever they need. I have to get to the hospital to see how Malden is doing."

Bishop looked at me, and affirmed, "You got it, Boss." The police officers followed him to the main entrance of the store while I rushed to my own vehicle parked on the side of the building. I accepted now the worst, but hoped for the best for young Malden.

I made my way out of the store parking lot, and headed over to the urgent care facility only about ten minutes away. I reached the medical facility, and found a parking spot that was literally a quarter mile from the emergency entrance.

I rushed through the parking lot, and wondered, what if Malden was actually hurt. I realized this was entirely my fault. I told myself over and over again, you dumb ass Travis. I continued the conversation in my mind while I said, nice job, Travis! Oh sure, you can find this boy's family, and all will be peaches and cream. I called myself a dumb ass all the way to the emergency entrance.

I walked in, made my way over to the head nurse's station, told the nurse I was Travis Scott, and explained, "One of my store associates was just transported here by ambulance."

The head nurse looked up, and stated, "Oh, yes, Mr. Scott, the young man is being attended to as we speak. I just have a few questions for you if you don't mind."

I replied, "Whatever I can do to help."

The nurse continued, and explained, "Well, the young man had no ID on him, or even a wallet when he was brought in. The only information we had, was from the initial police report that told us his name, address, and age." The nurse looked up at me, now suspicious, and said, "I found that unusual." She paused, and added, "Don't you, Mr. Scott?"

I looked back at the nurse, and answered, "Maybe he forgot it at home, or something, ma'am. I really can't say."

The nurse replied, "Well, that leads me to my next question. I looked up the address given to us to look for a phone number to call his parents, and what do you think I found, Mr. Scott?"

I sighed, stared back at her, all the while knowing where she was going with this, but tried to divert her attention, and offered, "Look, if this is about insurance, I'll make sure all of this is taken care of." I reached into my back pocket to get my wallet, produced a gold Master Card, and placed it on the counter.

The nurse stared back at me, and shook her head while she said, "Not quite the answer I was looking for, Mr. Scott." She continued, "It's funny because when I looked up the address, I found it listed to you. When I questioned young Malden about this, and who we should call, he would only give us your name." The nurse paused still looking at me, and confirmed, "That's the only reason why we're having this conversation right now, Mr. Scott."

I looked away for just a moment, and pleaded, "Can I please see, Malden, now?"

She answered, "No, Mr. Scott," and paused, while she stared at me, when she said, "But you can take him home when the staff doctor is through with him. Malden's injuries turned out to be just some minor scratches, bruises, and a bloody lip that required a few stitches. He will be sore for a while, but you should be able to take him home soon."

I looked at the nurse with relief, and thanked her so much for taking care of the young man. I turned to walk to the waiting area, and thanked God in my mind, for taking care of Malden. I hadn't felt this much joy since the birth of my first child, but soon my thoughts turned to anger when I saw him in a wheelchair being pushed in my direction. I got up, approached him, and asked, "You okay, Malden?"

He looked up at me with those innocent eyes, and said, "Yes, sir."

I turned to the head nurse, and said, "Thank you."

She motioned for me to approach the nurse's station where she handed me back my gold card, and advised, "A bill will be sent to your home address, Mr. Scott."

I thanked the nurse again, walked back over to Malden, and asked the nurse pushing him,

"Can he walk, or should we keep him seated for now?"

The nurse looked at me, and explained, "Malden is fine, Mr. Scott. This is just formality," referring to the wheelchair.

I looked at Malden, with the bruises on his face, a few stitches on his lip, and asked, "So are you all set to go home, Malden?"

He just replied, "Yes, sir."

I went and got the car, so he didn't have to walk a mile. I drove up to the front emergency entrance, and let him into the passenger seat for the ride back to my house. We arrived home with little said about the whole incident. I was mostly angry the whole drive home, determined to find out who had done this to this young man, and what I was going to do when I found these sons of bitches.

I parked the car in the driveway when we arrived, and both entered through the front door. Gretchen was in the den, heard the front door open, and walked out to see what was going on. She gasped, and held her hands up to her face when she saw Malden all cut up, and bruised. I looked at Malden, and said, "Just sit here in your favorite spot, okay."

I looked at her, when she said, "Oh my God, Travis. What happened?"

"It looks worse than it is, Gretchen. I'll explain later, but for now, can you look after Malden until I get back." Now with determination in my voice, I announced, "I have some unfinished business to attend to." She nodded, and walked over to him. I left the house more pissed off than I was earlier, but was relieved Malden would be well cared for now that he's with Gretchen.

I drove back to the store, and nothing but hateful images raced through my mind. I mean, who the hell would do something like this to another human being. My God, what kind of world do we live in?

I pulled into my parking spot at the store, entered the employee side entrance, made my way over to, and up the stairs to my manager's offices. I saw Mary pacing in her office, side to side, no doubt waiting for me to arrive. I reached the top of the stairs, and noticed Mary had stopped pacing, and was looking directly at me. I conceded to the moment, and decided, let's just get this over with. Why delay the inevitable.

I entered Mary's office without saying a word while she walked past me to close her office door, clearly upset. I leaned on the side of her desk with arms folded, and listened as she spoke.

"Are we done here now, Travis? My God, police, fire rescue, EMTs." Mary's voice was clearly agitated over this whole mess, and slightly shouting her words with conviction. She continued, "Bishop told me Malden got into a fight in the parking lot, and had to go to the hospital." She paused while she walked around her office in circles with one hand covering her forehead, and continued her rant. "Oh my God, Travis, if this gets back to the home office!" Mary with determination now shouted, "This young man doesn't belong here. He needs to be with his family, Travis!"

I listened to all she had to say, spoke up now, and shouted, "Don't you think I know this, Mary? Don't you think I know all that?" I paused for a moment, looked at her, and continued to shout, "You don't see what I see when I look into this child's eyes. I don't see a loving family out there looking for their missing child. I only see disappointment, sadness, and a whole bunch of nobody gives a crap about this kid!" I paused for a moment, and said, "Well, Mary, I will not abandon this child."

She stood there with arms folded, staring at me after my rant, and spoke in a much softer tone. "Look, Travis, I can understand if you've forged some bond with this child, and that's okay, but are you willing to throw away everything you've worked for your entire life over this kid? I'm looking at your entire career circling the drain right now." She paused a moment, leaned over to get my attention, and continued to say, "And by the way, in case you haven't noticed, Travis, you're taking me down with you!"

I stood from leaning on Mary's desk, looked at her, and explained, "Mary, I need you to find a way we can keep this child around here a little longer. I need more time to figure this all out."

Mary, in disbelief of what she heard, shook her head, and said, "Are you serious, Travis? Can you hear what you're saying?" She walked over to her office window, turned back to me, convinced now, and responded, "You're asking for the impossible, Travis, seriously."

I was back leaning against her desk, arms folded, and simply replied, "Nothing is impossible, Mary!"

She looked at me, chuckled some, and was dumbfounded by what I had implied. She turned to look out her office window, turned back around, and said, "All right, Travis, let's approach this from a different angle. Oh, better yet, let me paint you a picture." I listened while Mary's rant was filled with condescension over the whole situation.

She went into a mime-like scenario as she lifted an imaginary phone, and said, "Ring, ring." I stared at her improv now while she continued her imaginary phone conversation.

"Hello, Mrs. Corporate. Yes, this is Mary in HR from your North Carolina store. Well, thank you, I'm doing just fine. Listen, the reason I've called is this. I need permission to hire a young man, but here's the thing." She paused. "We're just not sure where he lives, nor do we know where he lived previously."

She again paused when asked an imaginary question from Mrs. Corporate. "No, we have no social security number, nor any previous workplace experience. No, no references for that matter either. Oh, and by the way." She paused again, and stared at me while she continued. "We're not entirely sure how old this young man is either. But leaning on the side, perhaps under the legal age to work here, so we'll need you to arrange a rewrite of the child labor laws for the State of North Carolina. Just in case, so we can accommodate this young boy."

"Oh wonderful, that's awfully generous of you. Thank you so much," and added, "Click!" while she mimed hanging up the imaginary phone. I finished listening to her fictitious conversation when she looked at me, and said, "Oh, and if you didn't hear that last part before I hung up, Travis, yeah, that was corporate wishing me much success in my future endeavors outside our company." She looked at me, nodded, and said, "Do you get it now, Travis?"

I stood, turned to her, and said, "Look, Mary, you are one of my oldest and dearest friends. I trust no one more, outside of my wife, and know in my heart if anyone can make this happen, it would be you."

She looked at me again, shook her head, and simply said, "I can't do that, Travis."

I spoke adamantly to her. "Yes you can, Mary."

She repeated, "No, I can't."

I again said with determination now, "Yes, Mary, you can!"

She ended this, you can, and you can't, conversation, stood there, shook her head, and stared at me. I finished my talk with, "I know you, Mary, and you can make this happen because you are the best."

I turned to walk away when she spoke up, and exclaimed, "You know, Travis, those words mean nothing to me anymore."

I stopped after I heard that, turned around almost out of her office, and asked, "What means nothing, Mary?"

She stood there with arms folded, and said, "You say that to everyone, Travis. I hear you all the time say to other people, you are the best. It has no more meaning to me."

I paused for a moment, and considered what she just said, looked at the frame of the doorway to her office, turned to her, and stated, "That's true, but what you don't know," while I paused, and explained, "I only mean it, when I say it to you."

She stared at me, shook her head one more time, and said, "Just go."

I was still reeling with anger in my mind against the individuals who had hurt Malden when I entered Bishop's office. He could see the look I projected, a face of determination that clearly said, don't cross this man's path without a damn good reason.

He greeted me with his usual, "Hi Boss," as he continued to say, "I took the liberty to make a copy of the video we found earlier of the incident out in the parking lot. I burned a DVD for the Police to look into, but not sure they will be of any help though, Boss. My original estimation of the distance from the main camera was pretty spot on. You really can't make out who the kids are that hurt Malden."

"I want you to bring up the video feed, so I can look for myself."

"Are you sure, Boss? It's really hard to watch."

I stopped my forward motion toward the video camera system, turned to him, and said with an angry tone, he's never heard before, "Just show me the damn video feed, Bishop!"

He was taken back by the stern request, and responded, "Yes, sir." He walked over to the CCTV system, and brought up the video feed while I watched three teenagers approach Malden in the parking lot. I saw no indication whatsoever that Malden initiated this in any way. It had just looked like these three individuals wanted to inflict pain on whoever they ran into. My anger grew while I watched these three boys kick, and punch Malden, mercilessly.

"Okay, Bishop, I've seen enough."

I stood away from the monitor thinking about what I just saw when Bishop swung his chair around toward me, and said, "You know, Boss, maybe this means something, or maybe it doesn't," but he waited for me to respond.

I stopped thinking for a moment, looked at him, and said, "Just spit it out, Bishop."

"Well, Boss, yesterday when Malden worked in my department, while I checked in on him occasionally, he came to me at one point, and said he thought some kids were in the store trying to steal stuff. But when he brought me over to where he saw those kids, they were gone, so I thought no more of it. I wonder, Boss, if those are the kids who beat up Malden."

I looked at him, and firmly said, "I want you to scan the video of your department for yesterday, and look for those three teenage boys. Scan the whole damn store if you have to, Bishop. I want those individuals to be accountable for what they did to Malden. Are we clear on this?"

"Yes, Boss. I'll get on it right away."

As I left his office, I realized how I had treated him. I knew none of this was his fault, and turned around to address him. I called out his name now while he was reviewing video feed, heard me, and swung around to acknowledge. I looked at him, and said, "Thanks for all your help on all this stuff, but do me another favor will you?"

"Sure, Boss."

I demanded now, "Don't ever call me, sir." I smiled, and watched him smile back as I turned to head out of his office.

I was hell-bent on finding those kids, and wanted to hang them up by their buster browns if ever given the chance, but wanted to get home to check on Malden. I started my descent down the stairs when Mary popped out of her office, and called out, "You missed your weekly store manager's conference call, Travis."

I heard that, stopped on the stairs, turned to her, shook my head, and said, "Crap, crap, crap." I said to myself now, how much more crap can get piled onto this day?

She looked at me, and explained, "Don't worry about it, Travis. I covered you in the meeting."

I dropped my shoulders while I listened to her, and said, "I don't know what I would do without you, Mary." She smiled, and headed back into her office. I resumed heading down the stairs, and could hardly wait to get home to make sure Malden was all right.

I arrived home finally, and parked my car in the driveway, so I could enter through the front door. As I walked in, I could see Malden in the sitting area while he stared at his book closed, and fumbling the pages with his fingers. I shut the front door, dropped my briefcase, walked over to him, and asked, "You okay, buddy?" No response from him when I noticed Gretchen standing at the kitchen entranceway while she stared over at us. I looked at her, and asked, "Everything all right, Gretchen?"

She looked at me now, and declared, "Oh, everything is just fine, Travis," with a sarcastic underlying tone in her voice. "Young Malden there has developed an inherent male attitude typical in most male species."

"What do you mean by that?"

"I mean, Travis, he's been stubborn all afternoon, wanted nothing more than to sit there, and wait for *you* to come home."

"Oh, I see," while I thought, and was relieved that something else might be wrong.

I no sooner finished my talk with Gretchen when Malden looked up at me, and said, "I'm sorry, Mr. Scott. I didn't mean to make those boys mad at me."

I turned to him, saw that look of disappointment in his eyes, and lowered myself down in a baseball catcher's stance, so I could talk eye to eye with him. I put my hands on his knees while he looked down at his book, fumbling the pages, and said, "Hey, Malden, look at me." He looked up at me while I spoke. "You know what? You did nothing wrong! I watched a video of what happened today, and can only say there are some bad people in this world who just don't care about anything. I know you didn't do a darn thing wrong!"

He looked down again at the book in his hands. I spoke again. "Hey, Malden, look at me." He stared back at me while I continued to say, "We're buddies, right? You're my buddy, and I'm your buddy. Can we agree on that, Malden?"

He responded, "Yes, sir."

I continued, "Okay, so what we need to do is come up with a code word we both agree on, so if there's ever any trouble one of the buddies can say the code word, so the other one can help him. Do you follow me so far, Malden?" He looked at me, and nodded. "Excellent, so now we both agree, we're buddies, and just need to come up with a code word."

I looked down at the book Malden stared at, and said, "All right, how about we use," as I turned my head, and leaned sideways so I could read the title of the book in Malden's hands that read, *LIKE A WITCH'S BREW*. I thought not quite one word, but that's okay. "So, Malden, our code word will be *LIKE A WITCH'S BREW*. There, we have it now."

"So Malden, look at me. If I ever get into trouble, I'll say the code word *LIKE A WITCH'S BREW* so you'll know, because you're my buddy, that I was in trouble. And if you say the same I'll know you were in trouble, so I can help you. Do you understand, Malden?"

He looked up at me, and said, "Yes, sir."

I looked over to Gretchen while she stood there in the entrance way to the kitchen, watching me work my magic with Malden, and saw her all choked up over the whole code word conversation. She wiped her eyes, and said, "Come on guys, dinner is getting cold."

I stood, looked down at him, and said, "Let's have dinner. You don't want to piss off Gretchen." I smiled for both of us while we both walked toward the kitchen.

CHAPTER 7

It was the next morning after breakfast. I was in the kitchen cleaning the dishes after I made sure Malden was okay. He was content just reading his book in the great room, in his favorite chair by the front door. I could tell Gretchen wanted to start a conversation with me, guessed it was about Malden, and how hard we've fought to make things right for this young man. I knew deep down in my heart we needed help in trying to resolve this matter.

I looked at her while I dried my hands, and already knew what she'd been thinking, and didn't need it to be said. I realized this was born out of the many years of being with the one you love. You just know at times what the other person is thinking, and need not say a word. I looked into her eyes, and declared, "Way ahead of you, Gretchen."

I finished what I was doing, and was walking out of the kitchen when she asked, "Where are you going, Travis?"

I turned around, and said, "I'm going to make a phone call." I headed into my study, and closed both entrance doors to the room, so I could have some privacy during my call.

Monday morning had come quickly. Malden was positioned in the same place he always was, and waited for me to announce we were off to work. Gretchen walked me out to the great room, was visibly nervous of what might happen today, and looked to me, for support. I looked back at her, and said, "You know, you're welcome to come with us."

She replied, "I can't do that, Travis."

I looked at her, and affirmed, "I know, honey. Don't worry, nothing bad will happen today, I promise." I kissed my wife goodbye, turned to Malden, and said, "You all set, buddy?"

He turned to me, got up from his seat, stowed his book away, and said, "Yes, sir."

I opened the front door to let him exit. I looked back to Gretchen, and said, "I'll see you later, all right?"

She nervously replied, "I'll see you both, right, Travis?"

I questioned for a moment that maybe this was the day Malden might not be coming home with me after all, but couldn't bear to see her cry again, so I just blurted out, "Absolutely, honey." I left the house, and closed the door behind me, while I looked out to see Malden waiting for me by the passenger door of the car.

I was distraught over what I was about to do, but realized, as Gretchen did, this needed to be done. Okay, Travis, let's think positive thoughts here. I walked to my car, and announced, "All right, Malden, let's get this show on the road."

As we drove I began to realize how emotionally attached I'd gotten to this young man I just met, and barely knew. I dismissed the thought, and continued to drive. Malden and I finally arrived at our destination, the main police station in town, and drove around the lot to look for a parking space.

Malden looked up at the Police Department sign as I pulled into a parking space, put the car into park, and nervously said, "*LIKE A WITCH'S BREW*, Mr. Scott."

I looked in his direction, and responded, "No, no, Malden, no one is in trouble here." He continued to stare at the sign when I said, "Look at me, Malden." He turned to me while I spoke, and repeated, "No one is in trouble here. We talked about this yesterday. Gretchen and I want to better understand some things, and need a little help, okay, Malden." I continued to look into his eyes, and added, "That's all this is, I promise."

He replied, "Yes, sir," and looked away. I could see the unknown in the young man's eyes, but knew this had to be done.

I turned the car off as we both exited the vehicle to make our way to the front entrance of the police station. I held the door open for Malden as we entered, and headed over to the dispatch officer who looked at us while we approached him. "Morning, Officer, my name is Travis Scott, and I have an appointment with a Detective Cody."

The officer responded, "All right, Mr. Scott, have a seat over there, and I'll let the detective know you're here." I thanked the officer, and walked to the waiting area with Malden.

Several minutes had passed when an officer came out from the back of the precinct, and announced, "I'll take you to see Detective Cody, sir." Malden and I got up, and walked through the doors to the main squad room that was all a buzz from many people working the room. I looked around, and hadn't expected such a large group of officers here.

A man approached us, and introduced himself as Detective Cody.

I responded, "It's a pleasure to meet you," and shook his hand.

Detective Cody looked down to Malden, and said, "You must be, Malden."

He looked up at the detective, and acknowledged, "Yes, sir."

Detective Cody suggested to me now, "I thought we might talk first, so let's have young Malden here have a seat over at that bench until we're done. My desk is just over here, Mr. Scott."

I guided Malden over to the bench, and said, "I'll be right over there talking with the detective." He acknowledged, sat down, and took out his book to read.

I walked to Detective Cody's desk, and had a seat. The detective started the conversation with, "That was quite a story you told me on the phone the other day, Mr. Scott. I've got to say, this is a first for me. I didn't quite expect, however, what walked into my squad room when you arrived."

I was perplexed after hearing that, and responded, "What do you mean by that, detective?"

"Well, you never mentioned the young man was black, and when you said you were bringing in a sixteen-year-old child, that's what I expected. This young man looks nothing north of thirteen years old."

I looked at the detective, and responded, "Wait, a second, what does Malden's skin color have anything to do with this?"

The detective looked back at me, and simply said, "It doesn't, Mr. Scott. I think it best at this point I take Malden out back to one of our conference rooms to have a chat."

I implied, "You mean an interrogation room."

The detective responded, "No, Mr. Scott, a conference room. You can wait here until I'm through, so we can have a followup conversation."

The detective and I got up from our seats, and walked over to Malden. I leaned over, and said, "Malden, I want you to go with Detective Cody, he just wants to talk to you. I'll be right over there at his desk waiting for you when you're done." He stared at me the whole time, and fumbled his book in his hands. He got up a little reluctant, but followed my direction, and walked away with Detective Cody, and exited the squad room.

I made my way back to Detective Cody's desk, and sat back down. I felt a bit weird like some emotion of guilt that started to take over my mind. I dismissed that, and questioned who wouldn't feel like this sitting in a police station. I mean, it's natural to feel like that, right? I surmised there had probably been murderers and rapists who sat in this very chair. Plus the fact, my initial conversation with Detective Cody made me feel a little like I was the one on trial here for some heinous crime.

That uneasy feeling continued, and wished Gretchen had been here to keep me focused on the main reason that brought Malden and me to this place. I just felt like everyone in the room was staring at me. I wondered now, are there that many criminals in this town that necessitate such a large police force? I questioned myself for a moment. Do I live in another world, and just don't see what goes on around me?

I sat there for what seemed like hours, but only twenty minutes had passed when I saw the detective, and Malden reenter the squad room. I stood as they made their way toward me, and watched Detective Cody motion to a uniformed female police officer who acknowledged him. The officer approached us all standing at the detective's desk. Detective Cody looked down to Malden, and suggested, "So, Malden, how would you like to take a tour of our booking area with Officer Gates here?"

Detective Cody looked to Officer Gates, and asked, "Can you show Malden here where all the bad guys we catch get booked, show how we fingerprint, and take their picture?" Detective Cody looked back to Malden, and asked again, "Is that something you might like to do?"

Malden looked at me as if he wanted my approval while I added, "That sounds like fun,

Malden. Why don't you go with Officer Gates, and I'll be right here when you get back."

He continued to look at me, and responded, "Yes, sir."

Officer Gates turned to Malden, and said, "Come on, Malden, I'll show you where the booking room is." I watched as he walked away with the officer, and exit the squad room.

Detective Cody and I sat down at that point. I was anxious about whether the detective could shed any light on this whole situation after his talk with Malden. "Well, Mr. Scott, I had a nice little chat with Malden." The detective paused a moment, and said, "But I still can't figure something out that's bugged me this whole time since we spoke on the phone."

I looked at him, and asked, "What would that be, detective?"

He responded, "I've been doing this job for a long time, and can read just about any situation thrown at me, but this one thing," while he paused again, and said, "I just can't get past." I now felt more uncomfortable with the detective after he spoke, but continued to listen.

He went on to say, "Given the same set of circumstances, and assuming what you've told me is true, most people would've called the police that evening." The detective paused for a moment, and said, "But you didn't." He paused yet again as he leaned back in his chair, stared at me while he interlocked his hands and fingers together across his stomach, and asked, "Can you explain that, Mr. Scott?"

I continued to stare back at him. I thought about the question posed to me, kind of shrugged my shoulders while I looked away for a moment, and tried to answer his question.

I replied, "I don't know, detective. I guess maybe you had to have been there. I've asked myself that question a bunch of times. I mean, you didn't see what I did that night. I just don't know. Maybe it was my Christian upbringing that kicked in when I saw another human being who needed help, a child no less, so I helped him. That's what you're supposed to do, right, detective?"

Detective Cody, after listening to me, leaned forward, and said, "So, Mr. Scott, you want me to believe that you're some sort of patron saint of everything that's right." He paused again, and repeated, "Is that what you want me to believe, Mr. Scott?"

After I listened to the detective's comments, I decided he had crossed that line, and now had pissed me off. I thought that's it, done listening to this crap. I got up from my seat, extended my arm, pointed my finger in the detective's direction, and shouted angrily, "Screw you, detective! Let me tell YOU something. God forbid one of your kids finds themselves lost out there in this unforgiving world. I can guarantee this, detective. While you're on your hands and knees, you'll pray to God for someone like me that finds your child, who keeps them safe and protected, instead of some freakin' pervert out there."

All was quiet now in the squad room while everyone stared at me after my outburst. The detective got up slowly from his seat, looked straight at me, and said, "Have a seat, Mr. Scott," while he paused, and added, "Please." I was still visibly pissed off, but composed myself, complied with the detective's request, and sat back down.

The detective continued to observe me, apologized, and said, "Look, Mr. Scott, I don't know you from Adam, and needed to confirm to myself, you are who you say you are. I believe what you've told me, Mr. Scott." I looked at Detective Cody while he shook his head, and murmured the words, "Strange, strange, and strange."

I spoke up, and said, "Yeah, well, welcome to my world, detective. This hasn't been easy for me either. I'm this close." I showed the space between two fingers to the detective, and said, "To losing my job. Not to mention a dear close friend of mine wants to kick my ass over all this crap."

He smiled at me after he listened to my comments, and stated, "Well, Mr. Scott, children just don't fall out of the sky. We'll find where his family is. In the meantime, young Malden didn't want to share much of anything when I spoke with him, but I did find out one thing though."

Those words sparked significant interest in me as I listened to the detective. I looked over at him, and anxiously asked, "What's that, detective?"

He responded, "I found out he's very fond of you and your wife, Mr. Scott." He paused, and said, "For that reason alone, I'm willing to release the young man back to you, as sort of temporary custody, for now, if that's what you want."

I looked at the detective like the weight of the entire world had been lifted from my shoulders, and confirmed, "Of course. I don't want to see the young man end up in foster care, or some halfway home. I'm fine with taking care of him until we can find his family."

"All right then, Mr. Scott, let me explain to you how this works. My department will search our database with Malden's fingerprints to see if he shows up in the system anywhere, and circulate his photo around as well. I'm sure we'll have something concrete in a short amount of time.

"One other thing, Mr. Scott, we'll need to open up a missing child case with the DCS here in North Carolina, which is standard, until we can locate the young man's family. They have ultimate authority over the child until this is resolved. They'll be contacting you, most likely visit you at your home to meet with you and your wife, and talk with Malden. Do you have any questions, Mr. Scott?"

I answered, "None at the moment, detective." The detective and I stood as we concluded this matter for now, and saw Malden walking in our direction with Officer Gates. I looked at him, smiled, and knew just by his facial expression what he wanted to hear. "You all set to go home, Malden?"

He looked up at me, not exactly smiling, and responded, "Yes, sir."

I thanked Detective Cody, and Officer Gates as we both left the squad room.

I looked down at Malden, and announced, "Let's get the hell out of here."

I reflected on the past few hours while I drove Malden back home, and wondered again why I was chosen for some unknown reason to help this young man out of his unfortunate circumstances. I looked over at him sitting next to me reading his book. I felt like it was okay it was me, and guessed maybe some things in life just don't need to be explained.

I pulled into my driveway, parked the car, turned to him, and said, "Let's find Gretchen, and let her know what's going on." He turned to me with a look of approval, but didn't say a word.

I entered the front entrance to my home with Malden in tow, and saw Gretchen waiting to see if I had returned home alone. I saw the expression on her face turn from concerned to happy when she saw Malden come out from behind me as we entered the room. I looked at her, and confirmed, "Yes, he's here with me."

She looked relieved, and said, "Well, all right then." She enquired further, "How did it go, Travis?"

I looked at Malden, and proposed, "Hey, buddy, why don't you go into the den, and watch

TV, or just read your book if you like, so I can talk with Gretchen."

He looked up at me, and responded, "Yes, sir."

He walked past Gretchen while she announced, "It's good to see you, Malden."

He paused, turned to her, said, "Yes, ma'am," and turned to walk down the hall to the den.

Gretchen and I sat in the great room while I brought my wife up to speed on what transpired at the police station, and the meeting with Detective Cody. I could tell she was a little miffed over the way Detective Cody handled all of this with me, but knew she was relieved by the end result with Malden coming back home until they could locate his family. I exclaimed, "Look, Gretchen, I have to get to the store. Are you okay with Malden for the next few days until I can figure out what to do with him?"

She looked at me, and explained, "I've got that covered, honey. I already called the urgent care facility, they scheduled an appointment for this Thursday to have me bring Malden in to remove his stitches, and do a follow-up exam. I had also hoped for some alone time with him this week to maybe coax him into telling me something, or anything about himself, or his family. So, to answer your question, Travis, yes, and you should go now, so you can see if you even have a job waiting for you at the store."

I looked at her, and confessed, "Well, I guess I worried about how Malden would spend his time for nothing." I smiled at her as we both got up. I kissed my wife goodbye, walked away, but stopped, turned, and hesitated for a moment.

"What is it, Travis?"

"I don't know, Gretchen. I just feel like I should have Malden with me when I go to work."

"I'll explain to Malden he needs to be here this week to rest up, and heal before we let him back into the world."

I smiled, said, "Thanks, honey," and left the house to go to work, I hoped.

I arrived at the store, and all looked normal. I parked my car, and entered the employee store entrance, all the while feeling a bit apprehensive. I thought, well, so far, so good. I see no, 'You got no job anymore' police waiting to escort me out of the building. I smiled, and decided that was funny. I made my way into the store, greeted a few of my staff, and eventually made my way up the stairs to my office.

I walked past Mary's office, saw her busy at work, and knocked on her door. "You got a minute, Mary?"

She looked up from her desk, and responded, "Sure, Travis, come on in." I entered her office, set my briefcase down, and had a seat. She looked at me now, and said, "Please don't ask if I've come up with a plan yet to bring Malden back to the store."

I looked back at her, and affirmed, "No, Mary, I understand that will take some time, and a small miracle, I'm guessing. I won't bug you about any of that, and will wait since I know you'll approach me if you have anything new to add to the situation."

"Well, thank you, Travis. So how is Malden doing? I was so upset last week over what happened I never asked how he was."

"He's doing fine, Mary. I just wanted to let you know I met with the police this morning." I brought her up to speed on what transpired, and explained, "Gretchen is looking after Malden this week to make sure he's okay, and heals up."

Mary thanked me for keeping her in the loop, and said, "I'll try to be more tolerant of this whole matter involving young Malden."

I got up, and concluded, "Thanks, Mary. I appreciate what you do."

As I was leaving her office, she interrupted my departure, and said, "Hey Travis," while she leaned back in her office chair.

I turned, and acknowledged, "Yes, Mary."

She explained how she pitched an idea to corporate that might allow Malden to be back here at the store, but wouldn't give any details right now. She further commented, "It's a long shot, and just as soon save myself from the embarrassing details of the request, and leave it at that for now."

I looked at her, smiled, and said, "All right, I respect that," and added as I turned to walk out of her office, "You truly are the best." She chuckled, and resumed what she was doing work-wise.

***

I made my way to my office, set my briefcase down, and sat at my desk. I thought, finally some normalcy. I turned to stare out my office window, and saw two lot attendants working the parking lot. My mind shifted to thoughts of Malden, and that place in the woods I found him living a few weeks ago.

As I mulled that over for a moment, I realized I found this young man who had absolutely nothing. I mean, literally, just the clothes on his back, struggling to live from day to day. Living outside in the woods, and most likely, scavenging for food from the dumpsters in the back of the building.

I thought about myself now, what it was like growing up with two loving parents and a roof over my head every single night when I went to bed. I realized how blessed I was to have excelled, and achieved the things in life, I now enjoy. I recalled my earlier thought of normalcy, and said to myself, "Shame on you, Travis."

My thinking was interrupted when I heard a knock on my door, and turned to see Bishop standing in my doorway while he held something in his hand. "Hi, Boss, do you have a minute?"

"Sure, Bishop, what's up?"

"Well, Boss, I did what you told me last week, and I'm pretty sure I found those boys responsible for that whoop ass on Malden. I burned a DVD for the police on Friday afternoon, and called them, but they never showed up before I left for the day."

I replied, "Figures."

He continued, and stated, "The police showed up this morning, so I gave them the DVD, and they said they would get back to us if they find out anything."

I looked at him, got up from my desk, and announced, "Let's have a look at what you found," as I walked toward him.

He stopped me holding a DVD in his hand, and explained, "I burned an extra copy, Boss. You can look at it right on your office PC."

I stopped, gave way to him, motioned to my desk, and said, "Have at it." He sat at my desk, and loaded the DVD into the drive while I leaned over to watch what he was doing. The video started, and I could see the three teenage boys in his department.

Bishop spoke up, and confirmed, "This has to be them, Boss. I mean, we can't see Malden, but look at their reaction as they stared at something down the aisle. That must have been Malden who looked at them." Bishop and I continued to watch the video as all three boys walked away now.

"Good work, Bishop. I agree they look like the same three kids from the parking lot video I watched last week. Well, let's see what the police can come up with for now."

Bishop got up from my seat, and said, "Let me know if you need anything else, Boss."

"Thanks again, Bishop. I appreciate all you've done." I watched him leave my office, and sat back down to focus on my work.

***

Several days had passed while I felt like I recouped some of the lost time from the past few weeks. I was happy Malden had healed nicely while he spent time with Gretchen at home. I was still sad in some respect, not able to spend much time with him, but knew I couldn't risk having him at the store without some legitimate and proper means to allow it.

It's midday, and wondered why I hadn't heard from Gretchen, who said she would call after Malden's doctor's appointment to have his stitches removed. I said to myself, well, let's stay focused here, and maybe, just maybe by the end of the day, I can say I was caught up.

Meanwhile back at home, Gretchen had just pulled into the driveway with Malden after his doctor's appointment. All went well, stitches removed, and you could hardly notice he had any, to begin with. Both got settled in the house while Gretchen noticed him head for the den, and surmised what he was about to do.

She walked past the den entrance, looked in, and said, yep, there he is, sitting quietly just reading his book. She headed into the kitchen, thought back to when her children were around Malden's age, and can't ever remember either one in the den reading a book. She figured the only reason our kids were ever in there was to watch TV. It dawned on her now, all this time Malden had been here, she can't recall one time seeing him watch TV. She put her bags on the kitchen island, walked out of the kitchen, and made her way into the den.

She walked over to the sofa, and sat next to Malden, still staring at his book, reading away. She started a conversation, and said, "You know, Malden, when I was a little girl about your age, and something was bothering me. I would find my mom and sit down like we are now so I could talk to her about what it was." She stared at him while he read as she spoke, and could tell he had listened to her conversation by the way he just held the book.

She continued, "I'm not sure why, Malden, but it didn't matter what the problem was, or even what it was all about. It was just, I guess, my mom being there, who listened to what I had to say that made me feel better. Do you understand what I mean, Malden?"

He looked up, and away from his book in his hands after he listened to what she just said. He spoke after a moment or two in a soft voice, "My mother died a long time ago."

"Oh, Malden, I'm so sorry." He didn't respond, and just continued to stare straight ahead while she placed both hands on his knee, trying not to shed any tears after she heard that.

He looked at her, and asked, "May I go into the other room, ma'am?" She saw the sadness in his eyes as he stared back at her that was heartbreaking.

She continued to stare at the young man, and responded, "Of course you can, Malden," while she removed her hands from the young child's knee. He got up, and walked away while she straightened out some magazines in front of her on the coffee table. He stopped just before he left the room, and stood there with his back to her, while she sat on the sofa. Gretchen looked up, stopped what she was doing, and asked, "What is it, Malden?"

He just stood there, but didn't say anything. After a moment he spoke. "You remind me of her, ma'am." After she heard that, she knew he had referred to his mother, but couldn't find the words to respond. He said nothing else, and walked out of the room. Gretchen wiped her eyes, and sat there thinking about what just happened when she was startled by the phone.

She got up, made her way to the kitchen, and answered it. She finished her conversation, and turned to walk out of the kitchen when the phone rang again. She turned around, and answered the call. "Hello? Hi, Ash, how are you doing, honey?" Our youngest daughter was on the other line, which was surprising since Gretchen usually initiated the calls ninety-nine percent of the time to either of our children.

She sat at the kitchen island now while she talked, and listened, catching up on everything going on in our youngest daughter's life. She finished the call after some time had passed, and remembered she was supposed to call me after Malden's appointment. She blurted out, "Crap, Travis will be pissed."

She quickly called my work number. I answered, and heard her say, "I'm so sorry, Travis, this call is so late. I've been straight out all day."

I replied, "That's okay, honey. I wondered why you hadn't called, but have been busy myself, and figured you would call when you had the time. So how is, Malden, doing?"

"He's doing fine. The doctor removed the stitches, and you can hardly tell he had any."

"Awesome, honey, that's good to hear."

She added, "The doctor gave him a thorough physical, and said everything seemed normal for a boy his age."

"Even better news, Gretchen."

"Well, I do have some bad news to tell you. You want to wait until you get home?"

"*No!* I would prefer you told me now."

"Okay, well I sat down with Malden earlier to see if he would talk with me."

She paused while I responded, "And?"

"Malden told me his mother passed away some time ago."

After hearing that, I sadly responded, "Ah, geez, Gretchen."

"I know, Travis, it broke my heart when he told me."

"Did he talk to you about anything else?"

"No, that was all he told me. I mean, you should have seen the sadness in his eyes. I'm about ready to cry now just thinking about it."

"Hang in there. I'll be wrapped up here soon, and we can talk when I get home."

"Wait, Travis, there's more. I got a call from the Department of Children Services, and they're sending a caseworker over to the house tomorrow around ten a.m. You have to be here, so please make sure your schedule at work will allow it."

"All right, Gretchen, I hear you, and will make sure I'm there. Is there anything else?"

"Well, this could probably wait, but I talked with Ash this afternoon."

"Is everything okay?"

"Yes, but I told her about Malden. You know as well as I do that over-protective, over-the-top personality kicked in, so she's concerned for us."

I curiously responded, "How so?"

"Ash is afraid we'll be tomorrow's front page news, and be the victims of a mass murder at the hands of young Malden."

I laughed after I heard that, and announced, "Typical Ashley, my God." I remembered back when the kids were younger, and in particular Ashley. I can't figure out where she developed that type of personality. My oldest daughter Ava didn't act like that. I speculated now, someone could light a match in a room, and Ash would look at that as a four-alarm fire.

I turned my attention back to Gretchen on the phone, and added, "Well, you just made my day, honey. I needed a good laugh. Well, let me finish up here, so I can redo my schedule for tomorrow."

"All right, Travis, I'll keep dinner on hold until you get home, so we can all sit down together."

"Okay, love you."

"Love you back, Travis."

The following morning Gretchen and I sat, and enjoyed our breakfast with Malden. Gretchen asked me, "So, Travis, how were things at the store this week, any fallout from the events of last week?"

I looked at Malden eating his cereal quietly, turned to my wife, and answered, "No, everything seemed like business as usual. I was nervous at first that perhaps the thing that happened last week would bite me in the ass with corporate. I won't lie to you, Gretchen, I walked around most of the week on eggshells just waiting for someone to approach me, and say it was nice working with you, Travis. But, Mary would have told me if there had been a problem."

She looked over at Malden, and replied, "Thank God."

I turned my attention back to Malden who sat across from me, and said, "So, Malden, your lip looks okay. I can hardly tell you had any stitches. Not much of a battle scar, however."

He looked up, and replied, "Yes, sir." I chuckled and smiled, thought to myself, you just have to love the respect this kid has toward adults.

Gretchen spoke up now. "So, Malden, it'll be all about you this morning, right?" She had taken Malden aside last night to explain to him what was going on this morning, and a person would be here to have a chat with him. Malden being Malden didn't react to that any different than anything else she had observed in the short time she has known this young man. She added, "So, Malden, maybe later you can help me with some errands I need to get done."

He looked up at her, and answered, "Yes, ma'am."

I finished my breakfast, turned to Gretchen, and stated, "I need to get some work done before the DCS person shows up, so I'll be in my study. Just let me know when he or she arrives."

"All right, Travis. I know this meeting is taking precious time away from your work at the store, so I'll do the dishes so you can get right to it."

I stood, and said, "Thanks, Gretchen, I appreciate it." I have a strict rule in my household I've had since the first time I met her. The rule was pretty basic with no gray area. Gretchen did the cooking, and I do the dishes. It's as simple as that.

I was busy at work in my study when I heard the doorbell, and looked at my watch and saw it was 10:00 am, give or take a minute or two. I got up while Gretchen answered the door. She greeted the woman, who introduced herself as Aiesha from the Department of Children Services. She let the social worker in while Aiesha exclaimed, "What a beautiful home you have, Mrs. Scott."

She replied, "Well, thank you, we enjoy it very much." I walked past the den entrance, and saw

Malden sitting on the sofa reading his book when I entered the great room while Gretchen handled the introduction. "Travis, this is Aiesha from DCS."

Aiesha and I exchanged greetings.

Gretchen addressed Aiesha now. "Malden is in the den, but we thought you would have more privacy using my husband's study."

She responded, "That would be fine, Mrs. Scott."

Gretchen led the way to the den where Malden was, and introduced Aiesha to him when we all entered the room.

Gretchen announced, "So, Malden, why don't you, and Aiesha, head into the study. Travis and I will wait for you here."

He got up, stowed away his book, and answered, "Yes, ma'am."

He walked out of the den while I looked to Aiesha, and said, "He's showing you the way." I followed Aiesha and Malden into my study, and told Aiesha she was welcome to sit at my desk, or the computer desk, or on the leather sofa. I stopped my dissertation, and conceded, "You're welcome to sit wherever you like, Aiesha. I'll be with Gretchen in the other room."

"Thank you, Mr. Scott." I left my study and closed both entrance doors so Aiesha and Malden could have some privacy.

I joined Gretchen in the den while we started the waiting game for this to be over. Gretchen and I tried to make the best of our time together under the circumstances, but waiting seemed to be the hardest thing we needed to deal with. At one point while I sat next to her, I turned, and said, "How you doin'?" to imply I spoke with a New Jersey accent.

She responded the same way, and answered, "No, how you doin'?" We looked at each other, realized this took all of five seconds off the clock, and left it at that. We both waited and waited, and even waited some more. Gretchen looked up from the sofa at one point, and announced, "Travis, please, you're going to wear out the carpet if you keep pacing like that, plus it's starting to annoy me."

I ignored her comment, looked at my watch, and said with some aggravation in my voice, "Three freakin' hours, Gretchen," and repeated, "Three hours. I mean, what the hell? I can't have a two-minute conversation with this kid, and she's been in there for three hours, my Lord!"

She responded, "Please, Travis, just read a magazine or something," but just as she finished her sentence, we both heard one of the study doors open as Aiesha was headed our way toward the den.

Aiesha sat down in one of the recliners while I joined Gretchen on the sofa when she said, "I asked Malden to give us some privacy, so we could talk. He's reading a book in the other room."

Gretchen looked at Aiesha, and commented, "Wow, you were with Malden for a long time."

Gretchen and I stared intently at Aiesha at that point, and awaited a response to hear what she had to say. Aiesha spoke, and explained, "Well, I had a nice talk with the young man, and frankly," as she paused for a short bit, and finally conceded, "Who am I kidding? I got nothing from that child."

Gretchen and I looked at each other as I got up from the sofa, and said in an agitated voice, "Three hours? I waited three hours, Aiesha, for I got nothing, my Lord!" I paced again with one hand covering my forehead, and asserted, "I'm thinking this kid, *did* just fall out of the sky."

Gretchen, stared at me, and said, "Travis, please," looked at Aiesha, and asked, "What do you mean, Aiesha?"

Aiesha continued to stare at me, and spoke. "I'm sorry, Mr. Scott. I understand your frustration," and added, "Look, if Malden is the cause of some stress within your family, we have facilities we could place him in until we can find his family."

I stopped my pacing, looked at her, and answered defiantly, "No, Aiesha, that's not why I'm upset." I further stated, "Malden is welcome in my home for as long as it takes. I'm upset over the fact, with all the resources we should have at our disposal, no one can tell us a damn thing about this child, or where he came from, geez!"

"Look, Mr. Scott, I have a Ph.D. in behavioral psychology, and I've never met a person in such a regressed state of mind. This child is so closed off from the world. I don't get the sense he has any psychological issues. Quite the contrary, he appears to have a high level of consciousness.

I'm just not sure what he's been through. It's different with children at this age, if we compare the same with an adult, children will compensate for some trauma, or tragedy in a much different way. I just have no answers for you, Mr. Scott." She continued to say, "I threw everything but the kitchen sink at this young man, and couldn't breach that barrier he's put up."

Gretchen interrupted her, and asked, "What about his mother who passed away, Aiesha?"

She looked at her, and answered, "Mrs. Scott, honestly, I'm shocked Malden even shared that bit of information with you."

Gretchen stared up at me while I laughed now, and said, "Wow." I added, "I'm glad we're not paying you by the hour, Aiesha."

Gretchen, again said, "Travis, please," while she addressed Aiesha, "So where do we go from here?"

She explained, "We're in close contact with the police, specifically the detective who met with your husband and Malden, but nothing has been determined yet."

I interjected my two cents, "I don't think anyone has tried hard enough."

Aisha responded, "Mr. Scott, Malden's fingerprints didn't show up anywhere in the system, and they've cross-checked missing persons nationally. They even checked to see if, for some unfortunate reason, maybe a set of parents died unexpectedly somewhere, and somehow a child got missed, but still nothing."

I looked at Gretchen, and said, "Ashley will be happy to hear Malden isn't a mass murderer." She looked back at me, and dropped her shoulders to let me know she was not happy with my comment.

Aiesha weighed in again, and said, "Look, we'll continue to pursue this as aggressively as we can, I'll make sure I stay in contact with you folks, and get you regular updates."

Gretchen stood, and responded, "Well, thank you, Aiesha. We appreciate any help you can give." She added, "Please don't misunderstand my husband. We both want what's best for Malden."

"I know that, Mrs. Scott."

Aiesha was shown out by Gretchen while I gathered work from my study, and spoke to Malden, "Hey, buddy, I have to go to work, but will be back later on if you want to talk about any of this." He didn't respond, and continued to sit on the leather couch reading his book.

I figured he was probably not happy with not accompanying me to the store, but had to dismiss that thought. I walked out to the great room where Gretchen was, and announced, "I need to get to the store, honey."

She looked at me, knew all of this was torture on my OCD type of personality, and said, "All right, Travis, I have errands to run, and will make sure Malden is occupied."

"Thanks, Gretchen, love you."

"Love you, too, Travis."

CHAPTER 8

I was still aggravated over the wasted morning I just endured as I pulled into the supercenter parking lot, and realized how frustrated I was over all of this. I parked my car, walked into the store trying to level my emotions, and decided maybe this was all just a byproduct of my OCD nature. I had a conversation with myself, and said, come on, Travis, you should be happy. How devastated would you be if you found out something horrible was associated with Malden. I rationalized that, and determined I've got to rid myself of this OCD crap.

I did a walkthrough of the store to get my mind off the unknown associated with Malden, and all the wonderful people who've tried so hard to help us find his family. Yeah, right. I concluded. The only people who are going to make any difference in Malden's life were Gretchen and me. I saw Walter, my grocery department manager off in the distance, and headed over to speak with him. "Hi, Walter, how are you?"

He responded, "I'm doing fine, Travis," and asked, "How is Malden doing?"

"He's fine, Walter, and getting better every day. So how are things going in your department today?"

"Excellent. I just hired two additional people who'll start next week to help with the summer vacations that will be starting soon."

"That's awesome, Walter."

"So, Travis, are you spending any time up at the lake this summer?"

"As a matter of fact, I am. I'm taking the last two weeks off in August. My girls will be spending some time with their boyfriends for a few days with us, and depending on what happens with Malden, I expect he will be with us also."

He looked at me, perplexed, and said, "That's so weird, Travis, that no one can find his family." I realized with such a large store with 200 plus employees, I'm amazed how word gets around about things, and people I imagined should be less traveled at least when it comes to my affairs. I concluded I guess it's just human nature for people to want to gossip.

"Yes, Walter, it is weird. Well, I have some business to attend to in my office, so take care, and keep up the good work."

"Thanks, Travis, I will."

I made my way across the store to the entrance to the management offices, and headed up the stairs. I noticed how quiet it was, and thought that was a bit unusual. I passed by several of my manager's offices, and saw them empty. Well, that explained the quietness.

I made my way to my office, dropped my briefcase on my desk, and walked over to my office window to zone for a few minutes. I reviewed in my mind the events of the day so far, was still troubled by some of the things Aiesha had to say about Malden, and his state of mind. I wished I could have him around the store since that seemed to be one of the highlights of his young life. I dismissed the notion since I'd only aggravate myself more knowing I can't have him here right now.

I turned to head back to my desk when I saw Mary as she walked into my office with a smile, and shook her head. I sat down, looked at her, and asked, "Why are you so happy today, Mary?"

She looked straight at me, and announced, "You have to be the luckiest S.O.B. on this planet, Travis." She continued to smile, and added, "They bought it, Travis. I don't know why or how, but they bought it."

I stared at her, confused, and asked, "Bought what?"

"My idea I pitched to corporate earlier this week that would allow Malden to be here at the store. I figured out a way we could have him here sanctioned by corporate. Isn't that great news, Travis?" I tried to take that all in, and stared down at my desk with no reaction, or emotion. She asked, "What's wrong, Travis? I thought you'd be happy over the news. That's what you wanted, right?"

I looked up at her, and said, "I'm sorry, Mary, it's just I'm so happy at this moment, and didn't want you to see me cry."

"Oh, Travis, that's better than any thank you could've ever said."

"Please, Mary, sit and explain to me how you pulled off this small miracle."

She sat, and explained her idea she pitched to our corporate office that stemmed from some local interest of parents with children in the area who wanted to work at the store, but not necessarily be hired in the traditional manner. More like a summer internship for children of parents struggling who wanted to give their kids something to do over the summer months. She continued, and concluded. "There are rules we need to follow, but since you have custody of Malden, and he has a fixed address, we can justify him being here under this summer program."

I looked at her, and commented, "You're amazing! I would've never come up with that in a million years."

She continued, "We can have Malden here at the store, but he can only work a four-hour shift, Travis. You might arrange it, so Gretchen could drop him off around 2:00 in the afternoons. He could ride home with you when you leave for the day. I can't imagine Gretchen wouldn't agree to that except for the fact she'd have to get used to seeing you regularly before it gets dark outside."

I chuckled, "Haha, Mary," since I got the funny comment interjected into our conversation. I was still in shock, and declared, "I just can't believe you got this done, Mary. I mean, Malden will be so happy. I don't know what it is about the store this kid levitates to. I can't wait to see his face when I tell him later." I was hoping for a moment, maybe, for the first time, I may actually see him smile.

She looked at me somewhat perplexed, and said, "Come on, Travis, you still think that?"

R.P. Christman

I looked up from my thought process, and asked, "What do you mean? Think what, Mary?"

"Oh, Travis, you need to walk out of that world you live in sometimes. It doesn't sit well with you, especially at a time like this."

I still had no answer to my question, and repeated with open arms, "Think what?"

She paused for a second, and informed me, "It's not the store Malden wants to be at, Travis!" She paused yet again, and declared, "It's you he wants to be around, *at* the store!" I was taken back by her assessment of him, and questioned, did I miss this? Is she right about all that, and I just didn't see it?

I responded, and said, "Huh, maybe you're right, Mary."

She looked at me, leaned her head slightly to one side, and chuckled, "Duh, Travis, I know I'm right."

"Well, Mary, all I can say is well done. If we were at a bar right now, I'd buy you a drink."

She got up, and pointed out, "Yeah, well, you can buy me something from the vending machine, Travis. I doubt I'll ever see the inside of a bar anytime soon, especially since I know you don't drink."

I smiled at her, agreed, and said, "Fine. A Snickers bar it is, next time we're in the break room." She turned to leave when I interrupted her, and asked, "So Malden is okay to start work here on Monday? Is there any paperwork I need to fill out that has to go through your office?"

She turned to me, and stated, "He can start on Monday. I took care of the paperwork for you already." She turned, walked out of my office, and only got about five feet down the corridor when she heard a loud, "YES," coming from my office. She paused a moment, and continued walking toward her office with a smile.

I was so excited about the news, and felt like a kid on Christmas morning after I just unwrapped the best present I ever received. I called home to let Gretchen know the good news, but no answer. I recalled now, she did say she'd be out doing errands. Well, that's all right. I'll surprise Malden when I get home, and maybe see that smile that I'd wished for.

I felt reenergized, and said to myself, "I'll kick this work's butt on my desk, and be caught up by day's end, by God, even if it kills me." I held true to my promise, and finished all the work I had scheduled for the day. I said a small prayer to thank God, for the positive news I received, how grateful I was for letting Malden into my life, and giving me the opportunity to help the young man. I looked up while I walked out of my office, and said, "I won't let you down, sir."

I made my way to my car, was happy how my day turned out despite the way it started, and wouldn't let anything change that. I figured, after all I'd been through, I felt deserving of the right to be happy, and couldn't wait to get home.

I opened my car door, tossed my briefcase in the front seat, stood there for a moment while I looked up, saw blue sky, and thought, this is nice. I saw Marshall in the parking lot off in the distance while he did his thing. Despite my wanting to get home at that point, I shut my car door, and walked out to the main lot to see him. Marshall could see me walk toward him from a distance, and met me half way. I approached him, and greeted him, "How are you, Marshall?"

He responded, "Just fine, Mr. Scott," and enquired, "How is, Malden, doing?"

"Well, Marshall, he's doing well. He had his stitches removed, and is back to normal."

"That's good, I kinda miss seeing him, plus I don't have to work so hard when he's around."

I smiled at the comment, and said, "Well, Marshall, you'll get to see him more often starting on Monday."

"Really," he responded, and added, "That will be cool."

I replied, "Yup," while I continued to explain, he'll be put on the schedule to work during the afternoons. I stated, "Look, Marshall, just wanted to see if my original favor was still in play here once Malden is back working at the store."

He confirmed, "Absolutely, Mr. Scott. I'm looking forward to working with him again, and I'll make sure I keep a close eye on him."

"That sounds great, Marshall, I truly appreciate it. Well, have a good night, and try to leave some work for Malden on Monday."

"Don't you worry, Mr. Scott, I already planned on that." I walked back to my car, and thought, what a funny guy I am.

***

I arrived home, parked in the garage, headed up the stairs, and found Malden in the kitchen with Gretchen. She was fixing dinner when she turned to see me enter the room, and said, "Hi, honey."

I looked at Malden who sat at the kitchen island, and said, "Hi, Gretchen."

She asked, "How was the rest of your day?"

I walked over, and stood beside her while I leaned against the counter. I looked at Malden, folded my arms, and elaborated on the day's events. "As a matter of fact, Gretchen, it went well. I got a ton of work completed, and can honestly say I'm up to date mostly."

She was peeling potatoes at the kitchen sink, turned her head to me, and smiled, "I'm glad, Travis. You were pretty aggravated when you left the house earlier."

I continued, and said, "Well, something else happened that doesn't affect me as much as someone else."

I continued to stare at Malden engrossed in his book when she turned to me, and asked, "What's that, honey?"

I explained, "Well, Mary came to see me this afternoon with some good news." Gretchen, still peeling potatoes in the sink, glanced over to see my intense stare while I looked over at Malden. She turned to see what Malden was doing, saw him sitting quietly reading, and resumed what she was doing.

I continued, and said, "Yeah, it seems like she came up with a plan that would allow a certain individual to start work back at the store on Monday." I now saw Malden look up from his book, as Gretchen stopped what she was doing, and looked to me while I said, "I knew you were listening, Malden." She turned around to look at Malden who stared at me with an almost happy expression, and knew it was him I had referred to. Not quite the smile I had wished for, but said to him, "I'll take that Malden," and added, "Cool stuff, huh?"

He replied, "Yes, sir."

Gretchen nodded in agreement, looked to me, and asked, "How on earth did you manage that?"

I looked at her, and explained, "This was all Mary. She figured out a way Malden could be at the store legitimately." I contemplated for a moment how great this will be, and how I wouldn't have to sneak around the fact he was there anymore.

I looked at Gretchen, and announced, "Well, there is one caveat to this whole thing, and it will be dependent on how Malden gets to the store each day." I continued, and explained, "He can only work a four-hour shift." I said now, "Mary thought someone could drop Malden off at the store each day around 2:00, and I could drive him back home." I looked at him while he stared at Gretchen, now.

She turned to Malden after she heard me, and said, "Yes, Malden, I'll drive you to the store."

He was still staring at her, and responded, "Thank you, ma'am."

She smiled, looked at me, and stated, "I guess you had a pretty decent day after all."

I leaned over to her, and whispered softly, "I thought for a second there I saw Malden smile. Damn it, I must have blinked, and missed it." She smiled, turned back to prepping dinner, and just shook her head.

The following Monday I was at work in my office, wondering how Malden spent his morning, and probably couldn't wait to be here at the store. I got up from my desk to start my morning ritual to walk around the store, but decided to stop by, and see Mary first. I walked up to her open door, saw her at her desk, and announced, "Just wanted to thank you again for helping out with Malden," and added, "Gretchen also thanks you, Mary."

She replied, "Well, I'm glad you're happy, and maybe now you'll get the chance to figure out what's going on in this young man's life."

"Hopefully, Mary, and again, thank you for everything you've done."

"Oh, by the way, Travis, I have you scheduled for a diversity workshop with Winette's people the week after the 4th of July. It's not what you had requested, but because of your vacation schedule in August, and the upcoming audit, I couldn't take the chance of not slotting you before the deadline."

"Oh yeah, that's right," I remembered. "The audit, I did receive notification of this. I'll let you know, Mary, as well as the rest of the staff the schedule, and who will be here for that. The home office hasn't given me the finalized date when we should expect this though. As for the workshop schedule, because of everything you've done for me, Mary, I'll attend whatever day, or time you tell me to."

She smiled at me, and said, "Thanks, Travis."

I was out on the main floor walking the aisles, checking out the store shelves, and the usual things I looked for when I ran into Winette. I was excited Malden would be working in her department, and started to explain Malden's schedule moving forward when she interrupted me.

She informed me, "Mary already came to see me, and gave me the heads up. I'm glad Malden will be working in my department. He's a good kid, and works hard."

"Thanks, Winette. I know we didn't quite start off on the right foot with Malden, but appreciate the feedback. I'm hoping, maybe having him here might trigger something that will help us all understand things about the young man."

"Well, Travis, I'll keep you posted if we hear, or see anything that could help us in that regard."

"Thanks, Winette. I'll stop by later after he is here to check in, and make sure all is going well."

"All right, see you later, Travis."

I heard the code announcement over the loudspeaker that signaled my presence was required in the main office. I made my way to my office to handle a phone call from corporate to discuss the upcoming store audit.

Later on in the day, Gretchen showed up with Malden to drop him off at the store, and walked in with him, so she could speak with me. She noticed Winette by the front registers while she walked into the store, and proceeded over to talk with her. Malden rushed to grab a store smock, and headed out to the parking lot to meet up with Marshall.

She and Winette talked for a bit while Gretchen filled her in about the change in her home life since Malden came into our lives. Winette got called away for a store-related issue, so Gretchen cut the conversation short, and said, "It was nice talking with you, Winette," and headed up to see me in my office.

Gretchen was greeted by some of the store staff as she made her way to my office, and saw me finishing up a phone call. She wanted to say hi to Mary, but she had some meeting going on in her office. She sat while we talked a little about the upcoming 4th of July holiday. She suggested, "I think we should try this year to take in the town fireworks. Malden might enjoy the show."

I agreed, and said, "Let's do that." I elaborated, and stated, "Malden will probably get a kick out of seeing them. So how is he doing today?"

She got up from her seat, walked over to my office window, looked out, saw Malden out in the parking lot working with Marshall, and answered, "He's fine, Travis." She pondered for a moment, and asked, "Do you think we'll ever know anything more about him other than what we know now?"

I wondered about that for a second, and said, "Well, to this point I would have to say no, but if I think about it logically, how is it possible that we wouldn't at some point, I guess. Why are you asking this now, Gretchen?"

"I don't know, Travis. I kind of feel bad that I feel good that he's in our lives, but all the while feeling guilty for not knowing whatever it is he's going through. I wish I could find a way to help him get out of that funk he's in. I don't know, Travis, not sure you can understand what I'm trying to say."

I thought about that for a moment, and said, "I understand what you mean, and feel the same way I guess. I'm just glad he's not being forgotten anymore, has people around him who care, and want what's best for him. The rest will come, I suppose, at some point."

She turned to me, and smiled. "I guess you're right. I'll leave you to your work, and will see you and Malden when you get home." Gretchen and I kissed, said our goodbyes as she left, and I was back to work on my computer.

I made a few stops during the day while I worked the store, checked in on Malden to be sure all was okay, and on occasion would get an update from Winette. I was still trying to balance the workload of all my responsibilities at the store, including trying my best to figure out what I could do to better understand Malden's situation.

Later in the week, Malden was at work in the store stocking shelves with merchandise in housewares alongside Catie, and one of Winette's tenured associates, Marcia, who's a supervisor in her department. He had just finished working the parking lot carriages, so Winette placed him and Marshall in the store to help with some other merchandising duties.

Malden was busy working when he was approached by a customer looking for assistance. Marcia could see him down the aisle with the customer holding a store flyer open to show him something. Marcia, noticing this, walked down to assist young Malden while she speculated it's probably just a customer who needed help to find a product. She got about halfway down the aisle when she saw the customer close the flyer she had shown him, and walked away. She eventually got to him, and asked, "Everything okay, Malden?"

He turned to look at Marcia, and explained, "The woman was looking for something in the store ad."

She reflected for a moment, decided, well, I'm here, so I might as well just help the woman find what she wanted, and dismissed the idea Malden could have known anything more. She walked to the end of the aisle, looked for the woman, saw her in the distance, and walked quickly to catch up with her, so she could assist. She approached the woman, and asked, "Can I help you find something, ma'am?"

The woman looked to Marcia, and replied, "No, I found what I was looking for. The young man I asked knew just where to find these plastic quart containers I looked everywhere for." Marcia was perplexed over the conversation she's had with this customer when the woman added, "The young man said you were out of the clear plastic ones, but this blue one will do." The woman thanked her anyway, for her help, and walked away. She stood there thinking about what just happened, and wondered how Malden knew where these were in the store.

Marcia ran into Winette later on in the day while Malden and Marshall were back in the parking lot doing their thing, collecting carriages to the storefront. Marcia explained to Winette what had happened with Malden earlier, and was shocked he knew where a random product was in the store, plus he knew we were out of a certain color of that product.

Winette thanked Marcia for telling her this before she walked away, and saw Malden at the front entrance pushing some carriages into the store. She turned to grab a store flyer from one of the registers, walked out by the front doors, and waited for him to see her. Malden noticed Winette, and walked toward her.

She stared at him while he approached, and said, "So, Malden, I ordered some smaller size smocks for the store." She did this because the smallest size smock Malden wore was still huge on him, and looked rather uncomfortable. She explained, "They should be here in a few days, Malden."

He responded, "Thank you, ma'am."

"You're welcome, but that's not why I wanted to see you." She asked, "Can you do me a favor?" as she opened the store flyer, scanned the ad to pick out some obscure item, leaned over to him, and asked, "Can you get me one of these?"

He looked at the ad, the item Winette had pointed to, and responded, "Yes, ma'am," and turned to walk into the main store. She watched him walk away, and headed back to the front registers. She figured it would take some time since she knew exactly where Malden had to go to retrieve the item, and carried on what she was doing working her department schedule at the supervisor's desk.

She was called over to one of the registers by one of her associates to ask about a price not reading properly from a barcode. She turned to walk back to the supervisor's desk when she almost knocked Malden over who was standing there in front of her, and blurted out, "Oh geez, Malden, you startled me." He looked up at her, and held his hand out with the item she asked him to retrieve.

She was taken aback by this, not only because it's what she asked him to get, but how fast he could retrieve the item that was halfway across the store. She took the woman's leg shaver from his hand, and was a little freaked out about the whole situation. She said, "Well, thank you, Malden. That will be all."

He replied, "You're welcome, ma'am," and turned to walk away while she tried to figure out how he knew where to find what she's looking at in her hands.

Not satisfied, she called out, "Wait a second, Malden," as he stopped, and turned around while she walked past him. She grabbed the store ad she had on the supervisor's desk, opened it again, scanned for another object, and walked over to him. She found what she was looking for, and said, "So, Malden, do me one more favor," leaned over to show him what she was looking at, and asked, "Can you grab me one of these?"

He looked at the ad, responded, "Yes, ma'am," and walked away. He stopped after a few moments while she continued to observe him. He turned to her, and stated, "I need some help, ma'am."

She walked over to the young man, leaned over, and asked, "What do you mean by that, Malden?"

He explained, "They're on a pallet in the receiving area, and I need help getting to them."

Winette, who already knew this, crouched down closer to him. Her facial expression in almost a state of shock, looked at him, while he stared back at her, and asked, "How do you know that, Malden?" He didn't say a word, and shrugged his shoulders. She was speechless when she heard one of her associates call out to her from one of the registers, and said, "Okay, Malden, why don't you go about what you were doing."

He replied, "Yes, ma'am," and walked away.

Winette was still crouched while she watched him walk away when she heard her name again, and stood to go assist one of her associates.

Meanwhile, I was in my office talking with Gretchen on the phone, while she explained we were all set for the fireworks display that evening. I announced, "I can't believe how fast this year has gone by, and tomorrow is the 4th of July already."

She responded, "Well, we aren't getting any younger, Travis, and you know what they say, as you get older, the days, months, and years accelerate."

I replied, "Hey, we're not getting older. If anything we're getting better."

"Okay, Travis, you keep telling yourself that."

I smiled after her comment, and asked, "What time do the fireworks start?"

"They start at eight p.m., Travis."

"Okay, sounds good. I'll just see you when I get home." I hung up, and left my office to see Bishop on some store business.

Meanwhile, back at the front of the store, Winette was still perplexed. She couldn't understand how Malden knew she had referred to a store item we ran out of the previous day. Or that it was delivered yesterday afternoon, and still on a skid not broken down yet in the receiving area. She was constantly being interrupted by her work, so she tabled that for the time being since she was no closer to figuring it out than when she started.

Malden and I finished our day, and were driving home when I enquired, "So, Malden, when was the last time you saw some fireworks?" He just sat there with no response, so I rephrased the question, "You have seen fireworks before, right, Malden?"

This time he turned to me, and replied, "No, sir."

I thought, no way, how's that possible, realized who I was talking to, and announced, "Well, Malden, I think you'll be impressed by them."

I was home in my study after dinner when Gretchen walked in, tried to ask me a question when I interrupted her, and announced, "Gretchen, did you know Malden has never seen a fireworks display?"

She looked at me, and replied, "No."

I just shook my head after her response, and thought my God, where did this kid come from? "I'm sorry, Gretchen, what did you want to say?"

"Well, Travis, I didn't want to discuss this at dinner with Malden there, and just wanted to tell you Aiesha called after we spoke on the phone this afternoon. She wanted to give us an update on Malden." I spun my chair around to look directly at her while she continued. She explained, "Aiesha stated they're still looking, and didn't have any new information on him."

I replied, "I'm shocked, Gretchen," and shook my head.

She added, "Well, just thought you should know," and turned to walk out of my study, reminding me, "It's getting close to the time we need to leave, so don't get wrapped up in anything you can't finish later."

I spun my chair back to my PC and confirmed, "Yes, dear."

***

I was driving everyone to the town park in anticipation of the fireworks show we'll soon see. I looked into my rearview mirror, and observed Malden sitting quietly in the back seat. For some reason that reminded me of the night at work when I saw him enter the woods behind the store.

I turned back to the road while I drove, and wondered what his life would be like today if I had never waited at the store that evening to find this young man. Gretchen interrupted my thought process, leaned over the back seat, and said, "So, Malden, Travis tells me you've never seen a fireworks display."

He looked at her, and replied, "No, ma'am."

She responded, "Well, I think you are going to enjoy them, Malden."

We arrived, and found a parking spot. I was helping Gretchen now while we carried our belongings to a spot we picked out in the middle of the park. I took the blanket she packed, and spread it out on the ground for us to sit on. Malden dropped the small cooler Gretchen put together with some snacks in case anyone got hungry. I sat, looked around the park, and commented, Geez, honey, there are a lot of people here."

She looked up, and said, "Well, it's a nice night for the fireworks, so I'm not surprised," while Malden sat between her and I on the blanket. It wouldn't be long before the fireworks show would start. It was about 8:30, the sun had set, and the evening sky had taken shape. I looked up when I saw, and heard the first fireworks shoot up into the sky.

I looked at Malden, and announced, "Here we go, buddy." The first fireworks went off while the rest followed in sequence.

After hearing the first reports, I was like "Wow, those are loud," and said to Gretchen, "They're going off low this year."

I glanced over at Malden, who sat closer to Gretchen since the show started, and looked at her as she whispered, "The loud booms, Travis." I stared at Malden on occasion, and noticed no reaction, or emotion, but saw an intense stare, and amazement at what he watched.

I listened to the crowd's reaction around me as each firework exploded into a beautiful pattern of light in the sky. I heard the children and adults say wow, and ooh as each one exploded. I was more amazed at the reaction, or non-reaction, in this case, of the young man who sat next to me than the beautiful display of colors exploding in the sky in front of us.

The night air was perfect as the fireworks display continued, and I could smell the sulfur in the air coming from them. After a while, I could tell the grand finale was about to take place, and announced to Malden, "Watch this, buddy." The sounds of dozens of rockets were heard ascending into the sky all at once, and with that, the entire skyline exploded with an intense light show better than any I'd ever seen.

I took a moment to look at Malden, who sat even closer to Gretchen now. The sounds of the reports were deafening, but the display of color, and light patterns in the sky were magnificent. The spectacle of lights ended, the last of the reports were heard, and all I could hear were the claps and whistles of the company around us as the show ended. I got up, looked at Malden and Gretchen, and blurted out, "That was awesome!" I asked him now, "How'd you like the fireworks? Pretty cool, huh?"

He stared back at me, and responded, "Yes, sir."

I stared at Gretchen, and commented, "Yeah, well, this was a good one, buddy."

She got up while I talked, and said, "Ouch, my butt is killing me."

I looked at her, and smiled, "You have to think younger thoughts, Gretchen."

"You do that, Travis." She paused a moment, and said, "Next year we're bringing chairs!"

I laughed, and looked at the young man still sitting there. "Come on, Malden, let's pack this stuff up."

It was the following week after the holiday. I was working in my office when I heard a knock on my door, and looked up to see Winette. "Do you have a moment, Travis?"

"Sure," I said. "Have a seat. Is everything okay?"

"Yes, Travis, but I've been meaning to tell you about something that happened last week. I should have said something sooner, but I guess I thought it wasn't anything urgent, and we got so busy last week."

I interrupted her, and stated, "Just tell me what's on your mind."

She explained to me what Marcia had told her when she worked with Malden last week, and what she had done to test him after the fact. She explained all this to me, and said, "I'm still a little spooked over the whole thing. What do you think, Travis?"

"I don't know, Winette. What you've told me is pretty amazing, for which I have no single rational answer for."

"I know, it's so weird, it's as if he knows where everything is in the store. How is that possible?"

"Not sure, Winette, but don't spend so much time thinking about it. I'm sure there's a logical explanation for what you've shared with me."

At that moment I saw Mary approach my office while she leaned in, and announced, "You folks ready?"

I answered, "Ready for what?"

She looked at me surprised, and said, "Please don't tell me you forgot about the diversity workshop, Travis."

I lost track of time, looked at my watch, saw it was 3:30, and said, "Crap! All right, Mary, I'm on my way."

Winette got up, turned to her, and confirmed, "I'm on my way as well."

Winette and I followed Mary out of my office to make our way to the employee cafeteria which had been modified to section off an area to conduct the diversity workshops. I looked at the setup in the makeshift area, and commented, "This looks nice." I added, "Very professional looking classroom." I was in front of the room with Mary and Winette, and said to Winette, "I hope Malden can sit through this hour-long class without reaching for his book to read."

She looked at me, and stated, "I didn't schedule him for the workshop, Travis."

I simply replied, "Why not?"

She answered, but had a hard time while she tried to explain her reasons, gave up, realized she had made a mistake, or should have enquired about that, and responded, "My apologies, Travis." She noticed Marshall come into the classroom, made her way over to him, and asked him to please get Malden to join everyone here.

He replied, "Sure thing," and left the room to find him.

I worked my way past some of the associates who had filed into the room, paused while I walked past Winette, and whispered, "Thank you." I looked straight at her, and said softly so no one could hear, "That's why you're one of my department managers. Don't ever forget that." She looked back at me, and acknowledged with a smile.

I made my way to the back of the room, and reserved three seats while I waited for Malden and Marshall to return. After a short bit as they entered, Mary, at the head of the room, announced, "Okay, everyone, let's get started, shall we?" I motioned to Malden and Marshall to have a seat next to me while Mary continued to say, "We have a lot of material to cover in the next hour."

The meeting went well with the expected information as it pertained to the subject of diversity in the workplace, and I had a good opportunity to see its effect on the associates. All in all, I thought the material was presented well, and everyone in the room looked to have benefited from something covered in the class. I concluded, well, Malden was his quiet self, and appeared to appreciate the subject matter as best as I could tell.

As the meeting ended, I looked at my watch, and said to myself, well it's 4:50, not quite the hour Mary had scheduled the class for, but we started late, and the class participation was probably more than expected.

I turned to Malden while everyone got up, was leaving the room, and said, "I'll meet you at the front of the store in about ten minutes so we can head home."

He acknowledged, "Yes, sir."

I made my way to the front of the room, and congratulated Mary for a job well done. Just as she was about to respond, I saw something in the corner of my eye, turned around to see Marshall helping Malden up from the floor outside of the room, and immediately headed over to them. I stood outside the room in front of Malden, who was upright now, standing next to Marshall, and one of the new hires in Winette's department.

I looked at all of them, and announced, "What's going on here, guys?" I listened to silence as I looked at Malden who just stood next to Marshall looking over now at the new employee. I looked at the young man I didn't know, and asked, "What's your name, son?"

The young man responded, "Bill."

I looked at him, and said, "All right, Bill, you know who I am, right?"

He responded, "Yes, sir."

"Okay, so can someone explain to me what's going on here?" Again silence while all three boys just stood there.

Mary came out to the hall at this point, and enquired, "Travis is there a problem?"

I looked at her, and answered, "No problem, Mary. I got this."

I turned back to the three young men still standing there, and again repeated, "Gentlemen, I'm waiting for an answer." I looked to Marshall while he stared at Bill, and called his name, "Marshall."

Bill spoke up at that point, and said, "He bumped into me," while he stared at Malden.

I looked to Bill, and said, "All right, Bill, I don't know what happened here, but what I did see was Malden being helped off the floor from being knocked down obviously. So why don't you apologize to him, so we can go about our business. Okay?"

He looked at me, and in a disgusted tone responded, "I'm not apologizing to him."

I looked at him after he spoke, nodded in agreement, walked toward him, and said, "Okay, Bill, maybe you're right. Why don't you and I take a little walk, so we can discuss this further?" I placed a hand on his shoulder to move him in the right direction to start our walk toward the front of the store.

I walked out of the store with him, and made sure we were off to the side of the building, so we wouldn't disturb any customers making their way through the main entrance.

I looked at him, and firmly said, "Look, you only have two options here, Bill. I'm not sure what your beef is with Malden, although I've got a pretty good idea of what that might be." I continued, "You can apologize to him, or I can call your parents, and have them meet me here at the store, so I can explain to them why you lost your job. Pretty simple, Bill, so what's it going to be?"

After he listened to what I had to say, he looked up at me straight in the eye, and responded, "Do what you want, I don't care," and added, "My father would whoop my ass if he found out I apologized to some black kid. Go ahead, call him, I don't care." I was taken back by the response, looked at him, and knew this reaction resulted from an ill-intentioned manipulation of a child, for many years at the hands of some stupid racist parenting.

I held back my anger, and stated, "All right, Bill, two things. One, you're done here, and two, when you get home and tell your folks you lost your job today, just tell them you aren't sure why, and have them come see me. Make sure they ask for Travis Scott, okay, son?"

He took his store smock off, threw it onto the ground, and murmured the words as he turned to leave, "This job sucks anyway. Who needs you?"

I watched the young man walk away, and couldn't help but feel sorry for the boy while I walked over to retrieve the store smock from the ground. I made my way back into the store, dropped the smock at the front registers, saw Malden waiting for me, and said, "I'll be right back, Malden, just hang here for a bit."

He replied, "Yes, sir."

I walked to the back of the store to see Mary when I passed Marshall, and announced, "You don't have to work with that one anymore."

I heard Marshall say while I walked past, "Best news I heard all day."

CHAPTER 9

Gretchen and I had finished cleaning up after dinner one evening when she suggested, "Why don't we go out onto the patio, relax, and just take in the view."

I looked at her, and agreed, "That sounds like a great idea." Gretchen and I live in the valley, and have a picture perfect view of the mountains in the distance from our patio. It's not that long ago when we both would spend at least a few days a week just sitting, and talking about the day's events. But since Malden has been introduced into our lives, this routine had been broken up somewhat.

I walked to the kitchen entrance, saw Malden sitting in the great room reading his book, and let him be while I turned my attention back to Gretchen, now pouring herself a glass of wine. We both proceeded out back to the patio area, and sat down.

I wondered about the young boy I fired several weeks ago, and said to her, "I can't get over why, as a parent, you would raise a child to be so negative toward another human being because of his skin color. I don't get it, Gretchen."

She responded, "Well, Travis, thank God there are more people like us who shift the balance of that kind of thinking, otherwise we would've never gotten past slavery, I suppose."

"I guess." I looked up, and said, "I miss this. I could sit here for hours just staring at the mountains."

"It is nice, Travis. So, are you looking forward to our vacation at the lake house? It's just around the corner."

"I am, and excited about Malden being with us. I want to take him fishing, show him how to water ski, and do all the things we did when the girls were growing up." I answered the question again, "Yeah, I'm excited about it."

She sipped her wine, and added, "I brought up our vacation to him, but, alas, no real reaction from the young man."

I rationalized that, and all that we've been through with Malden, and said, "You know, Gretchen, it's like Malden is waiting for something." I turned to look at her, and asked, "Do you feel the same thing I've felt?"

"I don't know. I'm at the point where I'm just tired of trying to figure this all out. I can't believe it, Travis! We're getting voicemail messages now from DCS with updates that are basically the same week in, and week out. I mean, my God, this is a child, and they're leaving messages on our answering machine just to say we have no information to report on."

I responded with a cliché I've used on a regular basis, and said, "Why am I not surprised by that."

***

I arrived at the store the next morning running late, made my way to my office when I passed by Mary's open door, and stopped to say, "Good morning." She was working diligently at her computer, and hardly noticed me as she acknowledged the greeting. I perceived, that's odd, and asked, "Everything all right, Mary?"

She replied, "Yes, Travis," but still didn't look up while she continued typing on her keyboard, and added, "You have someone waiting for you in your office."

I glanced down the hall to my office, looked back at her, and asked, "Who's in my office, Mary?"

She just responded, "Home Office CPA."

I stared at her while she continued to type away, and asked, "Would you like to join us?"

She answered now with one word, "Nope!"

I was a bit confused, and responded, "Why not, Mary?"

She continued to stare at what she was typing, and announced, "Already met him, Travis," while she continued to type away.

I said, "Okay, then," and proceeded to my office. All the while thinking this doesn't sound like the way I wanted to start my Monday morning.

I walked into my office, placed my briefcase down on my desk, and introduced myself to the gentleman waiting. "Hi, I'm Travis Scott."

The gentleman stood, shook my hand, and acknowledged, "I'm Matthew Silverman, Senior

Corporate Certified Public Accountant from our Home Office."

"A pleasure to meet you, Matthew, and I apologize if you've been waiting long. I was running behind this morning."

I made my way to my office chair when Matthew responded, "Well, Mr. Scott, I have been waiting a while," as I sat down slowly now after I heard that.

I looked at Matthew, and started the conversation with, "Well, I hope you had a nice trip from New York, and welcome to North Carolina. I trust the hotel we set you up in is to your liking."

I was interrupted now by Matthew, who said, "Yeah, look, Mr. Scott."

I interrupted him, "Please, call me Travis."

He remarked, "Okay, Travis," as he now continued, and explained, "I only have one week here to complete a lot of work, and would just as soon skip the introductory small talk if you don't mind. I'd just like to start the process of getting this audit completed." I now realized why Mary was acting the way she did earlier after this brief conversation I've had the pleasure of speaking with Matthew.

I nodded in agreement, and confirmed, "All right, Matthew, I believe we've allocated space for you to set up in our conference room."

He stood at that point, and stated, "I've already spoken with your HR manager, Travis, and she's explained all that, so if there's nothing else, I'd like to get started if you don't mind."

I just sat there while I stared at him, and responded, "Okay, Matthew, let me know if you need anything."

With that, he turned around to leave my office when he stopped, turned back, and said, "Oh, by the way, Travis, I noticed a safety issue at the front of the store when I arrived this morning. I would have thought something like that would've been addressed, or at the very least brought to your attention. However, since that's obviously not the case, and since it poses quite a problem for our customers who shop here, I'm advising you of the potential problem, so you can take the appropriate action."

I stared at him now after I listened to his dissertation, and responded, "What safety issue, Matthew, are you referring to?"

He explained, "There's a bee's nest, of significant size above the front entrance doors before you enter the store that shouldn't be there. I would suggest, for our customers' sake, it be removed as soon as possible if you don't mind."

I reviewed what he just said, and responded, "All right, Matthew, I'll look into it," as he now turned to leave my office. I interrupted his departure while he turned around again, and decided, "I changed my mind, Matthew. I would prefer you address me as Mr. Scott," and after a slight pause I added, "If you don't mind." He stared at me while I completed my request, said nothing, and turned to leave my office. I looked at my computer monitor, and said to myself, PUTZ.

***

I finished several hours of work on my computer, mostly emails, and now it was my favorite time of the day to start my tour of the supercenter. I walked the aisles, enjoyed a few moments away from my office PC while I continued to take notes, and just bask in the endless variety of merchandise all around me.

I surmised for a moment about Matthew, whom I only met briefly, and made up my mind I didn't care for him much. I concluded he must be good at what he does, for the home office to keep such a person employed.

I continued my walk of the main store, ran into Marcia stocking shelves in housewares, and stopped to ask her how everything was going. Marcia is a pleasant young lady who always has a smile on her face. She's worked hard over the years, and deserved the supervisory position she had earned.

She greeted me, and responded, "Everything is going well, Mr. Scott."

I replied, "It seems you are correct. I can see your area of the store is well maintained. So, Marcia, I wanted to get some input on Malden working in your department. How's he doing in your estimation?"

"Well, sir, he's a hard worker. A little shy, but some people are like that I guess."

I explained to her what Winette shared with me about what happened a few weeks back with Malden, and a customer he helped.

"I know, Mr. Scott. I was shocked he could help that woman out like he did."

I looked at her now, and said, "We should all be so lucky to have a Malden in our department, right?"

She laughed at my comment, and said while I left, "Have a good day, sir."

I finished up my walk of the store, and stopped by to see Winette by the front registers to say, "Good morning."

She greeted me, and asked if I had met Matthew yet?

I responded convincingly, "Oh yes, I have."

She commented, "Well, I guess you don't care for him much either."

I didn't wish to bring myself down to my subordinate level, so I just diffused the conversation with, "Well, Winette, some folks are just harder to read, and get along with than others, I suppose." I made my way to my office, and sat at my desk when I noticed Matthew approach my office. I looked at my watch, saw it's only been four hours since he's been at the store, and whispered, "Terrific."

He knocked on my door, and asked, "Mr. Scott, do you have a moment?"

"Sure, Matthew, what is it?"

"Well, Mr. Scott, I would appreciate it if you would ask your staff to be a bit more conscious of the scheduled meeting times for this audit."

I was confused, and asked, "What exactly are you referring to, Matthew?"

He explained, "When a meeting is scheduled for eleven o'clock, it means eleven o'clock. It doesn't mean eleven-ten, or eleven-fifteen, or--."

I interrupted him at that point, and said, "I get it, Matthew, and I'll speak with my staff. I added, "Anything else?"

He replied, "No, Mr. Scott," while he turned to leave my office.

I shook my head while I moved my mouse to clear the screen saver on my monitor, and said in silence, my damn vacation can't come soon enough.

Later on in the day, I took a break while I stood at my office window, staring out over the parking lot to watch Malden working with Marshall, and concluded they make a good team. I stopped my staring, and turned to see Bishop and Steve at my doorway waiting, for guess who. Both in unison asked, "You have a minute, Travis?"

I looked at both of them, and said, "Let me guess, it starts with an M, and ends with a W."

Bishop was first to respond, and shouted, "Bingo, Boss!"

I just shook my head, and said, "Guys, come on, what's the problem?"

Steve spoke up first, and announced, "He's telling me how to run my department, Travis."

Bishop weighed in, and echoed, "Ditto."

I responded, "Look, guys," while I was somewhat irritated now, and questioned, "What do you want me to do? Last time I checked we all, including Matthew, work for the same boss. Do you agree with me on this, gentlemen?" I continued, "So, please do me a favor, be patient with the audit process, and try to be on time when you're scheduled to meet with Matthew. Can you both please do that?"

They looked at each other, back to me, and acknowledged what I had asked. As they both left my office, I could hear Bishop say to Steve, "I picked the wrong week to be on vacation."

I sat back down at my desk when I got a call from Gretchen. I answered, "Hi, honey. What's up?"

"How's your day going, Travis?"

"You don't want to know, Gretchen."

I heard her on the other end whisper, oh boy, when I asked, "What's the problem?"

"We got a call from Aiesha at DCS, and she'd like to meet with us tomorrow at the house."

"What's this all about?"

"Not sure, Travis, she wouldn't elaborate, so I'm nervous."

"What time, honey?"

"She said she would stop by around nine a.m."

"I'll make sure I'm there, Gretchen. Just don't worry about it. We can talk later when I get home."

"All right, Travis. I'm sorry if this added more stress to your day."

"No problem, honey, I don't sweat that stuff. I'll talk with you soon." After I hung up with her I leaned back in my office chair, thought about what I said trying to make my wife feel better about the whole DCS thing, and realized, I do sweat that stuff!

The following morning Gretchen and I patiently awaited the arrival of Aiesha from DCS. We were in the great room while Malden read his book in the den. I was pacing now like I'd done the last time we met with Aiesha, looked at my watch, and stated, "It's 9:20, Gretchen. Where is she?"

"Travis, please be patient. She'll be here soon."

"Just saying, Gretchen, it's 9:21 now," and confirmed, "I now understand what Matthew was talking about."

She looked at me, and asked, "Who is Matthew?"

"No one, it's not important." I observed Aiesha's car pull into our driveway now, and declared, "It's about time." I made my way to the front entrance, and opened the door as she came up the stairs. I greeted her while she extended a good morning to Gretchen as she walked into the great room.

She apologized for running behind when Gretchen said, "Malden is in the other room, but I can get him if you'd like to speak with him."

"Not right now, Gretchen." She explained, "There is something we need to discuss before I speak with him if it gets to that."

Gretchen turned to me with a nervous look, turned back to Aiesha, and said, "Please have a seat," while we all sat down.

Gretchen continued, "So what's this all about, Aiesha?"

She apologized for the last few weeks with just leaving a voice message with her updates on the search for Malden's family. She added, "It seems we have more kids than we can handle. That's no excuse, mind you, but thought I would mention it just the same."

Gretchen enquired, "That's okay. I assume you still have no new information."

"That's correct, Gretchen." She explained, "Although it's only the beginning of August, we need to arrange for Malden to be in school the beginning of September in the event we can't locate his family."

I spoke up now, and said, "Crap! I never thought of that."

She looked at me, and implied, "I can't imagine you ever thought Malden would be here this long, or to think you needed to place him in a school program, Mr. Scott." She continued, and said, "This is a state mandate, so I need to get an idea if things have changed from the last time we met."

I looked at her with some confusion, and asked, "What do you mean? What things would've changed?"

She cautioned now, "In my experience, most people who find themselves in similar circumstances, with the best of intentions, could handle a short period of time, and maintain the welfare of a child, but--"

I spoke up again, and announced, "Wait a second. This isn't just about Malden going to school is it, Aiesha?"

Gretchen looked at me all confused with an anxious tone, and questioned, "What are we talking about here, Travis?"

Aiesha stared at me, and responded, "No, Mr. Scott, it isn't just that."

Gretchen, still nervous, looked to Aiesha, and asked, "What are you talking about, Aiesha?"

She looked at us both, and said, "Can I be honest with you folks, off the record, for a moment?"

I got up now all frustrated, and shouted, "Geez, Aiesha, just spit it out."

She looked at me, and continued, "Look, folks, I've experienced nothing like this before. It's been, what, over two months now, and we know as much about this child as we did on day one. I just think it's possible we may never have any answers to the whereabouts of this young man's family. If that's true, I need to know now if your intentions would change toward Malden, and whether or not it's the right thing for the child to be here with you moving forward."

I sat back down after she spoke with determination, and said firmly. "Look, what I said the last time we met, do you remember what I said, Aiesha?"

"I do, Mr. Scott."

"Well, Aiesha, that hasn't changed, and won't change as far as Gretchen and I, are concerned." I looked at Gretchen for a moment, and saw in her eyes what she need not say with words, turned back to Aiesha, and concluded, "Let's discuss what we need to comply with the state mandate for Malden's education, shall we?"

I surmised, as Aiesha looked at both of us, and saw what she didn't see often in life, just two loving, and caring people who only wanted what's best for Malden. She conceded, "Okay, then, let's discuss some options."

Gretchen looked at me, and said, "Well, between you and I, the school system in this area isn't the best. I'm not even sure, what's available, for private schools." She added, "My God, it's been forever since we homeschooled our children."

With that said I looked to Aiesha, and asked, "Is that a possibility, Aiesha, to maybe homeschool Malden versus putting him into a public or private school?"

I looked at Gretchen for approval. "I mean, if that's something you'd want to do."

She thought about that briefly, turned to Aiesha, and said, "I think I could do that, Aiesha."

Aiesha responded, "Well, Gretchen, you would need to have a state certified teacher's certificate, current of course, but yes, I suppose I could make that happen."

I looked at Gretchen now, and asked, "Are you sure this is okay with you?"

Her mind was racing, trying to remember all that went into the process many years ago when she did that for our children, looked to me after a moment, and decided with a smile. "We can do this, Travis."

I looked back at Aiesha, and commented, "My children are smart as a whip, and I know this is all due to Gretchen who set that foundation for what they know now."

"All right, Mr. Scott. If you and your wife can make this happen within the state mandated guidelines, I see no reason it shouldn't be this way."

Aiesha turned to Gretchen, and added, "I'll send you some paperwork the state will need, and your certification documents when you receive those."

"Thank you, Aiesha. I'll get on this right away."

I thanked Aiesha for stopping by, and sat with Gretchen after she left to discuss all of this. I knew Gretchen, and could see the wheels spinning in her head mapping out what she needed to do to get Malden homeschooled. I mentioned we only have three weeks left before September, and offered, "Look, we can push our vacation out if we need to."

She looked at me as she took a break from her thoughts, and responded, "We'll do no such thing. I'll manage what needs to get done in the time frame we have, and if I have to study for the certification exam during our vacation, so be it." I stared at my wife while she spoke with admiration and respect, for this undertaking, and was so proud of her. Well, I knew one thing for sure, as I looked at her, if anybody can do this she can.

She looked at me, and said, "Why aren't you at work? *Go!* I have things to do, Travis." I smiled at her, leaned over to hug her, and got up to go say goodbye to Malden.

The next few days I found myself dodging my staff, and felt like a ping pong paddle just whacking my staff back into the game during this audit. I couldn't stop thinking about my wife at home probably knee deep in the process to get her teacher's license renewed, and was so proud of her.

I was on the main floor of the store, heard my signal over the loudspeaker, and thought, what now? I made my way up the stairs to my manager's offices, and stopped at Mary's door to find out what I was paged for. I greeted her. "Hi, Mary, what's up?"

She looked at me, and said, "Someone is waiting for you in your office."

I thought for a moment, looked around, and prayed out loud. "Please, God, not this Deja vu again."

She smiled, looked at me, and offered, "Well, I could lie to you if you'd like."

I dropped my head, and said, "Please, Lord, give me strength."

R.P. Christman

She was still smiling, shook her head, and announced, "Two more days, Travis," and repeated, "Two more days."

I looked back up, and responded, "Thanks, Mary, I think."

I made my way down to my office, and walked in to see Matthew sitting there waiting for me. I sat down, and asked, "What can I do for you, Matthew?"

"Well, Mr. Scott, its midweek which is the time I normally schedule during the audit, for our stores, to update the store manager of the current progress of said audit."

I looked at him, and asked, "Do you always talk like that, Matthew?"

He looked at me with a somewhat perplexed expression, and replied, "I'm not sure what you mean, Mr. Scott."

I continued to stare back at him, and said, "Never mind, Matthew. So how have we done so far?"

He responded, "Excellent, Mr. Scott."

I waited a moment, then another moment, heard silence, and no further explanation on the answer to the question I posed to him. At that moment I thanked my lucky stars I never majored in accounting in college. "So, Matthew, that's good and--?"

"Well, Mr. Scott, I could expound, and discuss specific figures by department if you'd like."

"No, no, Matthew, I trust your judgment, and expertise on these matters. Is there anything else then?"

He got up from his seat, and stated, "Not related to the store audit, Mr. Scott, but I wanted to follow up with you regarding the other more serious matter we discussed when I arrived on Monday." I sighed, and thought, not this again.

I stopped him, and said, "Look, Matthew, I've been informed, and will address it in due time, so if there's nothing else."

He didn't say a word, and turned to walk out of my office. I got up from my desk, walked down the hall, and walked past Mary's office when I heard, "How'd it go, Travis?"

I stopped, doubled back to her door, and saw her leaning back in her chair smiling. I stated, "I have a headache now, Mary. What does that tell you?"

She replied, "You don't know the half of it, Travis." I just shook my head as I turned to leave, and make my way down to the main floor to see Winette.

I walked through the store when I saw Malden down one of the houseware aisles busy at work with Catie, breaking down a pallet of merchandise, and smiled while I watched them work together. I made my way to the front register area where I saw Winette with her supervisor Marcia. I walked up to her, and requested, "A moment of your time when you have a second, Winette."

She finished her talk with Marcia, turned to me, and said, "What's up, Travis?"

I curiously asked, "Winette, have you had any complaints from anyone about any bees around the storefront entrance?"

She looked at me after I said that, and almost burst out laughing. She extended her hand out to me while she said, "I'm sorry, Travis, I meant no disrespect."

I was confused, and asked, "Did I miss something?"

"No, Travis, I'm sorry, but this whole bee thing with Matthew is hilarious."

"What do you mean by that?"

"Well, he's complained all week to everyone about the bees. I get to see a show about it every morning when he arrives at the store, and every night when he leaves."

"Not sure I follow. What's he doing?"

"Travis, I swear to God, Matthew waits outside the front entrance about fifteen feet away from the building. He'll stand there until the automatic doors open when someone either leaves the store, or enters. He literally will run into the store, Travis, and does the same thing when he leaves. I almost can't stop laughing right now, seeing the image of Matthew with his briefcase running in and out of the store."

After I heard all that, I looked at Winette, and said, "You're kidding, right?"

"I swear to God, Travis, you can't make something like that up."

"Okay, Winette. Thanks, I appreciate what you've told me."

I walked past the front register area, made my way to the front entrance, and walked out of the store to check on what Matthew reported as a safety hazard. I walked out past the automatic doors, looked up to the front of the building, and scanned the area for a bees' nest, but couldn't see anything right off. I was interrupted by some carriages being pushed past me to the front doors by Marshall. He greeted me, and asked, "What are you looking at, Mr. Scott?"

I returned the greeting, "Hi, Marshall." I looked back up, and asked, "Have you had any issues with any bees bothering you, or anyone else around the front door area?"

He looked at me, and answered, "No, sir."

I looked back up, and now saw a hornet's nest about the size of a golf ball, maybe even smaller than that, and said, "Oh, for God's sake."

Marshall had looked up at the same thing I was staring at, and correctly pointed out, "That's a hornet's nest, Mr. Scott, not a bee's nest."

I turned to him, and said, "Thanks for the clarification, Marshall." He continued into the store with the carriages while I walked behind him.

I'm somewhat of a nature enthusiast, and have a special place in my heart for anything 4H related, not exclusive of flying insects like bees and hornets. As a matter of fact, one of my favorite places to visit at the state fair I enjoy going to is the bee house. My staff is very much aware of all this, and they've seen on many occasions where I'll see a spider, or some other creepy crawler in the store, and rescue it to the outside. It's just one of those quirky things with me.

There was even a time my staff found a field mouse by the loading docks, and got it cornered. I just picked up the mouse with my bare hands, walked outside with it, and released it back into the woods. Don't even try to step on an ant around me unless you want to spend a whole lot of time having me explain to you why I shouldn't stomp on your butt.

I walked back into the store a little aggravated over this whole bee incident. I wondered how a grown man could be so scared of such a tiny insect, and all the wasted effort and time even just to talk about it, my Lord. I said to myself, "Matthew, be damned, I'll take that hornets' nest down when pigs fly."

I was out by the loading docks with Steve and Walter discussing business when I noticed Bishop making his way toward us. He approached, looked at me, and said, "You have two police officers waiting in your office, Travis."

I felt somewhat uneasy while he explained that to me, and told him, "I'll be right there."

He acknowledged, and said, "All right, Boss, I'll let them know."

I turned back to Steve and Walter, but hesitated, and called to Bishop, "Wait," and said, "I decided to come with you."

I turned to Steve and Walter, apologized with, "I'm sorry, we'll need to table this, gentlemen, and I'll get back to you."

Steve looked at me, and responded, "Sure thing, Travis."

Bishop and I walked back to our offices while I enquired if the police officers mentioned what this might be about.

"No, Boss, they just said they were here to see you."

I made my way to my office while Bishop headed in the opposite direction to his when I announced, "Thank you, Bishop."

I walked into my office to the two police officers waiting, and stated, "Hello, gentlemen, I'm Travis Scott. Can I help you?"

I stood behind my desk when one of the officers declared, "This is just a follow-up call on the incident that took place outside your store a while back. Detective Cody asked us to stop by to let you know we found the three boys responsible for the injuries to Malden Crenshaw."

I stared at the officer, and replied, "I see."

The officer continued, "The three boys are minors, and we did what we could to punish them, but like I said, Mr. Scott, they're all minors."

I saw where this conversation was going, and interrupted at that point to say, "I get it, Officer."

The officer added, "If it makes you feel any better, Mr. Scott, I'm sure their parents will do more to them than anything we could have done to punish them." The officer looked at me, and asked, "How is the young boy doing? I understand we're still looking for his family."

I walked over to my office window, saw Malden outside in the lot with Marshall, motioned the police officers to my window, and said, "Have a look for yourself, gentlemen." The officers walked over to my window, and saw Malden out in the parking lot pushing some carriages.

One officer commented, "Well, Mr. Scott, Malden looks like he's doing just fine."

I replied, "I assure you he is."

The officer concluded by saying, "Well, we just wanted you to know there was closure to the incident."

I looked at the officers, and said, "I appreciate you coming by to let me know. When you see Detective Cody, please pass on my thanks to him."

Both officers responded, "We will, Mr. Scott."

The officers left while I stood at my office window, and reflected on what they had said about the closure of the Malden incident. I worked the rest of the day in my office except to finish up some business with Steve and Walter, interrupted earlier in the day when the police stopped by to see me.

I drove Malden home that evening, all the while thinking what plausible punishment those kids received that could've been severe enough to satisfy the anger I had toward them. I realized now after looking at Malden who sat next to me, apparently unaffected over time by the whole incident, should suffice as I now closed this chapter in my mind, and life.

I drove to work that Friday morning reviewing the work schedule I had on my plate when something dawned on me. I smiled, and felt good about my morning when I remembered, it's Matthew's last day at the store. He'll conclude his business with the audit, and be out of my hair. "Yay, for me," I said to myself with a sense of relief that business would finally get back to normal after he's gone.

I arrived at the store, and pulled into the parking lot when I saw Matthew standing by the front doors with his briefcase. He stood there exactly the way Winette had explained it to me earlier in the week, waiting for the doors to open.

I drove slowly into the lot, making my way to the side entrance of the store by the access road. I continued to watch Matthew waiting when I saw the automatic doors open, and observed Matthew run into the store. I shook my head in disbelief of this, and laughed at what I just witnessed.

I eventually parked my car, but was still amused by the image of Matthew running with his briefcase. I tried to compose myself before I left the private confines of my vehicle. I exited my car, all the while thinking, well if nothing else, this will keep me smiling all day. I decided I'll keep the details to myself if asked why I'm in such a good mood.

I walked into the store through the side entrance, and made my way up to my office. I could sense a noticeable difference in my staff's demeanor throughout the day, and attributed this to the anticipated departure of our dear friend Matthew. I concluded, well, as different as he was, and had been, it's nice to know we did well in the overall scheme of the store audit.

I was by the main store entrance by the checkout registers when I saw Gretchen pull up to drop Malden off to start his afternoon shift. I made my way out of the store to meet up with her, and announced, "Hey, buddy," while Malden walked past me to make his way into the store. I leaned over the open passenger window, and said to her, "Good timing, honey."

She smiled, and responded, "Well, it is if you're someone with time to shoot the breeze, Travis."

I looked at her, and agreed. "I know you're busy, and need to get home to work on the homeschooling thing and all."

She responded, "It's all right, Travis, I'm only kidding," and added, "I'll always have time for you."

I responded with a smile, "Aw, that's so nice of you to say, Gretchen. I tell you what. I'll see if I can arrange for Malden to be dropped off at the store for the next couple of weeks before we go on vacation." I continued, and said, "If anything, for at least a few of the days during the week, so you don't have to stop what you're doing to bring him here."

"Travis, it's not a problem, trust me."

"I'm sure it's not. Let's try it out for a few days, and see what happens."

"Fine, I'll see you when you get home. Love you."

"I love you too," and watched while she drove away.

I stood by the front entrance, saw Marshall with Malden out in the lot, and walked out to see them both. As I made my way to the boys, I greeted Marshall, and said, "Hey, Marshall, I have a question for you." I got his full attention while I explained that I wanted to know if he knew someone who could pick up Malden a few days a week at my home to bring him to the store if their schedule would allow it.

Malden stood next to Marshall when he offered, "Well, I could pick up Malden on the days I work the afternoon to early evening shifts, Mr. Scott." He also stated, "Your home is only like ten minutes away from the store. I could always use my break time to get him on the other days I start in the mornings if that's okay with you."

I looked at him, smiled, and said, "Well, Marshall, it's pretty cool that you've offered that. I tell you what, for now, maybe you can just coordinate with Malden your afternoon scheduled days." I looked at Malden, and continued to say,

"So he can let my wife know you'll be stopping by the house."

"Sure thing, Mr. Scott, be happy to do it."

I pulled my wallet out of my back pocket, and took out two twenty dollar bills, handed them to him, and explained, "This is for your time, and gas for helping me out, Marshall."

He spoke up, and responded, "You don't have to do that, sir." I stared at him after he spoke with a look on my face that said, you better take the money, don't argue with me, and just say thank you. He conceded, and said, "Thank you, Mr. Scott," while he took the money.

"All right then, I'll go grab a piece of paper, so I can draw you a map of where I live, Marshall."

As I was about to turn and leave putting my wallet back into my pocket, Malden spoke up, and said, "I can tell him where we live, Mr. Scott."

I turned to look down at Malden after he said that, and concluded, I've never heard him refer to my home as his home. I just smiled, and responded, "Okay, Malden, just be sure you let Gretchen know which days Marshall will stop by to pick you up."

He stared at me, and replied, "Yes, sir," while I turned, and walked back to the front of the store. I contemplated what Malden had just said, smiled, and announced, "I'm having a good day."

***

I finished up the afternoon with Walter in his department going over some receivables he had questions on when he spoke up, and said, "So we did well on the audit, Travis?"

I was still reviewing the way bills in my hand, and responded, "As far as I know we did very well, Walter."

"Well, that's good news," and added, "Doesn't quite make up, for the way it was conducted however, but am glad to see him go."

I looked at Walter surprised, and asked, "Matthew, left already?"

"Yup, I saw him leave about forty minutes ago."

I looked at my watch, saw it was 5:40 in the afternoon, and said, "Crap! I hadn't realized the time, and never got to see him before he left."

I shook my head after that being said when Walter commented, "Really, Travis? You should be jumping up and down that he's gone." He continued, "This is one guy you don't want to delay his departure."

I chuckled while I finished up the paperwork I had reviewed for Walter, handed the clipboard to him, and said, "Have a good evening, Walter." He acknowledged me, and turned to walk away while I was still smiling. It wasn't because of what he just mentioned though. It was because of the image of what I saw when I came into work this morning with Matthew running into the building.

I made my way to the front of the store by the checkout area, saw Marcia, and asked, "Is Malden in, or out of the store?"

She answered, "He's in the front parking lot, Mr. Scott."

I made my way to the front entrance, walked outside, and saw him in the distance collecting carriages from one of the carriage corrals. I shouted out, "Malden, ten minutes." I watched him acknowledge my request, and turned to head back inside the store. I walked into the store, pass the automatic doors that just opened, stopped for a moment, and turned around to walk back out.

I was outside looking up above the front doors, but didn't see the hornet's nest any longer that was torturing Matthew all week. I continued to scan the area, and said, "Huh." I walked back into the store to make my way to my office to grab my briefcase.

I walked to my manager's office entrance still curious where the hornet's nest disappeared to, and speculated no way Matthew got rid of it. I could see the image of Matthew running into the store this morning still making me laugh to this very moment.

I reached the entrance to the manager's offices, and opened the door to ascend the staircase. I could hear some of my managers upstairs carrying on a conversation, and laughing. I thought it's nice to hear laughter again. I made my way to the top of the stairs, and turned past Mary's office. I could see Winette and

Bishop in her office, but as they noticed me walking past, the room went quiet. I thought little of this while I continued to my office, but heard the sound of laughter start up again coming from her office when I entered my own.

I grabbed my briefcase, did a quick scan of my desk to be sure I had everything, and exited my office. As I approached Mary's office I could still hear my managers laughing, but when I neared closer, the sounds of laughter turned to silence.

I stopped at her office, and walked in to see her standing in front of her desk. Winette was standing to the right of me, and Bishop was directly ahead sitting on the credenza Mary had in front of her office window. I spoke up over the quiet in the room, and said, "I'm leaving for the day, but was wondering," while I explained to everyone I had just come from the front of the store, and didn't see the Hornets' nest above the front doors.

I looked at my store staff in the room, still quiet after I spoke, and asked, "Does anyone know what happened to it?" Again, I'm hearing nothing but silence when I looked at Mary, and said, "Mary?"

She answered awkwardly, "Well, Travis, I did have a hand in that, but it was really a group decision. My input was so minimal, and to take credit for something someone else did would just be wrong." She looked over at Winette, and said, "It's actually Winette who deserves the credit for that."

I stared at Winette while I placed my briefcase on the floor next to me, and said, "Winette?"

She looked away from Mary, then to me, and explained, "I did come up with the idea originally, Travis, but it was really Bishop who orchestrated the actual engineering of the idea."

I stood with my arms folded, looked away now from Winette, turned to Bishop, and said, "Okay, Bishop."

He turned to look at Mary, and said, "I really don't want to take anything away from Mary, Boss, so--."

I interrupted Bishop to announce, "Look, folks, I hate to break up this little mutual accreditation thing you got going on, so will someone please just tell me what happened?"

I stared at Bishop now while he spoke, and said, "Well, Boss, we decided, I mean, we all decided that maybe the hornet's nest would grow to be a potential problem for our customers entering the store, so we called an exterminator."

I continued to look around the room at each of my managers trying their best to avoid eye contact with their boss when I realized something, turned to Bishop with a concerned stare, and asked, "You had them killed, Bishop?"

Bishop, after hearing that, saw the concerned look on my face, jumped up off the credenza, and said, "No way, Boss, we would never do something like that!"

I looked back at him, and asked, "Well, what did you do with them?"

He continued, "We asked the exterminator if the Hornets could be relocated, which he said they could, Boss, and we asked if we could have the empty nest when he was done."

He finished talking while I continued to look around the room with some confusion, and responded, "To do what with it?"

Bishop was looking at Mary and Winette while he continued to answer the question, and said, "Well, Boss, we boxed it up, and had it shipped." He paused a moment, and added, "Anonymously of course."

I stared around the room again at my managers all avoiding eye contact. I looked back at him with a perplexed stare, and asked, "Shipped it where, Bishop?"

He responded, "We gave it a good home, Boss."

Aggravated now, I shouted, "WHERE?"

He looked at me, and simply answered, "We had it shipped to our home office, Boss, to Matthew's office in New York."

I looked at him when he said that, and could barely get the words out in a much softer tone, "You sent it to, Matthew?"

He added, while Mary and Winette were one syllable away from laughing their butts off, "We just wanted to send Matthew a token of our appreciation, you know, Boss, for being so nice and all to us." With that said Mary and Winette lost control, and couldn't hold back their laughter any longer. Bishop was now enjoying a nice laugh as well after seeing me smile, thinking about what he just told me.

I reached down to pick up my briefcase, and turned to walk out of Mary's office talking to myself, "You sent it to, Matthew," shaking my head the whole time. All the while my managers were having the laugh of their careers behind me. Enjoying the moment, I continued to laugh, walking down the stairs to get Malden to take home.

CHAPTER 10

The following two weeks had come and gone while Gretchen and I were preparing for our two-week vacation around her hectic schedule. Not to mention all the studying, for her upcoming state board exam to renew her teacher's license. She was grateful though, for the help from Marshall picking up Malden in the afternoons during the past few weeks, and taking him to the store.

She decided Marshall was a nice young man, but didn't forget to tell him every time he showed up for Malden to be sure they both wore their seatbelts, and told him he'd better drive responsibly. She recalled how overprotective she'd been with our girls when it came to their safety, and paused a moment to think about that. She realized she now includes Malden in that thought process as if he were her own son. She smiled, and decided, I'm okay with that.

She was prepping dinner when she heard Malden and I pull into the garage, and stopped herself from thinking so much, to concentrate on what she was doing. I entered the kitchen with Malden in tow, greeted my wife, and asked, "What's for dinner, honey? I'm starved."

She responded, "Hi, Travis," and answered, "Pork chops," while Malden walked past her heading for the great room, no doubt.

"Let me guess, and applesauce." She looked at me, and smiled, just shaking her head. I announced to her now, "So, look, after dinner, we should spend some time out on the patio, so we can finalize what we need to get ready for our vacation." I paused, and said, "In three days, whoo hoo!" and continued, "For two weeks away from the mayhem."

She looked at me, and said, "Wow, you are excited about our vacation."

"I need a break, honey. I'm so looking forward to spending some time at the lake."

"Okay," she responded. "After dinner, the patio, it's a date."

Later on, Gretchen and I were relaxing on the patio discussing some last minute items we needed to address before we head out in a few days to the lake. I let her know I already spoke with Mike, and he'll have our boat docked at the pier before we arrive on Saturday.

She acknowledged what I had said, and added, "We should look into maybe having Mike build that overhang thing we discussed a few years ago, so the boat stays dry when it rains."

I thought about that for a moment, and agreed, "Maybe we should, honey." I looked at her, and said, "I'm sorry you have to spend some time studying for the state test."

"Oh sure, Travis, like you're not taking work from your office."

"You're correct," and added, "I have all these reviews I have to get done on my staff, and can't seem to find the time to do them lately."

She responded, "Gee honey, I wonder why," referring to Malden, who's now, or at the very least becoming a full-time member of the Scott family.

"I guess you're right, but you know what, I'm okay with all that. Work at the lake, or not, I'm going to relax, and have some fun." She seemed pleased to hear me in such a positive mood, and thought this will be a nice vacation. I said to her, "I'll see if Malden will help me Friday night pack up what we can into the SUV, so we can head out on time, or maybe even sooner on Saturday morning."

She chuckled, and said, "Yeah right, like he would refuse anything you ask of him."

I turned to her, and said, "What do you mean by that?"

"Travis, the kid is like a magnet around you. He would jump off a bridge if you told him to." She heard what she just said, and took it back. "I'm just kidding, and please, Travis, don't tell him to jump off a bridge." I smiled while she said that, and wondered, why I don't get what other people already know. Get with the program will you, Travis, as my mind was now telling me what to do.

The following day I was in my office putting together some paperwork I'll take with me to the lake including the stack of reviews I need to complete. I regressed back to the days when my parents took me to the lake house. Well, a cabin,

I suppose during those days, thinking not quite a house at that point during my summer vacations.

I remembered as a small child, my grandfather would rustle me out of bed most mornings when it was still dark out, so we could capture night crawlers to use when we went fishing. I remembered how awesome that was collecting worms out in the woods with a flashlight around the cabin, and heading out with my grandfather later to fish with the worms we caught. I recalled during some of the drier vacations we would have to break out the lawn hose, and spray the tree line, for a while, to coax the worms out of the ground looking for the rainwater, or in our case the hose water.

Fun times while I recounted all the vivid memories I had as a child. I thought about when my parents bought the lake cabin after my grandparents got older. I'm guessing it was probably too much upkeep for them. I tried to remember when that was, and surmised somewhere in the late fifties. Since then I bought the property from my parents in the seventies when my parents retired to Florida.

I remembered how the cabin looked back in the day. Gretchen and I have transformed it into a full house with many improvements, and a few additions to the original structure. I thought about my lake house with four full bedrooms, and two guest bunk areas that can accommodate a group of people comfortably.

The house sits high above a secluded cove on the lake, far enough away from any neighboring homes, so we have some privacy when we want it. It's a big lake, and there are a lot of vacation homes. Over the years we have met some nice people whom we call friends now.

I finished my trip down memory lane to refocus on the tasks at hand, and the work I have to complete before the end of the week. I left my office to get to a scheduled meeting in Mary's office. I greeted her with a stack of paperwork in my hands, and said, "We all set to go over some stuff?"

She looked up from her desk, saw the stack of paperwork in my hands, and said, "Oh, my God, Travis, all that?"

I answered, "Yup," and added, "You still want to be the highest paid person in the store?" while I dropped the stack of paperwork onto her desk.

She responded, "Not now I don't." I smiled while I sat to start the process of going over everything she'll need to know while I'm gone. She looked at me, and mentioned, "It's nice to see you in such a good mood." She added, "You should take more vacations, Travis." I looked up at her while I was lining up all the paperwork into small piles which were taking up the majority of space on her desk.

"I am in a good mood, Mary, and it's not just the vacation. It's a lot of things, I suppose."

"Let me guess, Travis, let me take a stab at this. Oh, I know." With a surprised look, she said, "Malden."

I nodded while I arranged the paperwork in front of me, chuckled, and said, "Ha, ha, I knew you'd say that, and guess what, Mary? I'm not surprised, for a change, by what you said."

She laughed, and said, "Well, Travis, you deserve time away from the store, and I hope you and Gretchen have a wonderful time." She paused, and added, "With Malden as well, of course."

Mary and I spent the next several hours going over the day to day business she must know while I'm away, and concluded the meeting when I announced, "Well, I think that's it, Mary."

She looked at me kiddingly, and said, "What, no encore?"

I got up, smiled, and reassured her, "Look, if you run into any trouble just call me. I'll have my number in service at the lake while I'm there."

"Not to worry, Travis. Everything will be fine, and all this will be here when you return."

I reflected on that, for a moment, and answered, "Really?"

She smiled, and said, "Go! I have my own work to attend to now." I left her office when something dawned on me. I stopped, and turned around as she looked at me.

With a perplexed stare, I asked, "Why do I still have a job, Mary?"

"What do you mean by that, Travis?"

Still perplexed, I questioned, "Well, with all that has happened with Malden, who wasn't supposed to be here technically, and got hurt on our property. I mean, we would've had to turn in some paperwork to corporate explaining the police, ambulance service, and knowing how strict the guidelines are for these sort of things coming from the home office." I paused, and restated, "How do I still have a job, Mary?"

She leaned back in her office chair while I spoke, and said, "I turned in all the appropriate paperwork associated with that, Travis."

I was still confused, and repeated again, "How do I still have a job?" I thought about that for a moment, looked back at her with a concerned stare, and asked. "You didn't falsify the reports, for my sake, did you, Mary?"

She responded while she shook her head. "I did no such thing, Travis. Everything I explained in the accident report I sent to corporate was true, and accurate." She continued, "I simply explained a young man in our parking lot was involved in an incident no one had any explanation for. I stated we knew nothing about this young man who got hurt, and who was transported to the hospital." She looked at me after she said that, and said, "Am I wrong, Travis, with that statement of the events that transpired that day?"

I smiled at her after hearing her account of the events she described, nodded in agreement, and said, "I owe you one, Mary."

***

Gretchen and I woke the next day to the realization it was Saturday morning, and the day had finally come that started our vacation. I turned to her, and said, "Morning," while I looked to the open blinds across the bedroom, and saw what a beautiful day it was outside.

I got up with her, and listened to her say, "Let's do this, Travis." She helped me clean up after breakfast while we discussed any last-minute agenda items. Everyone was showered, dressed, and ready to start our day while we prepared for any last minute packing for the three hour plus drive to the lake.

She was in the kitchen checking for anything she might have forgotten when I walked in, saw her scanning the room, and said, "Come on, Gretchen, if we've forgotten something, oh well."

She looked at me, and agreed, "You're right, let's just get going." Malden helped me pack any last minute items into the back of our SUV, and the last most important item, the cooler full of meats Gretchen shopped for yesterday afternoon. I was thinking about all the barbecues I would manage, and concluded this will be awesome.

We were all on the road now headed to our destination, for the long-anticipated two-week vacation that didn't come soon enough. Most of the drive was consumed with conversation about the itinerary Gretchen and I put together along with the anticipation of our two daughters, and their boyfriends arriving later that afternoon.

The drive to the lake was almost as beautiful as the lake itself while we drove through the mountains that were so picturesque. Gretchen and I talked all the while we were driving, and tried to include Malden in the conversation occasionally, but Malden being Malden, just acknowledged anything that was posed to him. I occasionally looked into the rearview mirror to stare at the young man. He just sat there in the back seat looking out the window the whole drive.

I was taking the last turn toward the lake, and drove down the private dirt road passing by our sign on a tree that read, "The Scott Family." Ahead we could barely make out through the dense trees the lake beyond the house.

I drove up to the side of the barbecue area adjacent to the house, and parked the SUV. Gretchen and I exited the vehicle along with Malden from the back seat, and felt a little stiff from the long ride. Despite the stiff joints, Gretchen and I walked out past the front of our vehicle with Malden in tow past the barbecue area. We stopped at the top of the stairs to look out over the cove, and the lake beyond the tree line. I looked down to Malden, and said, "What do you think buddy, pretty nice, huh?"

He looked up at me, turned back to the view we were all staring at, and responded, "Yes sir."

I looked down at the dock, saw my boat tied to it, and said, "Looks like Mike is a man of his word," while Gretchen looked down to the same thing I was staring at.

After a few moments of taking in the view, Gretchen decided, "We should open the house, and unpack the car."

I stood there enjoying the view a few more moments, and said while I nodded, "Okay, sounds like a plan." I started the process, and walked to the back of the SUV while Gretchen was unlocking the side door of the house that entered the kitchen area.

She checked the refrigerator, felt inside, and popped her head outside to say, "Travis, need the electricity turned on." I made my way to the backside of the house to turn on the main disconnect circuit, closed the NEMA enclosure, and could hear Gretchen shout from inside, "Thank you!" I pulled everything out of the back of the SUV with Malden who carried what he could to the inside of the house.

I finished unpacking the SUV with Malden's help. We then took out some patio furniture from the outside utility shed, and placed some chairs in the barbecue area next to the steel rod iron bench I leave outside year round. I stood there admiring my barbecue area, and how inviting it looked. I turned around to see the vantage point of the lake view I'd admired from this spot over the many years of being here.

I glanced over at Malden sitting on the rod iron bench, and said, "Let's see if Gretchen needs any help." He got up while we both walked toward the house now. He and I entered the side door into the kitchen, and heard Gretchen upstairs making up the rooms for everyone. I looked at the large cooler of food we brought with us, and announced, "All right, buddy, let's get this food put away."

I moved the cooler closer to the refrigerator, opened the door, and knelt while Malden handed the contents to me to put into the refrigerator. I inspected one of the packages he handed me, and said, "These are great steaks, buddy. I'll show you how to cook one of these babies this week."

I was still holding the package of steaks when Gretchen came down the stairs, saw the two of us by the refrigerator, and with a small gasp said, "What are you guys doing?"

Malden and I turned to look at her almost simultaneously when I said, "What? We're helping to put the food away."

She stared at both of us with her arms folded, and responded, "Travis, can't you feel how warm the refrigerator is?"

I turned back to the open refrigerator, put my arm in, pulled it back, and said, "Oh yeah."

She announced, "Put everything back into the cooler, Travis. The refrigerator needs to run at least a day before it's ready for food."

I dropped my head past my shoulders while my wife spoke, turned to Malden, and said, "When you grow up, and get married kid, I hope you find someone as smart as Gretchen who will point out your shortfalls in judgment."

She called out, "Come on, Malden, I'll show you where your room is."

I looked at him almost face to face, and said, "Don't make her wait, son." He immediately got up, and walked to a waiting Gretchen while I pulled out everything I had just put into the refrigerator back into the cooler.

Later in the afternoon, Gretchen and I had completed the opening of our lake house, with the help of young Malden, and waited in anticipation, for the arrival of our daughters. I was arranging some of my store paperwork by my desk in the corner of the living room while Malden sat on the couch reading. Gretchen came down the stairs almost running with an excited look, and exited the house at the kitchen entrance.

I looked over at Malden staring at me, and said, "They're here, Malden." I could hear the screams of my daughters outside greeting their mother, no doubt to a flurry of hugs while I got up, and said, "Come on, Malden, let's meet the other half of your family." I walked through the living room into the kitchen, realized what I had said to him, and smiled. We both exited the house to see my daughters with their boyfriends, and Gretchen.

The next ten minutes were consumed by everyone introducing themselves. I got a big hug from each of my daughters as well. I introduced everyone to Malden, now standing next to Gretchen, but he only stared, and accepted the introduction.

Gretchen diffused the awkward moment, and said, "Malden is a little shy, but I'm sure he'll open up to everyone at some point," while she looked down at him taking in everything as she spoke.

I looked to Malden, and said, "Hey, buddy, let's get the grill going, and cook up some grub, for everyone."

I prepped the barbecue, and grabbed some burgers and chicken from the cooler in the kitchen to put on the grill. Gretchen was inside the house with our daughters showing everyone where to put their stuff, and what rooms they would bunk in.

I was busy cooking while Malden was sitting on the bench next to me, and said, "Crap! I need a plate to put this food on." I looked at him, and asked, "Hey, buddy, can you grab me a big plate out of the kitchen?" He got up, and immediately went to get the plate I asked for.

I continued to cook, and said, "Ah crap!" again. I thought he won't be able to reach above the kitchen sink, for a plate, so I shut the barbecue lid to go help him. I turned around, and almost knocked him over while he stood there holding a plate toward me. "Geez, Malden, give a guy a signal when you come up on him like that." I smiled at him while I accepted the plate, and wondered how he retrieved it from high above where the cabinets are, but shrugged it off.

"All right, Malden, we're just about ready here." I heard Gretchen and the kids inside the house, and let him know, "The next few days of peace and quiet, not going to happen, buddy." I shut the barbecue off, grabbed the plate of food, and walked toward the house with Malden in tow.

The Scott family and guests were having a wonderful early evening dinner with great conversation, and a few compliments directed toward my cooking skills, for a job well done.

At one point I had taken the opportunity to grab some paperwork from my desk, and returned to the dinner table, so I could work on the annual reviews, for my staff. Gretchen normally wouldn't allow something like that, but she was so engrossed in her conversation with our daughters she didn't notice I had left the table, to begin with.

I was reviewing some of the paperwork in front of me, but occasionally would look over to check on Malden patiently sitting there taking in all the conversation going on around him.

At one point Ashley looked to me, and asked, "Dad, can I take Scott out on the boat tomorrow, please?" I considered that, but remembered there's a rule I had, for as long as I can remember. I always take the boat out initially from storage to make sure everything is running properly before I let my kids, or anyone else use it.

I was brought back to memories of my children long ago when I taught both my daughters how to drive the many boats my family had owned over the years, how skilled they had become navigating the lake waters, and the many coves and inlets that make up the lake as a whole.

I looked up, and said, "I'll see if I can fit some time in tomorrow morning to take her out for a spin."

Ashley responded with excitement, and thanked me.

I looked to Ashley's boyfriend Scott, and asked, "So, Scott, how long have you known my daughter?"

He looked at me, and answered, "About six months, sir." I looked at him, gave my approval, and thought why not? He said the magic word, *sir*.

Scott leaned past Ashley while he looked in Malden's direction, and asked, "So, Malden, I brought some baseball gloves with me if you want to get together tomorrow, and play some catch." Gretchen paused from talking off the ear of our oldest daughter Ava, and her boyfriend Peter, after hearing this to look over at him. I looked up now at Malden, and saw him not acknowledging Scott, just staring ahead.

Ashley turned as well to him sitting next to her, waiting for a response when he turned to Gretchen, and asked, "May I go in the other room, ma'am?"

Gretchen, staring back at Malden, could see in his eyes that maybe all of this was a bit overwhelming for the young man, and just nodded with a smile. He got up from the table, and walked away. There was only silence in the room now when Ashley called out, and said, "You don't have to be, so rude, Malden."

Gretchen spoke up immediately, and said in a stern voice, "Ashley!"

She looked over at her mother, and responded, "Well, Mom, that was rude. Scott was just trying to be nice."

Gretchen responded in a normal tone now, "You know nothing about what this child has been through, Ashley."

Scott spoke up, "It's okay, Ash, no big deal." I stared at my youngest daughter when she looked in my direction, and saw the look on my face she'd seen a thousand times before, the look that's already decided this conversation was over.

Ashley continued, "Well, I'm sorry," and ended it there.

The rest of the afternoon went wonderfully while Gretchen got a full update on everything going on in our daughter's lives, and was noticeably happy to be spending time with them with the whole family. I finished cleaning up, and had washed the dishes while Gretchen spent time with the girls. I looked out the side window in the kitchen, and noticed Malden sitting out by the barbecue area. I finished what I was doing, dried my hands, and walked outside to join him.

I made my way to where he was sitting on the bench, and had a seat next to him. I was taking in the view when I asked, "You okay, Malden?"

He stopped reading for a moment, and responded, "Yes, sir."

I nodded, staring at the view as the sun was starting to set, and said, "Don't let my youngest daughter get to you. She may be older now, but there was a time I remember well when she didn't act much different than you, Malden. You know something, Malden, despite that, she turned out pretty good." I patted him on the knee while I got up, and asked, "You want to take a walk down to the cove, and see if we can find some frogs before it gets too dark?" He looked up at me, and nodded okay.

The following morning I was in the main living room working on staff reviews at my desk. I have a great view of the cove, and the lake beyond from where I sat. I looked out the window down by the dock, saw Malden sitting there reading, and smiled thinking, if this place doesn't snap him out of whatever he's in, nothing will. I heard my youngest daughter coming down the stairs with Scott in tow with their bathing suits on when Ashley got my attention. "Dad, please, can I take the boat out, and show Scott around the lake?"

I turned to her, and stated, "I haven't had a chance to take her out for a spin yet, Ashley."

"Come on, Dad, please. It will be fine, I promise."

I continued to stare at my youngest daughter with the excited look on her face that made me cave in, and said, "Fine, but look, make sure you idle the engine for about five minutes before you head out of the cove. All right? The keys are in the boat, Scott, do what Ashley tells you, and make sure there are two life jackets in the boat before you leave."

Ashley was pouring with excitement, and replied, "Thanks, Dad," and added, "Come on, Scott, let's go!"

I turned my attention back to my staff reviews when I heard Ashley yelling for me to come outside. I got up while Gretchen came out of the other room, and asked, "What's wrong, Travis?"

I answered, "No idea, Gretchen." We both rushed outside to see Ashley and Scott at the top of the stairs pointing to the middle of the cove. I rushed over to them, and looked down to see my boat almost fully submerged in the middle of the cove away from the dock. I rushed down the stairs while everyone else followed, ran to the end of the dock, and shouted, "Son of a bitch!"

I stared at my boat, and everything that was in it, was floating around the cove. I said, "Son of a bitch," again. I walked back toward everyone now standing in the beach sand by the water's edge, knelt next to Malden on the dock reading, and asked, "Did you see what happened here, Malden?"

Ashley spoke up now, that diverted my attention, when I heard her say, "It's pretty obvious, isn't it, Dad."

I stood up, looked at her, and said, "Did you see who did this, Ashley?"

Ashley, in a defensive posture, responded, "No."

I walked toward her, and pointed out sternly, "I didn't raise you to accuse people of something you didn't see them do."

She stood there with her arms crossed, and responded, "Just saying."

I was still pissed, not exactly at Ashley, but at why I can't figure out what the hell happened here. I looked to Scott, and asked, "Scott, can you and Ashley grab the two kayaks," while I pointed to the utility shed by the house, "Paddle around the cove, and bring in anything to shore that's floating?"

Scott manned up, and responded, "Sure thing, Mr. Scott."

He looked to Ashley now, and said, "Come on, Ash, let's do this." They both headed up the stairs to retrieve the kayaks while I walked with Gretchen behind them trying to figure out how our boat ended up in the middle of the cove, under water.

I was on the phone with Mike at the local boatyard, in the living room sitting next to Gretchen, and explained what had happened. I finished my conversation, hung up when Gretchen looked at me, and asked, "So what did he say?"

I got up, looked out the picture window at the cove, saw my daughter and Scott in kayaks retrieving our stuff floating around, and answered the question, "Mike is sending someone over in a few hours to trail the boat back to his place."

Gretchen sat there staring at me while my attention was focused on Malden who sat on the dock reading his book when she asked, "What do you think happened, Travis?"

I turned around, walked away to go upstairs, and replied, "I have no idea, Gretchen."

I ascended the staircase as she enquired, "Where are you going, Travis?"

"I'm going to change into my swim trunks, so I can retrieve our damn boat."

Later in the day, I was with Gretchen outside, sitting on the bench by the barbecue. I had just finished up with the guys from Mike's boatyard to get our boat trailered. I stared at the view in front of me sitting next to her, turned all around, heard silence, and asked, "Where are the kids?"

She replied, "They all went for a walk around the lake."

"Ah, that's why it's so quiet. Where's Malden?" I stood, and didn't see him anywhere.

"Malden is in the house, in the living room, reading quietly."

I looked at her quietly sitting there going over some study questions for her exam, and said, "Man, I was hoping to take Malden out on the lake today."

She stopped reading, for a moment, looked to me, and said, "I know, honey, but tomorrow is another day, and you said Mike might have the boat back here tomorrow."

"I know, I know," while I sighed, and decided, "You know what? I won't let this get me down. As a matter of fact, I think I'll try, and bang out some more reviews with Malden inside."

She paused from reading, and said, "Good for you, honey."

The following morning came quickly. I was all showered after eating breakfast with the family, and came downstairs to see Gretchen in the living room studying. I stopped to look at her, looked out the picture window, and saw my daughters with their boyfriends swimming off the raft in the middle of the cove. I commented, "Honey, you should take a break from that, for a while, and go outside with the kids. They look like they're having a ball." I continued to hear the high pitch squeals of my daughters playing in the water.

She looked up, and confirmed, "I will Travis. I just need to get through a few more things here."

"Okay, but if I get back, you're not in the water having fun, I'll carry you down those twenty plus stairs, and put you into the water myself."

I saw my wife look up, and smile at me when she asked, "Where are you going, Travis?"

"I'm going to the boatyard to see Mike."

She suggested, "Malden is outside on the bench. See if he wants to take a ride with you."

I responded while I walked out to the kitchen, "Way ahead of you, honey." I walked outside toward Malden, and asked, "Hey, buddy, would you like to take a ride?" He got up immediately, stowed away his book, and accompanied me to our SUV.

Malden and I were pulling up to the boatyard, and finding a place to park while I reminisced out loud saying, "This place brings back so many memories, I just love it here." I felt a little jealous of Mike, who owns the boatyard, who gets to come to work here every day.

I parked, turned the vehicle off, and announced, "All right, buddy, let's see how our boat is doing." Malden and I walked to the storefront entrance that had a big bench outside when I suggested to him, "If you'd like, you can sit out here, and read until I'm done with Mike."

He looked up at me, and replied, "Yes, sir," while he pulled his book out, and sat on the bench.

I made my way into the store, and was admiring all the boat engines on display. I saw the new Yamaha and Evinrude engines along with all the boating accessories Mike had in his store. I looked over at the main counter, saw Mike, who looked up now, and greeted me, "How are you Mr. Scott, long time, no see?"

I looked at him, and said, "You tell me, Mike."

He chuckled, and stated, "Your boat should be ready later this afternoon."

I approached the main counter, pulled out my checkbook, looked back at him, and asked, "What the heck happened, Mike?"

He looked at me, and clarified, "Well, if you're referring to how your boat sank, I can tell you that."

I responded, "Please do."

He explained, "Well, first off, we had to drain the boat of all the lake water, then had to dry out the engine compartment. The reason she had submerged, we found, was because the drain plug was removed which allowed water to fill up in the engine compartment. The water then spilled into the rest of the boat, and hence, your submerged boat."

I listened to all that as Mike was talking, but was confused, and asked, "How did the drain plug get removed, or did it come loose or something?"

He looked at me, and explained, "Can't answer that, Mr. Scott. We didn't find it anywhere in the boat, but I can tell you this." He walked over to a display rack, and brought back something to show me. "This here is a drain plug like the one you had, and as you can see it has a locking mechanism attached to it, so it can't come loose."

I looked at what he had shown me, and asked, "So how is it missing then, Mike?"

"Well, someone would have unlocked it, and taken it out, I suppose. Can't think of any other reason why it would be missing."

I replied, "Huh."

He continued to say, "Your boat is designed, so it won't sink if the plug is removed, but it will fill up with water just the same."

I looked at him, and asked, "So how did the boat get free from the dock moorings?"

"That, I can't tell you, Mr. Scott."

He was finishing up the bill he'd been writing up, and slid it toward me as he now added, "You've heard the saying, Mr. Scott, an accident waiting to happen. Well, you sir, avoided a big one."

I stared away from the bill I was looking at with my checkbook now open, and said, "Really, Mike," while I glanced back down at the total, and announced, "I sure didn't avoid having to pay $669.00 dollars"

He replied, "And fifty-three cents."

I responded confused, "What?"

Mike restated, "The bill, Mr. Scott, $669.00 and fifty-three cents."

I said, "Oh, I see."

He explained, "I'm actually a little surprised at what I found because this is something I hadn't seen in a while."

"What's that, Mike?"

"Well, you have an inboard Evinrude engine, a nice one at that, but a few years back there was a recall for the fuel entry mechanism on that engine model. I replaced a bunch of those on that recall."

"Not sure I follow, Mike."

He motioned to me while he said, "Wait a second," and was talking while he walked into the back room then said, "You should have received a notice from Evinrude for this recall."

He walked back out front with something in his hand.

"Those things in the mail from Evinrude I get? You're supposed to read those things, Mike?"

"So I guess you did get the recall notice, and yes, you should read those, Mr. Scott." He showed me what was in his hand, and explained, "This was the fuel assembly attached to your engine that the fuel line was connected to." He turned it upside down to show me the wear, the break in the assembly, and further explained, "This happens when the engine gets hot, and over time because of the faulty design, it causes this hairline crack that eventually leaks the fuel out of the assembly."

He was staring at my confused look, almost eye to eye, while he leaned over the counter, and said, "Look, think of it this way, your boat is a sort of floating Molotov cocktail. When the engine heats up hot enough, that lights the rag inside the bottle. Now, as you're driving the boat the leaking fuel from the bad assembly travels back to the main fuel tank which is the fuel in the bottle. At some point, Mr. Scott, and I think we both know where this is going, BOOM!" I was startled by Mike's improv of my boat exploding when he stopped leaning over now, and said, "Hence, you avoided a big one."

I looked behind me to stare at Malden through the storefront glass sitting on the bench outside reading while I held my checkbook open on the counter with one hand, and a pen in the other. I was trying to process all of what was said while I continued to stare at the young man outside. Mike was still talking, when I heard him say something, "Well, you don't have to worry about that anymore. I replaced the assembly, and you should be all set."

I stopped staring at Malden, turned back to Mike, and said, "I'm sorry, what, Mike?"

He looked down to the bill in front of me, and said, "$669.00 and 53 cents, Mr. Scott."

I stared at him with a frightened look over everything I'd heard, and said, "Oh, yeah. Okay, Mike," wrote the check, and slid it toward him.

He looked at me, and asked, "You all right, Mr. Scott?"

I looked up to him, and answered, "Yes, I'm fine, Mike," and added, "Anything else?"

He explained, "I'll have one of my guys drop off your boat this afternoon at your dock." He was walking out back now, leaving me standing there imagining what could have happened to my daughter while I turned to stare at the young man on the bench outside.

Malden and I drove back to the lake house. I parked the SUV where I always do, watched him exit the vehicle, and settled in at the bench by the barbecue grill. I was still nauseous from the conversation I had with Mike, and couldn't talk the whole ride home with visions of a possible funeral for my youngest daughter, had all of this not happened.

I exited my vehicle, and walked over to where Malden was sitting while I stared out over the cove watching the fun my daughters were having with their boyfriends in the water. I had a seat next to him, sat there for a moment staring straight ahead, and asked out loud, "How did you know, Malden?"

He looked up and over at me for a moment, turned back to watch the kids playing, and didn't say a word. I sat there, and sighed while I nodded, thinking again about the whole situation. I patted the young man's knee, got up, said, "Thank you, buddy," walked toward the house, and entered the side door.

I stood in the kitchen wanting to update Gretchen on everything Mike told me, but saw a sink full of dishes I surmised were the kids, and said to myself, "Just like old times." I started to walk away, still staring at the sink full of dishes, but couldn't walk past. That inner OCD voice inside of me was telling me to wash them now. I shook my head, walked to the sink, and proceeded to clean the dishes.

I was still running everything Mike told me through my mind when I heard Gretchen come downstairs. I didn't stop what I was doing, looked over to see my wife in a bikini with a wrap around her bikini bottom while she entered the kitchen, and said, "Thanks for doing the dishes, honey."

I replied, "Yeah, yeah."

She stood there curious, and asked, "So how did it go with, Mike?"

I told her everything Mike explained to me while I finished cleaning the dishes. I ended my story while I dried my hands, and turned to see her holding her hands over her face with tears running down her cheeks. I didn't know what to say to my wife as she turned to look through the kitchen door window, and saw Malden quietly sitting on the bench reading his book. I could sense she knew now in her heart that somehow Malden knew all this, and did what he did to save our daughter's life.

She walked outside to where he was sitting while I watched from the window of the kitchen. I saw her kneel in front of him, and hug the young man tightly. I could see the tears still forming on my wife's face while she embraced him.

I stood there staring at my wife holding him close that seemed to last forever. I saw her pull back now, wiping the tears from her face, while she stared back at him. After a moment or two, she got up without saying a word, and walked away to join our daughters down by the cove. I stood there with the towel in my hand the whole time staring at him, still sitting quietly looking out over the lake.

It was midweek now, the girls and their boyfriends were all packed, and ready to leave for the next leg of their trip. Gretchen and I were outside the house saying our goodbyes, and I could tell she was a little sad to see our children leave so soon. She was talking with Ava, and wishing they could spend more time. But she knew they were all heading east for a long hiking adventure on a section of the Appalachian Trail they have been looking forward to all summer long. She said, "Well, we need to do this again soon." Ava hugged her mom, and Ashley followed.

Everyone was ready to leave when Ashley blurted out, "Oh, wait, I forgot something." Everybody looked at Ashley running over to see Malden, who was sitting on the bench by the outside grill. Ashley knelt in front of him to get his attention, and said, "I'm sorry, Malden, for anything I said this past week. I can see how happy my parents are when you're around, and I guess I might've been a little jealous."

He looked at her while she was saying all that when she added, "Well, I just wanted to let you know that. Also, Malden, in case you didn't know, you found the best parents anyone could have, just in case you don't have any of your own." He didn't respond while Ashley continued, "It's okay, Malden, I know. You don't have to say anything if you don't want to."

She got up, and said, "Have a good rest of your summer, Malden," while she turned to run back to everyone who just witnessed a really nice thing she did. Ashley hugged me, and said, "Bye, everyone," while Gretchen and I watched our daughters drive away.

I held Gretchen while we walked back to the house when I said, "I thought we weren't going to say anything to Ashley about what happened with the boat."

She looked at me, and responded, "I didn't tell her anything, Travis." I kept nodding, and smiled while we continued to walk back to the house.

CHAPTER 11

I finished loading the last of our gear into the SUV, and admired the view one last time beside my house before heading home after a great two weeks at the lake. I looked back, and saw Gretchen and Malden all set to leave. I said to myself, after breathing in the morning air coming off the lake one last time, "See you next year, house." We were on the highway now when I blurted out, "Damn good vacation," which interrupted Gretchen's studying from some of the paperwork she had in her lap.

She looked at me, glanced back to Malden sitting quietly in the back seat, and said, "You're right, Travis, we had a great time." She added, "I wish we could have spent a little more time with the girls, but all in all, it was terrific."

I elaborated further, "You know, next year we should take an extra week or two. Maybe I wouldn't feel so bad when it's over, and we have to leave."

She commented, "Well, Travis, you probably wouldn't be saying that if Malden weren't around," and added, "I know you, Travis. After two weeks you'd go stir crazy." I didn't feel what she said was deserving of a response, so I just continued to drive, and reminisced about all the fun we had.

I was brought back to that afternoon I got my boat back, and the apprehensive feeling I had about driving it. I got over it though, and was once again the skipper of my vessel, with pride, after the first spin around the lake.

I speculated the first time Ashley and Ava took the boat out was more troubling for me based on what happened. I soon got over that as the days went by, and everything was fine with smiles all around.

I was so proud of the days I went fishing with Malden, and the mornings I took him out to capture nightcrawlers. That was after I took him to a local sports shop, and bought him his own rod, reel, and tackle box. It was so awesome, despite the fact we didn't catch much fish. I attributed that to the lake not having a lot instead of our fishing skills.

It didn't matter, as I recalled. It was still nice, the whole experience being with Malden and all. I was taken back in time now to the day I went water skiing, and tried to recall how many years it's been since I did that, but couldn't quite remember. I critiqued myself, and felt like I did okay, plus it was fun seeing Malden in the boat responsible for shotgun in case I wiped out. I turned to Gretchen now, and said, "You know what, honey? I think I'm going to officially retire from water skiing."

"Why's that, Travis?"

"It took me almost three days to recover from the sore muscles I had. I should have never given you the signal to go around the lake for the second time."

She looked over at me, and said, "You were showboating, Travis, for the young man sitting in the back seat." I nodded in agreement, and couldn't think of anything different to say than what she did.

I blurted out again, "Damn good vacation!"

The next morning at breakfast I looked to Gretchen, and said, "It's nice to be home," but sighed while I looked over at Malden eating his breakfast quietly.

She looked up, and asked, "What's the matter, Travis?"

"Well, I have so much to do this week. I mean, you do as well, Gretchen." I continued, "But we can discuss this after breakfast." I looked at her, and nodded toward Malden.

"All right, Travis, I get it." She added, "Yeah, well, you don't want my life for the next week." She listed off all the things she had to do, plus prepare for the homeschooling of Malden that starts in a week. That, by the way, was all predicated on her passing the exam that would renew her teacher's license next Saturday. She continued as the list went on and on.

I offered, "Well, let me know if I can take anything off your plate, honey. I'm never too busy for my girl."

She looked at me, smiled, and responded, "Aw, you know just the right time to say just the right thing, Travis."

I nodded in agreement while I watched Malden finish his bowl of cereal, and said with confidence, "That's my job, honey."

Breakfast was over, and Malden had left the kitchen, I guessed, for the great room. Gretchen looked over at me while she cleared the dishes from the table, handed them to me to clean, and asked, "What did you want to say earlier?"

I was rinsing the dishes in front of me, and said, "The kids are back to school in a week, and I'm wondering how that will affect Malden being at the store since he's only covered under the summer internship thing that Mary got approved."

"I see. Well, you need to speak with Mary about that soon. I don't want to see Malden back in a depressed mood, not being able to spend time with you in the afternoons at the store." I had finished loading the dishes into the dishwasher, and stopped a moment to think about what she just said. I reflected for a moment, while I confirmed, Gretchen's assessment of Malden was the same Mary mentioned several weeks back. I just shook my head.

It was Monday morning and I was back at the store bright and early trying to avoid the anticipated welcome back conversations I would have to acknowledge eventually. I had decided later was better while I made my way to my office to acclimate myself back to the real world. I walked past Mary's office when I stopped, doubled back, and saw her working away. I peeked into her office, and announced, "Wow, you're here early."

I saw the big smile from her as she leaned back in her office chair, and responded, "Welcome back, Travis," and immediately asked, "How was your vacation?"

I smiled, and said, "It was awesome, Mary." I made my way into her office, and sat down. I started going on and on about what a terrific time I had, and all the things we did with the family.

Mary smiled while she listened, and said, "Wow, it sounds like you had a great time," and added, "The Scott family plus one now, I see."

I was so excited about the memories I was sharing with her, and said, "What, Scott family plus one? I didn't quite hear you, Mary."

She answered, "You heard me correctly, Travis. You said you and your family had a great trip. You didn't specify Malden any differently, so Scott family plus one."

I nodded now, and agreed, "I guess you're right, Mary." I got up, and said, "Well, I better get to it. I'm sure I have more than my share of work waiting for me in my office."

She graciously offered, "I'll give you a few hours to settle in before we need to get together to go over a few things."

I looked at her, and smiled. "Thanks, Mary, for everything," and walked out of her office to get to my own to start my day.

***

Gretchen was at home on the phone with Aiesha from DCS going over some details, for the upcoming state board exam. They discussed all the things they had talked about previously, as well as the sophomore curriculum that would be covered when she homeschools Malden.

Gretchen explained to her she's still unsure placing him in a sophomore curriculum was the right thing to do just because he said he's sixteen years old. Aiesha explained again to Gretchen this may be the trigger that could bring young Malden to the realization he wasn't actually at the age he says he is.

Gretchen was still apprehensive, and commented, "Well, we'll see soon enough." She went over everything she'd accomplished so far, and the assignment material ordered that should all be their midweek. Aiesha was impressed by the amount of work she'd completed in such a short amount of time especially throwing in a two-week vacation to boot.

Gretchen further explained, "Well, everything is going well, but I'm still praying I've done enough to prepare, for the exam, so I can get my teacher's license renewed."

Aiesha explained, "I have a contingency plan in place if something doesn't go according to plan," but still projected the confidence she had in her. Gretchen asked Aiesha to extend her deepest thanks to her friend in her office who had been huge in helping provide her with some of the guidance, through Aiesha, about the whole process to make this a reality.

I was in my office, finishing up with Mary, all the work I missed in the last two weeks, and completed the conversation with, "Well, that wasn't so bad."

She was set to leave my office, and said, "Yeah, well, do me a favor, and wait at least six months before you take another vacation, Travis."

I smiled, and interrupted her for a moment to discuss Malden's schedule for next week. She stood by my office door, could hear the concern in my voice while I spoke, walked back into my office, and sat back down.

"Well, Travis, we do need to address that, and you're right to assume the summer program ends as the kids go back to school next week."

I looked at her, and explained, "I just don't want to disappoint the young man. I mean, I've gotten so used to him being here." I tried to justify the benefits of having him here at the store, and that it wasn't just me being selfish.

She interrupted me, and confirmed, "I know all that, Travis, trust me. I think because of Malden's situation, the fact he lives with you now, and the authorities acknowledge all that, we might try something different." She paused, and suggested, "Like, just hire the young man."

I looked at her, somewhat surprised, and asked, "Could it be that simple, Mary?"

She answered, "Yeah, why not?" She continued to say, "All of this is positive stuff except for one thing, Travis."

"What's that?"

"You just need to get him an ID with a social security number. If you can do that, I'll hire him on the spot."

I replied, "Huh."

She got back up now, and explained, "I'll handle the other stuff that will surely come up with the staff."

I was deep in thought when she said that, and looked up while I only heard the second half of her sentence, and asked, "What about the staff?"

She looked at me, said, "Are you kidding me?" and paused while she continued, "Once I announce we're hiring Malden, every one of our department managers will be breaking down my office door requesting him in each of their departments."

I looked at her, nodded and chuckled over what she expressed, and said. "All right, Mary. I'll get back to you soon."

She smiled, and said, "Welcome back, Travis," while she walked out of my office.

I turned to pick up my office phone to call Gretchen. She answered while I said, "Hi, honey, I need the phone number for Aiesha, over at DCS."

She gave me the update on her call earlier with Aiesha, and some of the discussion points they covered while she looked for her number, and said, "Here it is Travis." She enquired, "What's this all about?"

I explained the meeting I had with Mary about Malden's work schedule, and she said, "All we have to do is get Malden an ID with a social number, and we can hire him to work at the store."

She curiously asked, "So, if that could be done, what birth date is someone going to give Malden?"

I thought about that, for a moment, and said, "You know, Gretchen that never occurred to me. Well, I guess, I don't know." I added, "I suppose we could ask him, but I'm not sure he even knows as sad as that sounds."

"Look, Travis, we can cross that bridge when we come to it, I guess."

"All right, Gretchen, I'll talk with you later. Love you." She hung up while I reviewed what we discussed, never thought about Malden not having a birthday, and felt a little sad over that.

I was on the phone trying to reach Aiesha, but had to leave a message on her voicemail. I hung up after leaving the message then blurted out, "Geez, what is with answering machines, and the DCS."

I worked the rest of the day, took a break here and there on the main floor to check on Malden, and saw the young man continue where he left off before our two-week vacation.

Later on, I was back in my office taking a short break, walked over to my office window to stare out, and watched Malden working with

Marshall. I wondered about the life Malden was living when I found him, am so proud of my family, for taking in this perfect stranger, and treating him with the decency every child in this world deserves.

I was happy now, and the thought of going back to my desk was less of a chore knowing I had work to do. As I started typing away on my keyboard, I couldn't remember if it was a thousand, or ten thousand emails I had worked up to that point.

I remained positive, continued to work when I noticed Mary approached my office, and say, "Travis, DCS is on line two for you."

I smiled at her, and said, "Thanks," while I picked up my phone, and pressed line two.

"Hi, Aiesha, thanks for getting back to me." I explained my call to her, and was hoping she could help me with the dilemma I faced with young Malden.

She thought about that, and answered, "To be honest with you, Mr. Scott, something like this has never come up, or at least in the fifteen years I've been working with DCS." She continued, and said, "It's a legitimate request, but I have no clue on how to respond to you. Give me a day, so I can get with my area manager, and figure out if this is something we can handle for you."

I thanked her, as I hung up, and appreciated the fact she would address this for Malden while I continued to get caught up with the work in front of me.

***

The next few days were consumed with more work to catch up on while Gretchen prepared herself for the state exam she'll take on Saturday afternoon. I had taken the opportunity on a few occasions to talk with Malden on what Gretchen was trying to do for him. Still, not quite the response one might expect when someone does what she was doing. But under the circumstances, since it was Malden, I gave him a pass every time.

It's Wednesday afternoon, and I was on the main floor of the store when I was called up to my office by an overhead page. I made my way to Mary's office, and said what I normally did, "What's up, Mary?"

She looked at me, and informed, "DCS is on the main line for you." She also enquired, "Does this have something to do with what we discussed on Monday?"

"It does indeed, Mary."

I made my way to my office, answered the main line, and greeted, "Aiesha."

She apologized, "I'm sorry I'm getting back to you a day late, but we had to scramble, and involve our state office with your request."

"That's okay, Aiesha, I understand. So what's the verdict?"

She responded positively, and said, "We worked everything out for you, Mr. Scott."

I smiled, and answered, "That's great news, Aiesha. You have no idea how happy you're making Malden, even though he knows nothing of this right now."

"Well, Mr. Scott, even our most tenured people at the state level were somewhat perplexed by the whole matter, and we're pretty sure this will be a first, for this agency addressing this for Malden."

"I'm so happy, and appreciative of you taking time out of your busy schedule to make this a reality."

She explained further, "Our state office is getting a social security number assigned for Malden, and we will use your address for now until we can--," while she paused before finishing her sentence.

I spoke up, and said, "I know, Aiesha, I know."

She continued, "Well, for now, we created the birthdate for Malden that coincides with the date the DCS file was opened until we can find out his actual birth date. I sent the photo of Malden taken when you brought him to meet with Detective Cody that will be used for the picture ID."

I said now, "Wow, you covered everything, Aiesha. I'm so grateful."

She concluded, "I tried to put a rush on it, but you know, or if you don't know, our state agencies run a bit slow. I suspect you should receive that by the end of the week with some luck."

"Awesome Aiesha, and thank you again." I hung up the phone, thought finally, something positive had been achieved associated with

DCS, and nodded in appreciation of that. I immediately got up to go see Mary. I was excited to tell her the good news, and enquire if she'll need a reinforced steel door installed in her office before word gets out Malden would be hired. I said to myself, you're one funny dude, Travis.

Malden and I were driving home later that afternoon when I started up a conversation about next week to see if he's excited about Gretchen homeschooling him. I got the standard response, "Yes, sir."

I chuckled when I heard that, and continued to say, "Well, Malden, we weren't sure if you'd be able to come back to the store next week, for reasons that aren't important now." I interrupted my talk when I saw him turn to stare at me with a disappointed look in his eyes.

I elaborated further, "Well, buddy, we don't need to worry about that anymore. We'll be officially hiring you at the store next week with all the amenities that go with that." I smiled, but he didn't say a word.

I diverted my attention from driving, looked back at him, rephrased my statement, and said this time, "So, buddy, you can keep coming to work with me next week, and the weeks after."

He turned toward me with a look of approval, I surmised, and now answered, "Thank you, sir."

I continued to drive, chuckling over all that was said, and suggested to myself, I need to work on my communication skills.

***

The next few days seemed like business as usual at the store, and at home except for some tense moments from Gretchen while she tried to psych herself up for her exam tomorrow afternoon. She was thrilled Malden was getting a picture ID, so he could be hired in the traditional manner at the store. She was excited to see what his response would be when we receive it, and present it to the young man. Gretchen and I were sitting on the patio Friday evening relaxing when I commented, "No wine tonight?"

She looked at me, then said, "No, I'm too nervous about tomorrow, and need to stay sharp."

I looked back at her, could see the uncertainty in her eyes, and offered, "You'll do fine tomorrow, honey, trust me."

"How do you know that, Travis? I mean I'm not even sure."

"Well, I know this, Gretchen, so listen carefully. Even if you don't pass the exam, and we can't homeschool Malden, it won't change a thing."

"What do you mean by that, Travis?"

I continued, "Well, if you pass the exam, then great, you'll have Malden. If you don't pass the exam, you'll still have Malden. If he has to go somewhere else to be schooled, you'll still have Malden. The way I figure it, it doesn't matter what happens," while I paused a moment, and confirmed, "You'll still have Malden."

She smiled now, looked at me, and said, "I love you so much, Travis."

I was staring over at the picture perfect view of the mountains in front of me, and said, "I know you do, honey."

The following afternoon we were en route to the satellite office of the state's Department of Education, about an hour away from our home, so Gretchen could take her exam. As I drove I looked at her sitting next to me, and asked, "So how does this work? I mean, does someone stay after the test is done to correct it to determine whether you passed or not?"

She responded, "No, silly, the test is electronic, and the test results are given to you at the end of the exam."

I further enquired, "So you need to get something like a B+ average to pass or something like that?"

"No, it's a pass or fail, and nothing in between, Travis."

I commented, "All right then, I'll keep quiet now, so you can study until we get there." We arrived, got settled in as I hugged my wife, and affirmed, "You'll do great." I looked down to Malden standing next to me, and said, "Wish, Gretchen, good luck, buddy."

She looked at him while he responded, "Good luck, Mrs. Scott."

She looked back into his eyes, remembered what I said to her last night, and confirmed, he's right, it doesn't matter what happens. I'll still have Malden no matter what. "Thanks, Malden, honey," then looked to me before she turned to walk away to the exam room announcing, "Let's do this, Travis!"

Malden and I waited outside the exam room in a small waiting area. There was no one else with us as I looked around. I could smell the air of a hundred years coming from the old furniture. I thought about all the money we pay in taxes, and wondered why they couldn't buy halfway decent chairs to sit on.

I looked at my watch, saw an hour and a half had gone by, and thought she should be done soon. I looked at Malden sitting next to me, and said, "Hey, buddy, let's take a walk, my butt is killing me." He and I exited the waiting area when I noticed Gretchen walking toward us, and stopped myself and Malden abruptly.

I looked at her with tears running down her cheeks while she stopped in front of me, and blurted out, "I passed, Travis," and put her arms around me for a big hug.

I blurted out, "Geez Louise, Gretchen, I saw those tears, and thought, fail for sure." She was still emotional while she tried to laugh when I said that. I hugged my wife back, and whispered softly, "I knew you could do it." She was staring down at Malden while she continued to hug me.

I drove the family home, and thought about whether Malden's ID would be in the mail today.

Gretchen was going on and on about the exam she passed, and all that went into the process with such excitement in her voice. She eventually turned to me, and apologized. "I'm sorry, Travis, for talking so much. I'm just so excited right now."

I interjected, "Well, you should be honey. What you did was amazing. I'm proud of you, and know once you get started teaching young Malden a thing or two he'll be the smartest sophomore kid around."

We arrived home, and parked in the driveway, so I could walk out to the mailbox. Gretchen was letting Malden into the house at the front door when I turned with an envelope in my hand held out to her exclaiming, "It's here, Gretchen!"

She smiled while she looked at my expression of joy, and said, "Good, let's celebrate, we deserve it." I nodded in agreement as I made my way up the paved walkway while she stood there waiting for me.

I was inside opening the letter from DCS, and knew they followed through with the request since I could feel the envelope with the ID inside. I finished opening it while I walked into the kitchen with Gretchen. She was at the refrigerator getting a bottle of wine while Malden sat quietly at the island. I had the ID out now, admired the professional look, and feel of the laminated surface with his picture.

Gretchen finished pouring herself a glass of wine, walked over next to me, looked at Malden's new picture ID, and nodded with approval.

I spoke up with excitement in my voice, and said, "Well, buddy, here it is, your very own State of North Carolina picture ID," and slid it over to him.

He picked up the ID, stared at it for a moment, and replied, "Thank you, sir."

"Well, I would have been a bit more excited, young fella, but that's okay. If everyone in this world were the same, it would be a pretty boring place." I leaned over to Gretchen while he was still staring at his new ID, and softly announced, "I've got to schedule some time to teach this kid how to smile." She smiled back at me before she took a sip of her wine.

Well, Monday morning came, and I didn't need to worry about whether I forgot, or not, today was the first day of school, based on all the school buses I ran into. I reasoned that, for a moment, and couldn't remember past years with so many buses when it dawned on me now this year was different. I realized with Malden around I didn't get up, and leave as early as I used to. Ah, that's why, and decided, I didn't care for this at all.

I recalled how excited I was when I left for work, and saw what Gretchen had done to transform half our dining room and table into a makeshift classroom for young Malden. It looked so cool with the memo pads, binders, and the school curriculum lined up by subject. I wondered to myself, and confirmed. I must have worn off on her since I didn't have to adjust anything to a ninety-degree angle. I smiled, and said to myself, you rule, girl.

Gretchen prepped Malden's first class assignment that morning. She reviewed the scheduled curriculum for Math, English, Geography, Social Studies, and History she would teach him. She laid out the first assignment that covered some basic questions on English that should take him approximately fifty minutes to complete.

She got up now, and went to get him since it was nine a.m. and the official start of the homeschooling program. She situated young Malden in the makeshift classroom in the dining room. She started by asking him to answer the English questions she had prepared, and placed the four-page document in front of him. She added, "This is so we can determine what we need to concentrate on moving forward. Okay, Malden?"

She smiled at him while he put his book down to accept the English assignment, and picked up the pencil in front of him. She got up, and announced, "I'll be back in a bit to check on you, Malden."

He interrupted her departure, and said, "Ma'am?" She turned to him while he spoke, "Thank you, ma'am," and started reading the questions in front of him.

She looked at the young man sitting there, and responded, "You're welcome, Malden," and turned to walk away now.

Gretchen realized, she could get a load of washing in before she had to come back to check on him, and headed upstairs to grab some laundry. She finished retrieving the laundry from both hampers in the master and guest bathrooms, and headed back downstairs. She walked past the dining room entrance when she saw Malden reading his book at the table.

She said to herself silently, "Oh boy," dropped the laundry in the kitchen for now, and headed in to see him to find out what the problem was. She made her way into the dining room, and saw him staring down at the book in his lap reading. She walked over to the table, and had a seat next to him while she noticed the English assignment upside down on the table.

Malden stared at her while she sat, and listened to her say. "Malden, honey, you can't just read your book. We need to work as a team here if this homeschooling is going to work. I know this may be different from what you were used to when you went to school in the past. I just need you to focus on what you need to learn, and if you don't understand something, you need to let me know. Do you understand what I'm trying to say, Malden?"

He stared at her, responded, "Yes, ma'am," closed the book in his lap, and placed it on the dining room table.

She smiled at him, and said, "So just try to answer what you can on these questions, and I'll be back so we can go over what we need to. All right, Malden?" She got up, but noticed him sliding the assignment toward her. She looked at him while he did that, picked up the assignment, and looked at the top page that had all the questions answered. She turned over the other pages, and they were all filled out as well. She sat back down while she read the questionnaire, and looked at him, while he stared back at her with a shocked look on her face.

Meanwhile, I was back at work doing my favorite thing walking the main store before we open, and wondered how Malden was doing at home on his first day of school. I remembered back to the days when my children were little, and went through the same homeschooling experience with Gretchen.

I headed over to the housewares department, looked at the large assortment of home furniture, and found what I was looking for. I noticed Marcia walking down an adjacent aisle, and called out her name. Marcia acknowledged, and walked over to me. I was still staring at the item I was interested in, and asked her, "Can you do me a favor. Please have one of your associates take this item out back by the employee entrance, deliver the ticket to Winette, and have her process this on my store account?"

She answered, "Sure thing, Mr. Scott."

I thanked her, and said, "I'll pick it up later when I leave for the day. Thanks again, Marcia." I continued my walk of the store, and was excited now, for what I just bought Malden.

***

I was in a staff meeting with some of my department managers later in the day when Gretchen dropped Malden off, and came into the store to see me after she parked out front. She and Malden exited her vehicle while he rushed into the store. She watched him pick up a store smock, and hurried back outside to start work with Marshall. She passed him while she walked through the front entrance, and announced, "Have a nice afternoon, Malden."

He rushed past her, and answered, "Yes, ma'am."

She made her way to the front registers where she noticed Winette at the supervisor's desk, and headed over to say hello.

Winette saw her, and said, "Hi, Gretchen, how are you doing?"

She answered, "Just fine, Winette," and asked now, "Is my husband in his office, or out on the main floor somewhere?"

Winette replied, "He's in a staff meeting behind closed doors, but I'm sure we can interrupt him if you need something."

"No, no, Winette, that's fine. It's nothing urgent."

Winette enquired, "How was the first day of homeschooling Malden?"

Gretchen sort of chuckled after she said that, and under her breath said, "Yeah, right, who's homeschooling who?"

Winette looked at her, and apologized. "I'm sorry, Gretchen, I didn't hear what you said."

She turned to Winette, and responded, "It's nothing, Winette. Malden did fine today. Well, I'll just see my husband when he gets home, but you can tell him I stopped by if you see him."

"I certainly will, Gretchen."

Gretchen replied, "Thanks, Winette," while she smiled, and walked away.

I was in my office after a long day of meetings. I kept thinking of the purchase I made earlier in the day, and whether Malden would be excited when he sees what I bought him. I looked at my watch, saw it's already 5:50, and said, "Crap!" I confirmed there are just not enough hours in the day. I quickly finished the email I was typing, hit the send button, got up to grab my briefcase, and headed on down to see where Malden was, so we could get home.

I walked up to the front checkout area, saw Winette, and asked, "Is Malden in, or outside the store?"

She responded, "Malden is outside with Marshall at the moment."

I thanked her while I headed for the front doors.

She stopped me, and told me my wife came into the store looking for me earlier after she dropped Malden off. Winette added that she told Gretchen I was tied up in a meeting, and would have interrupted the meeting, for her, but she didn't want to disturb me.

"Okay, Winette, and thanks."

She continued to say, "I had the item you bought earlier today put into the back seat of your car, Travis." She explained it took two of her associates to accomplish that.

I looked at her, nodded with a smile, and said, "That was nice of you, Winette."

"Well, Travis, you'll have to deal with it on your own when you get home."

I once again thanked her while I walked outside to get Malden to head home for the day.

I found him while we both walked from the parking lot to the side of the building. I was excited to hear how his first day of school went, but it was me who did most of the talking, and it seemed like business as usual for him.

"Well, buddy, that's all right, I can't quite remember any time I ever got excited when I went to school either." I was psyched now, and said, "I bought you something today, Malden. I hope you'll like it." As we approached my car, I could see the entire back seat taken up with the box put in there earlier. I said to him, "So what do you think. Pretty cool, huh?"

He looked up at me, and responded, "Yes, sir." I thought I can't wait to get home to put it together.

I pulled into the garage, and closed the door remotely while we both exited the car. I opened the back passenger door, and tried to negotiate the large box out of the back seat, but it was heavy and bulky, to say the least. Malden stood there watching me struggle with the box when I leaned back out of the car, and looked at him. I indicated now, "I may have miscalculated this, buddy," and now realized what Winette was talking about earlier.

He looked at me after I said that, and confirmed, "Yes, sir."

I turned to him, and blurted out with a smile, "No one likes a wiseass, buddy." I had an idea, walked around the car to open the other passenger door, and suggested, "Okay, Malden, you get on this side, and push, while I guide the box out of the back seat." He ran over to the other side, pushed the heavy box as I was grabbing it, and pulling it out. Within moments we heard a thud as the box hit the cement floor of the garage. I shouted out, "Hey, we did it."

I looked at him in the back seat, and said, "All we have to do now is figure out how to get it upstairs."

I negotiated the box over to the door to the stairs while I pushed it on the cement floor with Malden helping to guide the way. I looked at him, and said, "Okay buddy, this is what we're going to do. You're going to just guide the box up the stairs, and I'll do all the pushing."

He responded, "Yes, sir," and opened the door so I could push the box to the front of the stairs. We got the box up the first few stairs while Gretchen was in the kitchen, and could hear all the noise coming from the stairs to the garage. She stopped prepping dinner, walked over to open the door, and saw me on the backside of the box pushing this monster up the stairs.

She saw Malden guiding it in the front, and called out, "What the heck is that, Travis?"

Malden and I looked up to her at the same moment when she said that. I replied, "Isn't it great? It's a new desk for Malden, for school." She looked wide-eyed, and walked down the stairs to help young Malden and I get the box to the top of the stairs, and into the kitchen.

I looked at Malden, and said, "Thanks, buddy." I was out of breath now, looked over to Gretchen, and said, "Thanks, honey."

She was staring at the desk I bought Malden, and asked, "Where are you going to put this, Travis?"

I responded, "In my study," and added, "I just figured Malden should have his own desk, and this will be perfect right in front of mine. This way Gretchen, you can take back your dining room, and use my study to school Malden." I looked over at him sitting at the kitchen island taking the conversation all in.

She curiously asked, "So, you're going to put this together?"

I replied confidently, "Yes, I am," while she watched me push the box across the hardwood floor, moving quite nicely now.

She went back to prepping dinner, but added with a stern voice, "You better not scratch my hardwood floors, Travis."

I replied, "Yes, ma'am," while I headed out of the kitchen pushing the monster box.

***

Dinner conversation was great, and should have been mostly about Malden's first day of school, but the new desk I bought him seemed to take center stage. I hurried to clean the dishes after we ate, and was determined to have his desk put together by the end of that evening.

I grabbed a few tools from the utility drawer in the kitchen, made my way into my study, and started unboxing the new Executive Desk made of real mahogany wood. Malden was in the great room doing what he does, and reading quietly. Gretchen headed into the dining room to retrieve some paperwork she wanted to show me that I was unaware of at the time. She walked out of the dining room, and saw Malden reading his book in the great room while she made her way to my study.

She walked in on me after I had unboxed this huge desk, and had several pieces all around my study. She navigated her way to my computer chair, and had a seat. I was in front of her kneeling, looking over the instruction manual for the desk.

She announced, "We need to talk, Travis." I looked at her to acknowledge what she had said. "So, Travis, you used to say you were good at math in school. I want you to look at this, and tell me what you think." She handed some papers to me while I reviewed the first page, still kneeling on the floor in front of her. I looked at what appeared to be a math equation written at the top of the first page, and what looked like the work done to solve the equation below it that continued to the next page, filling that page up entirely as well.

I chuckled while I looked at that, and exclaimed, "Wow Gretchen, this is something else." I continued, and said, "You give me way too much credit," and paused when I indicated now, "I have no idea what I'm looking at." I was taken aback for a moment, and questioned, "Is this what sophomore kids are learning in school these days?" and added, "Malden won't be able to figure this out, Gretchen."

She explained now, "Travis, that's a college level calculus equation I printed off the Internet from your PC this morning." I looked at her while she spoke with some confusion. She continued, and said, "I gave that problem to Malden this morning. Travis, that work you're looking at is his."

I looked at the pencil work done, turned to the second page for the answer at the bottom, and said, "Huh."

"That's not all, Travis." She continued, "Everything I gave him to work on today was completed, and was one hundred percent accurate."

I was still looking at the math problem that spanned two pages when I asked, "How do you know this is right? It looks like jibber jabber to me."

"I have no idea if the work is right or not, but his answer is correct." She pointed to the page I was still staring at. She confirmed, "I had to look up the answer on your PC."

At that point, I said, "Huh," again.

She spoke up, annoyed, and asked, "Travis, can you please say something other than, huh?"

"I don't know what to tell you, Gretchen. I mean, obviously, the kid is smart, right?"

"No, Travis. Malden is way beyond smart. He is exceptional."

Still kneeling I looked at her, trying to justify what she just explained, and said, "Huh," again while she stared back with an aggravated look.

I got up from the floor, and announced, "Wait here, Gretchen." I walked out of my study and down the hall into the great room to ask Malden to come see Gretchen and me in my study. I walked back into the study with Malden in tow, and saw Gretchen still sitting at the computer desk. I made my way to my big desk, picked up a calculator, and said, "Malden, I want to ask you a few questions. All right, buddy?"

He looked at me, and responded, "Yes, sir."

I used the calculator, and asked, "What's the square root of sixty-four?"

He replied, "Eight, sir." I thought now, duh, that was too easy. Even I know that.

I said now, "Okay, Malden," while I used my calculator, "What's the square root of 15,625?"

He replied, "One hundred and twenty-five, sir."

I was more impressed by that, and said, "Okay, Malden, one more." Again I used my calculator, and asked, "What's the square root of 384,400?"

He replied, "Six hundred and twenty, sir."

I looked to Gretchen, and was as shocked as she was confirming he was correct. I put my calculator down, walked over to him, navigating around the many desk pieces I had laid out, knelt in front of him, and asked, "How do you know that, son?" Malden stared into my eyes while I asked the question, and just shrugged his shoulders. I paused a long time before I said, "All right, Malden, you can go back to the great room, and read if you like."

He responded, "Yes, sir," turned around, and walked away. I continued to stare at the young man leaving the room wondering what else he knew. I turned to look at Gretchen, still shocked, trying to figure out what we just witnessed.

CHAPTER 12

The weeks passed by as life went on at the Scott household. Gretchen continued her homeschooling of Malden which by the way, turned out to be one of the easiest endeavors of her teaching career. Gretchen and I often in the beginning days of Malden being homeschooled, would discuss how it was possible he was so smart given everything we knew about the young man, or at least where we found him.

I was so preoccupied with all of that, and would occasionally test Malden's brain. I was constantly amazed at the knowledge this young man possessed. Gretchen took another approach to all of this, and decided it was all right. Why shouldn't someone like Malden, who came from a bad environment or situation, not be coveted with such a special gift she saw day in, and day out?

Well, all of that had changed nothing in retrospect of the fact we love Malden very much, and are happy he'd been blessed with such a gift that will no doubt guide him in the future.

I was at work in my office, and looked at my watch to check the time. I was close to a scheduled meeting with Bishop in his office to go over some forecasted sales figures for the last quarter. I talked to myself out loud, "Cool, I have another ten minutes." I heard a knock on my door, looked up, and saw Mary standing there holding some envelopes in her hand.

"Hi, Travis, you got a minute?"

"Hi, Mary, yes I do, but have a meeting with Bishop in ten minutes. What's up?"

She walked into my office, had a seat while she handed me some envelopes, and assured me, "This won't take long, Travis."

I accepted a bunch of envelopes from her that were unopened checks from the store, and asked, "What are these, Mary?"

"Well, Travis, as you can see, those are unopened checks to Malden accumulating over the weeks since we officially hired him."

I counted the envelopes, and said, "Six weeks."

She responded, "Yup, every check since we started paying him. He just never picked them up at the end of each week, Travis."

I stared at the checks in my hand when I said, "Huh."

She added, "So, Travis, I'm just curious why he hasn't picked these up, or cashed them. I mean, what does he do for money, and how does he buy things?"

I looked up at her, reasoned that for a moment, and responded, "I have no idea, Mary. I mean, we provide just about everything for the young man. He eats three squares at our house, and I know Gretchen has taken him shopping a bunch of times over the months. I assumed he had money, and was drawing his paycheck like everyone else who works here."

"Well, Travis, as you can see that's not the case. I know you need to get to a meeting. I just wanted to drop those off to you, so you could talk to Malden about them."

"Okay, thanks, Mary. I appreciate you bringing this to my attention." She left my office while I continued to stare at the checks when I looked at my watch, and said, "Crap, late again!" I placed Malden's paychecks into my briefcase, and figured I'll address this later. I headed out of my office, for the meeting I'm now late for with Bishop.

Gretchen was at home, and had just finished another day of homeschooling Malden when she heard the doorbell ring. She assumed it was Marshall coming to pick up Malden to bring to the store. She made her way through the great room to answer the door, and now heard Malden racing down the stairs. She opened the door, saw Marshall standing there while he greeted her, and said, "Hi, Mrs. Scott."

She stared at him, and responded, "What did I tell you, Marshall, the last time you came to my house to pick up Malden?"

Marshall's facial expression was all defensive now while he tried to answer, "I'm sorry, Mrs. Scott, I'm not sure what you're talking about."

Malden was standing behind her while she explained, "I told you, Marshall, you don't have to knock, or ring the doorbell, just come into the house as if it were your own, okay?"

He looked much more relaxed after she spoke. She could almost see the relief that he wasn't in trouble, for something. He confirmed, "Yes, ma'am, I understand, and it won't happen again."

She smiled while he was apologizing for nothing as far as she was concerned, and asked him, "And what else, Marshall?"

He answered immediately, "Seatbelts, and I better drive carefully, ma'am."

She responded, "Very good, Marshall." She moved to the side to let Malden exit, and said, "Have a good afternoon, boys!" She stood there while the two walked away from the house, and got into Marshall's car when she heard the house phone ring. She shut the front door, and headed through the great room to the kitchen to answer it.

She answered, heard Aiesha's voice, and greeted her, "Hi, Aiesha. How are you? I feel like it's been forever since the last time we spoke."

She responded, "I know, Gretchen, and I'm sorry I've only been leaving voice messages again with updates on Malden."

"It's all right, Aiesha. You know how I feel about that, and it's all good, trust me." Gretchen was glad she had made peace with the fact we may never know anything more than what we know now about where Malden's family is, or if they even exist outside of his mother that is. "So what do I owe this pleasure, Aiesha?"

"Well, Gretchen, I'm just getting around to reviewing the school transcripts you've been sending weekly to my office, and again, I'm sorry, my caseload is significant these days."

"I understand, Aiesha."

She stated with a question now, "Gretchen, I'm not sure you understand what you need to send us with regard to these transcripts, so I just wanted to go over a few with you if you have the time?"

"Sure, Aiesha, and I apologize if I'm not filling them out correctly."

"That's okay we can make this right pretty quick. So what we need Gretchen, is the actual grade average for the curriculum you're teaching by subject, for Malden. It looks like you've filled out the grade average at 100% across the board."

"Those are correct, Aiesha."

"I don't think you understand, Gretchen." She continued to explain. "I know your goal is to get the young man to a 100% grade average, but we need to see the actual grade scores while we work toward that goal."

Gretchen now restated what she had just said, and affirmed, "You have that, Aiesha. I'm reporting Malden's actual grade average for all subjects within the curriculum I've taught." Gretchen listened to dead silence now.

After a moment or two Aiesha, asked, "Gretchen, you're teaching Malden at the tenth-grade level correct?"

"Yes, Aiesha, that's correct."

More silence when Aiesha asked her, "Maybe I should sit in on a homeschooling session with you, and Malden. I have an open window tomorrow around ten a.m. if that would work, for you?"

Gretchen realized she wasn't buying what she was selling, so to speak, and answered, "That would be fine, Aiesha."

"All right then, Gretchen, I'm looking forward to seeing you and Malden tomorrow at ten."

"Okay, we'll see you then, Aiesha."

Malden and I were home that evening when Gretchen came to see me while I was in my study working on my computer. She leaned against Malden's desk, and announced, "So, Travis, Aiesha called me today."

That got my attention pretty quick while I spun my chair around toward her, and responded, "Okay."

"Well, I guess she thought I was incorrectly filling out the weekly transcripts I have to send on Malden's grades. I told her they were right, and reflected the correct grade average, but I don't think she believed me. She asked to stop by tomorrow to sit in on a session with Malden."

"Well, Gretchen, if it were me you were talking to on the phone, and said your child was getting everything right, no exceptions, I'd be skeptical also."

"I know, Travis. I wanted you to know just the same. Can you grab Malden now? Dinner is just about ready."

I acknowledged, "Sure thing," and got up to go look for him.

The next morning I was running late, and remembered an important meeting with some of my staff. I chugged down the last of my coffee while I picked up my briefcase, saw Malden's paychecks, and said, "Crap!" I realized now that I had forgotten to speak with him about them last night. I took them out of my briefcase, and left them on the island to address with him later that evening.

Gretchen was walking into the kitchen when she saw me leave some envelopes on the island, and said, "What are those, Travis?"

I rushed up to my wife, kissed her, and said real fast, "Can't talk now, late for a meeting, Malden's paychecks from the store. I've got to go, honey, will explain later."

"Bye, Travis. Love you."

I was racing downstairs while I shouted, "Love you too, babe."

Later that morning, Gretchen had Malden all set up for the day's homeschooling lessons when she heard the front doorbell ring, and assumed it was Aiesha. She had explained to Malden last night she would be by this morning, but it didn't seem to interest him in the least. She answered the door, and greeted Aiesha.

"How are you, Gretchen?"

"I'm fine, Aiesha."

Aiesha said now, "I'm just glad I had the extra time this morning to stop by, and see how Malden was doing."

"He's doing just fine," and continued to say, "It's good to see you, Aiesha." Gretchen walked with her toward the kitchen when she offered, "Malden is busy working a class assignment at his desk in Travis' study. Would you like a cup of coffee?"

"That would be nice, Gretchen." They both entered the kitchen while Aiesha sat at the island, and Gretchen went to get them both a cup of coffee she had already made in anticipation of her visit. "So how is Malden's homeschooling going, Gretchen?"

"He's doing fine with it, Aiesha," and asked how she liked her coffee.

"Just black, Gretchen."

Gretchen now went over everything about Malden and her life experiences with the young man since the last time they spoke. She sat at the island with Aiesha, and stated, "Little has changed since the last time you met with Malden. He's such a terrific kid, and oh my God, Travis is so in love with this child." Aiesha was taking in everything she was saying, and smiling as she heard nothing but positive words about the life Malden had with her and Travis.

Aiesha concluded, what a great story, and thought Malden couldn't have found a more wonderful family to assimilate into. Gretchen continued, "I don't think I've ever seen Malden smile, or project any excitement over anything, but I made my peace with that since I can usually tell if the young man is happy or sad. I don't know, Aiesha, it's just that internal mother thing I guess that lets me know."

She explained how she found the special gift he is blessed with, and how some events surrounding the young man now make sense, which they attribute that to. She described things that have happened around him, including the miracle at their lake house that involved the averted boat accident.

Aiesha blurted out, "Oh, my God, Gretchen."

She smiled, and said, "Yup, of course, we have no idea what really happened, or what could have happened, but I know in my heart Malden protected my family that day, and I'll never forget it."

Gretchen was back to current events, and explained how Malden seems to have the correct answers to everything she presents to him. "It doesn't matter what the subject is within the curriculum, whether it's math, social studies, or geography, it's like he just knows, Aiesha. I can explain none of it."

Aiesha continued to listen to Gretchen talk while she drank her coffee. Gretchen added, "I'll sit with Malden while I give him a test, and watch him write the answers without pausing even for a moment, for anything. I don't even think he reads the questions, and just writes his answers down that are never wrong. It's amazing to watch, Aiesha."

Aiesha spoke, and said, "It sounds kind of spooky, Gretchen."

She looked at her, and asked, "You mean like Halloween spooky?"

"Well, yeah, I mean, I have goosebumps listening to you. So Gretchen, have you noticed anything else unusual about him other than that, or maybe something else in his behavior that's different?"

"You sound like a doctor now, with a Ph.D., asking me that."

Gretchen stared at the envelopes on the counter I left that morning, and wasn't sure what to make of them. Aiesha noticed the concerned stare while she looked at them, and called her name, "Gretchen?"

Gretchen had picked up the envelopes still preoccupied in thought over them when she heard her name called, and responded, "I'm sorry, Aiesha. What?"

Aiesha stared down at the envelopes she was fumbling with, and asked, "What are those, Gretchen?"

"My husband left these here this morning, but was in a hurry, and didn't have time to explain these paychecks Malden got working at the store."

Aiesha theorized about that, for a moment, and asked, "I'd like to try something with Malden, Gretchen?"

She replied, "Sure, the assignment I gave him earlier, under normal circumstances, would take about an hour to complete, but I know it only takes Malden about ten minutes. He's probably just reading his book at his desk." She got up, and said, "Let me take you to him."

They both entered my study when Aiesha commented, "That's an impressive looking desk, he's sitting at, Gretchen," as she chuckled slightly.

Aiesha addressed Malden, and announced, "Wow, that's quite the desk you have their, Malden."

He looked up from reading his book, and said, "Yes, ma'am."

She looked over at Gretchen again still amazed over the size of his desk when Gretchen said, "Don't even get me started on that, Aiesha."

Aiesha made her way over to look at the five-page questionnaire in front of Malden, looked to Gretchen, and said, "May I?"

She responded, "Sure," while Aiesha picked up the papers, and worked her way around Malden's desk to sit at my desk directly in front of him.

She reviewed the completed questionnaire, and commented, "Quite impressive, Malden." Gretchen stood behind him while she finished looking at the five-page questionnaire all filled out with the correct answers.

Aiesha called Malden's name to divert him from reading his book in his lap, and said, "Is it okay if I ask you a few questions?"

He looked at her, and responded, "Yes, ma'am."

She smiled at him, and began, "So, Malden, if you had a dollar, and wanted to buy an apple I was selling for fifty cents, how much money would you have left over?" Gretchen had walked over by her while she asked Malden that, and thought that's a dumb question, knowing how smart he is, but heard silence from the young man just sitting there.

Gretchen spoke up, and explained to her, "You'll need to rephrase that," knowing his personality when he doesn't answer a direct question.

Aiesha quickly responded, "Wait a minute, Gretchen."

She addressed Malden again, and asked, "So, Malden, do you understand what I've asked you?" Again, dead silence from the young man she stared at. She restated, "All right, Malden, let me ask you this. If you had 100 marbles in front of you, and gave me fifty, how many marbles would you have left?"

He immediately responded, "Fifty."

She answered, "That's correct, Malden," looking up now at Gretchen while she stared at Malden with a perplexed look.

Aiesha asked at that point, "Can we have a moment in the other room, Gretchen?"

She acknowledged, "Sure, Aiesha." She looked at Malden, and said, "You have thirty minutes left to finish this questionnaire that's already done." Gretchen realized how stupid that statement was, paused a moment, smiled at him, shook her head, and said, "Just read your book,

Malden, all right," while she followed Aiesha out of my study.

They both walked back into the kitchen when Aiesha asked, "So, what do you think?"

"I don't know, Aiesha. I guess the question should be what do you think?"

"Well, its obvious Malden doesn't understand money, which is strange. That might account for those uncashed checks," as they both stared at Malden's paychecks on the kitchen island. Aiesha smiled now, and blurted out, "Money is the root of all evil!"

Gretchen responded, "What?" after she heard that.

"God bless this child, Gretchen, for not understanding the concept of money!" She continued to say, "But on the other hand this could be an opportunity, for you to actually teach Malden something."

Aiesha left after a short while, and Gretchen was convinced she was satisfied now with the accuracy of the transcripts she's reported weekly to her office.

It was the day before Halloween, and Gretchen was getting set to run some errands after Marshall picked up Malden for the afternoon. Her first stop would be the bank to open an account for Malden, and deposit the many checks he had accumulated from working at the store.

She was brought back to that evening when we spoke after Aiesha stopped by the house. She recalled how I reacted, somewhat shocked, but not surprised after she explained how oblivious Malden was to the concept of money, and the look on my face after the conversation we had.

We both eventually decided to open an account for Malden to place his earnings in, so the money would be there for the young man someday. We knew he would eventually realize, at some point in his life, everything does revolve around the concept of having money.

Gretchen had just left the house, and was driving through our neighborhood. She saw all the wonderful Halloween decorations, and thought about our house not participating in this year's Halloween motif. She decided this year she'll spruce up the house for Malden's sake, and have fun with the trick or treaters who come by in droves every year.

She was in town after completing her banking business, and opened up a new account for Malden when she saw a party store ahead. She pulled into the parking lot, and was excited to go shopping for Halloween decorations for the house.

She exited her SUV, but hesitated after she was overcome by a feeling like she was being watched. She stopped to look around the parking lot, and only saw random people coming, or going to the store. She reflected for a moment, whispered aloud, "That's weird," but dismissed the feeling she had, and continued to walk to the store.

She bought a bunch of cool spooky decorations, was at home now to start the process of deciding where to put everything, and said aloud, "This is what Halloween is all about." She smiled while she retrieved the items from her bags.

I was back at the office wrapping up, for the day, and decided I'd had enough. I left my office, walked past Bishop's, and noticed all the Halloween decorations, plus a large cardboard picture of a ghost hanging on his door while I chuckled. I popped my head into his office, and announced, "Pretty cool, Bishop."

He looked at me, and responded in a vampire voice, "Welcome to my Transylvania crypt, Boss."

I laughed when he said that, and restated, "Really cool, Bishop."

"I thought you'd like it, Boss."

I shook my head, and smiled when I said, "Have a spooky good evening, Bishop." I was down on the main floor to find Malden, was still amused, and couldn't get Bishop's decorated office out of my mind.

I drove Malden home that afternoon, and had one of our many conversations, one-sided at least, since only I spoke, and asked, "So, Malden, you excited about Halloween tomorrow?" I heard silence and no response from him while he just sat there. I said to myself, come on, you have to know what Halloween is? My Lord!

I ignored the silence, thought about Bishop's office, and continued to smile while I drove home. I turned the last corner onto my street, but saw something different as we got closer to the house, and could see the front of it was all decorated for Halloween. I pulled up to the curb, put the car into park, exited the vehicle, and shouted, "Come on, Malden, you have to see this."

I stepped up over the sidewalk curb, and walked about halfway up the paved walkway smiling from ear to ear. I stood next to my lamp post that lights the pathway, saw it covered with webbing with some pretty realistic looking spiders along with orange and black garland wrapped around the post.

I looked up now to the front of the house, saw my ornamental shrubs decorated with more spider webbing and some makeshift gravestones on the lawn with the words RIP written across them. I looked up at the windows that were covered with stickers of pumpkins, bats, and some frightful looking black cats.

The one thing that got my attention most was the front door decorated with a pretty realistic looking cardboard cutout of a life-size witch with all that is associated with such. I smiled while I stared at it, and shouted, "Isn't this great, Malden?"

I looked down to my side expecting to see him, but he wasn't there. I turned around, saw him standing next to the open passenger door with the car still running, and repeated, still smiling, "What is it, Malden? Isn't this great?"

He didn't say a word, and just stood there. I heard the front door open, and turned to see Gretchen while she announced with excitement, "What do you think, Travis?" She looked over at Malden, and could sense something was wrong. Her smile turned upside down when she looked at the young man like he had just seen a ghost, or something. She turned to me, saw I was no longer smiling, and said with concern in her voice, "What's the matter, Travis?"

We watched the young man while he laid his head down low, walked past the car, up the driveway to the side of the house, and entered the side door to the garage. I immediately rushed over to my running car, closed the passenger door, and got in to drive it into the garage.

I finished parking the car, and went upstairs to see what the problem was. I met Gretchen in the kitchen where she asked, "What's the matter, Travis, and where is Malden?"

I looked at her, and said, "What do you mean, where is Malden? Isn't he up here with you?"

"No, Travis. I didn't see him when I came back inside the house."

Gretchen and I started looking for him, and calling his name while we searched the main level of the house. I told her, "I'm going back downstairs to see if I missed him in the garage.

You check upstairs." We both finished searching the rest of the house, when I came back upstairs from the garage, and saw her walk back into the kitchen. I saw that look of concern on her face, and said, "Oh, come on, I watched him come into the house, damn it. Where the heck is he?"

I glanced over at the door in the kitchen that goes downstairs to the laundry room, and asked her, "Did you leave that door open?"

She looked at the slightly open door, and responded, "No, I always close that door."

I walked over to the laundry room door, opened it while Gretchen was behind me, looked down the dark staircase, and called out his name, but only heard silence. I flipped the light switch on, went down the stairs, scanned the laundry room, and saw him sitting in the corner of the room next to the washing machine.

Gretchen was still behind me, saw him sitting there quietly, and asked, "What's the matter, Malden?"

I wondered what brought all this on, and have never seen him act like that. I walked over to him, stopped to kneel, and asked softly, "What's the matter, buddy, you okay?" He sat staring at nothing in front of him, and didn't answer me. Gretchen was standing next to me while I was crouched down talking with him. I tried to figure out what he was looking at when we pulled up to the house.

I asked him, "Did you not like some of the Halloween decorations around the house?"

He looked at me, and said adamantly, "Yes, sir."

I looked up to Gretchen, turned back to him, and said, "Maybe the witch on the front door. Is that what's bothering you?" He looked at me while I said that, and didn't say a word. I knew right away that's what spooked him. "All right, Malden, no problem. The witch is gone." I looked up to Gretchen, and said, "Right, Gretchen? We don't need that crummy old witch decoration."

She agreed, "Sure, Travis," as she turned to go upstairs, made her way out to the great room, and removed the witch decoration from the front door. She folded up the cardboard witch, and placed it in the trash when she heard Malden and I walk up the stairs from the laundry room. I closed the door, and watched Malden walk out of the kitchen while Gretchen announced, "All set, Malden. No more witches in the house."

I leaned against the island, looked at my wife for a possible explanation, but could see she was as perplexed as I was, and had no answer for why he reacted the way he did.

The following day after much thought, I figured, why rock the boat, and talked with Gretchen, who's still uncertain why Malden was so stressed out over a paper witch decoration. We decided to bag the Halloween tradition this year of passing out candy to the kids, and take him out for dinner to avoid the entire holiday. Gretchen and I had a ball with him that evening.

We made the decision to cross Halloween off our social calendar from now on because of the Malden incident we're sure we'll never figure out.

CHAPTER 13

Several weeks had passed since the Malden incident at Halloween over the witch decoration, and he seemed fine now as if nothing ever happened. Gretchen remembered how resilient our children were at his age, and thought he was no different in that regard.

She was so excited about the upcoming holidays, and was looking forward to spending Thanksgiving and Christmas with Malden. Our children had other plans this year, and weren't going to be around. She was sad over that, but remembered how awesome this time of year was. She smiled with anticipation, for the Christmas season that started the day after Thanksgiving, and all that's associated with her favorite holiday.

The holidays were fast approaching while she tried to figure out how she'd manage everything that included cooking, shopping, decorating, and wrapping presents. This year was so different from past years since Malden came into our lives, but it was nice to have a child around again to enjoy the holidays with.

She was a little concerned about how the days and weeks have flown by, and how busy her daily schedule is with homeschooling Malden. That alone took up most of her day, and left her with a short window in the afternoons to get everything else done. She realized, she'd better fine-tune her time management skills if she was going to get everything ready that needed getting done, and said to herself, you can do this, Gretchen.

I couldn't believe it was two days before Thanksgiving already. We were all sitting down having breakfast, enjoying one another's company, when I looked at Malden, and said, "So, Malden, tomorrow morning you and me will pick out our Christmas tree. Pretty cool, huh?" He looked at me, and didn't say a word while I tried to process the silence. My mind couldn't believe it either, and told me, no way, this child has to know what Christmas is!

Gretchen spoke up, and asked, "So, Malden, what would you like for Christmas this year?" In my mind I wanted to say, come on, it's not even Thanksgiving yet, but let her have her moment while he looked at her, and didn't acknowledge her either. She said, "Well, You think about that, Malden. We have some time before Christmas is here."

I shook my head now knowing his reaction when he doesn't answer a question. It's either because he's not happy, or he doesn't understand the question. I was sad over that, and said to myself, my Lord, where did this kid come from?

The following morning I was all set to take Malden out to the local hardware store to get our Christmas tree while Gretchen was busy in the kitchen prepping the turkey dinner we'll enjoy tomorrow. I kissed her goodbye when she said, "You two have a nice time, and pick out a full tree this year, Travis." I looked at her with a facial expression that confirmed what I brought home last year. I never could quite get the tree to look right with that huge hole in the middle of it.

I answered, "Fine, dear," while I walked out of the kitchen to get Malden who was in the great room.

I saw him quietly reading, and announced, "You all set to go, buddy." I watched him jump up from his seat, stow away his book, and walk toward me. We were on the road now having a one-sided conversation. I talked about all the past years Gretchen and I, with the girls, would head out the day before Thanksgiving to get our Christmas tree. I guessed it was just one of those holiday traditions that started one year, and had stuck to this very day even without the girls now.

I explained to him how the hardware store had changed over the years when they used to put out a few dozen trees in the front of the store. Since that time they've built a rather large tent-like wooden structure next to the store that held the trees every year now. "It's cool, Malden, and the smell of the spruce trees freshly cut is awesome." He continued to listen while I talked as we pulled up to the hardware store.

"Okay, buddy, let's do this." Malden and I were inside that huge wooden structure while I observed rows and rows of trees everywhere. I also noticed how busy it was, but watching the smiles on the children's faces with their parents picking out a Christmas tree was so precious to me.

I examined a tree when I looked down to Malden, and asked, "What do you think, buddy?" He looked at the tree, then to me, said nothing, and walked away. I reexamined the tree in my hand, and said, "You're right, this tree sucks," and leaned it back against the other trees that were all lined up.

I turned around, saw him on the other side of the tent, and walked over to him while he was staring up at a great looking tree. I smiled, and said, "Like father, like--," but didn't finish my sentence, looked down to him staring back at me, and said, "Wise choice, Malden." I looked back at the monster tree I was about to buy, realized for a moment, and guessed, I'll definitely have to help trim the tree this year.

Malden and I got the Christmas tree home that morning, and unstrapped it from the roof of the SUV. We unwrapped the tree from the restrictive wrap to let the tree sit out overnight to allow the branches to fall into place. I'd bring the tree inside after Thanksgiving dinner as was the tradition in the Scott family.

I stood there while I leaned the tree against the garage wall, looked down at Malden, who was staring at the tree, and said, "You'll have to explain this to Gretchen." He looked up at me, but didn't say a word.

We headed upstairs, entered the kitchen where Gretchen was busy, and heard her ask, "So did you get a good tree this year, Travis?"

I chuckled, and said, "We did indeed," while I walked past her.

She curiously announced, "Should I ask?"

Malden walked past me, headed for the great room, when I responded, "I wouldn't," while I exited the kitchen, and headed toward my study.

Later that afternoon I was still in my study busy working on my computer. Malden had relocated to the kitchen island to read. Gretchen was gutting the turkey, and prepping it for tomorrow's dinner. She'd get up early in the morning, and put the bird into the oven, so we could eat around midday.

Christmas preparation began promptly after dinner was over, which was my queue to bring the Christmas tree into the house, stand the tree, and string the lights. Gretchen would start decorating the tree as soon as I was done. I could see how excited she got at that moment just thinking about it.

Gretchen also enjoys those one-sided conversations she's had with Malden when he spends time with her while she's busy in the kitchen. I think he just likes to hear her voice, and is content to be in the same room with her. She won't deny that since she's perfectly happy to have Malden around even though he doesn't talk much.

She was having one of those one-sided conversations with him sitting at the island when she turned to him, and asked, "Would you prefer homemade cranberry sauce, or the jellied kind, Malden?" She smiled, staring at the young man, thinking yeah not going to get a response on that one, will I, Malden? She decided, "Well, let me ask, Travis." She dried her hands, and walked out of the kitchen to see me in my study.

She walked into the study when she heard me say softly to myself, "Crap, crap, crap."

She made her way over, leaned against Malden's desk, and asked, "What's the matter, Travis?"

I continued to look at my computer screen, and stated, "Everything is fine, Gretchen."

She questioned frankly, "Did you forget who you were speaking to? What's going on?"

I spun my seat around to look at her while she listened to me, and responded, "Why is it so hard to find out anything about Malden, where he was living, grew up, or anything else for that matter? I mean, it just doesn't make any sense."

She looked at the frustration on my face, and said, "Why are you doing this to yourself, Travis?"

"I don't know. It's just something inside me that refuses to let this go. I just don't know, honey." I could tell she was heartbroken over Malden's past being such a mystery to me. She probably knew in her heart the not knowing part was driving me crazy. I suspect she wished I would make peace with that as I know she had done. She placed her hand on my shoulder since I was back facing the computer screen searching for answers to Malden's past. She concluded at that point she would make the decision on the cranberry sauce on her own.

She walked back into the kitchen, looked at Malden sitting at the island, and reasoned, why not, when she decided to ask him now about his past, for my sake. She walked over to have a seat across from him, and started the conversation.

"Malden, can we talk for a moment, honey?" He stopped looking at his book, and stared at her while she spoke. "Look, Malden, you should know by now that we, Travis and I, love you very much. You've been here with us for a while now, and it's been great. You should also know this is your home, and will always be the place you can come to, no matter what."

She paused for a moment, and continued. "It's just we know so little about you, Malden. I'm okay with that, but you have to understand that truly bothers Travis because he loves you so much. You see, Malden, Travis isn't wired like you and I. It's the unknown, or the uncertainty of the past, I guess, or it's just a part of his chemistry. If he just knew something about you, honey, maybe it would be less of a burden on him. Do you understand what I'm saying, Malden?"

He stared at her after she said all that, with no emotion. He briefly paused, closed his book in his lap, spun off the bar stool, and walked toward my study putting his book into his pocket. She got up now to follow him to see what he would do. I was still sitting at my computer desk when I saw him walk into the room toward me from the corner of my eye.

I spun around to look at him, smiled, and said, "What's up buddy?" but never finished the word buddy when Malden wrapped his arms around me, and hugged me. I was startled by that, and couldn't understand what was going on. My arms were almost out straight while I saw Gretchen now standing at the entrance to my study.

He spoke in almost a whisper while he continued to hug me with his head on my shoulder, "It will be okay, sir." I felt paralyzed, for a moment while I stared at Gretchen, hugged the young man now, holding him, and patted him on the back. Malden released his hug, and walked out of the study using the other entrance toward the great room. I watched the young man leave, and looked back to see Gretchen wiping tears from her face as she turned to walk back to the kitchen.

The next day the Scott family enjoyed a wonderful turkey dinner, and now the long-anticipated moment had arrived, or at least from Gretchen's perspective. It was time to celebrate the start of the Christmas season after Thanksgiving dinner. All the dinner plates had been cleaned, and the pumpkin pie was ready for that evening when we'd all enjoy a slice. Shortly after we'd partake in another family tradition, and sit around to stare at our lighted Christmas tree.

I looked at Gretchen, and announced, "All right, I guess it's time to bring the tree in." I decided for a moment, if I tell her that Malden picked it out, I can save face, and avoid the conversation over the size of it. I told myself I shouldn't do that, but caved in, looked at her, and said quickly, "Malden picked out the tree." I said to Malden standing next to me, "Let's go, buddy," while we both walked out of the room hastily.

We eventually got the tree into the house, and set it in the stand. We all stood around this monstrosity of a tree in our great room now. Gretchen looked over to Malden, and said, "I think you picked out the best tree ever, Malden." She walked past me to retrieve the boxes of Christmas tree decorations from storage when I heard her say softly, "We'll have a talk later, Mister."

I heard that, dropped my head for a moment, realized I couldn't catch a break with this damn tree, looked to Malden, and said, "All right, buddy, let's get the lights." We walked out of the great room to go downstairs to the garage when I announced, "This will be the first time I ever needed a ladder to decorate a Christmas tree, Malden."

Gretchen had worked tirelessly on decorating the house for the holidays. It looked so festive and beautiful. She considered the Christmas tree, despite its size, the highlight of everything that represented the Christmas spirit in the Scott household.

She'd been so busy with Malden, and Christmas shopping that she hadn't had a moment to herself. Despite that, she was happy she was on schedule with everything she'd set her mind to.

She was in the middle of a class assignment for Malden, and was in the kitchen. She glanced over at the calendar, and said, "Crap!" She saw it was the 15th of December, and realized she hadn't wrapped, or sent our daughters their Christmas presents yet. She canceled part of her thinking process of being on schedule for everything, and rushed upstairs to get our daughters' presents to bring downstairs to wrap.

She decided that afternoon she would stop by the post office after she finished up some last minute Christmas shopping. She had our daughters' gifts all wrapped, boxed up, and finished filling out the shipping labels. She heard Marshall come into the house at the front door to pick up Malden. She shouted out, "How are you, Marshall?" as he walked into the kitchen, and Malden came out of the study.

"I'm fine, Mrs. Scott. Your house looks great!"

"Thanks, Marshall, it does look rather inviting, doesn't it?"

She asked Marshall if he was all set for Christmas when he responded, "Almost. I just have to do my shopping." She smiled, and alleged, typical for an eighteen-year-old, last minute, then realized, she was probably the same way at his age.

"Well, Marshall, you want to keep an eye on the calendar. It's less than two weeks away."

"I know, Mrs. Scott. I'll be doing some this weekend."

"All right, well, you boys have fun this afternoon. I have errands to run now."

"Okay, Mrs. Scott." He turned to Malden, and asked, "You all set?"

He answered, "Yes," and walked with Marshall out to the front door.

Gretchen was out and about, decided she'd stop by the post office last, and finish up her shopping while she drove to the main shopping center in town. She was at the mall finishing up in some stores buying more presents for Malden. She was so excited about all the stuff she bought for him, and couldn't remember now how many gifts in total, but realized there was a lot.

She finished her shopping, and left the store with bags in hand while she started her walk across the parking lot to her car. She thought, this is awesome, completed my last minute shopping, and can start to enjoy the next ten days before Christmas.

She walked down the row she had parked in, but out of nowhere, got that strange feeling again, like someone was watching her. She slowed her pace, stopped to look around, but saw nothing. She blurted out, "Huh," while she walked toward her SUV. She got to her vehicle opened the back passenger door when that same feeling came over her again.

This time, she turned around, and saw an older man about six or seven cars down just standing there staring at her. She was a little spooked by that, and looked behind her, thinking maybe he was staring at someone else, but no-one was there. She looked back, and saw the man still staring at her with a somewhat angry look about him. She turned, put her shopping bags into the back seat, looked back quickly, and shouted out, "What's your problem?" but the man was gone.

She scanned the parking lot where she just saw this older gentleman, and didn't see him anywhere. She shook it off, but was more than a little nervous. She quickly got into her SUV, and started the engine, so she could get to the post office to get our daughters' presents shipped.

She pulled into the town's post office, and said out loud, "Wow, it's busy here today." She concluded, well, it is Christmas time, and everyone is looking to ship their loved ones presents. She found a parking spot, opened the back of the SUV, retrieved the two boxes with our daughters' presents, and headed into the post office.

She was in line now with about fifteen people when she contemplated, I should have come earlier. Well, the line was moving fairly quickly, and only a few people were in front of her now.

She looked back to see how long the line was, and saw *him* again, staring at her with that angry look. She gasped silently, stared back at this man, turned away quickly, and said, "Crap," all the while thinking all kinds of horrible things.

She was frightened at that moment, and tried to tell herself she'd just imagined him. She took a deep breath, turned to look again, and saw the older man again staring back at her.

The person directly behind her asked, "Ma'am?"

She looked at him, and said, "Excuse me." The man motioned to her that she was the next in line to be helped. She looked over at the post office attendant waiting for her, and said to the man next to her, "I'm sorry." She walked over to the counter with the two boxes, leaned in, and said to the young man, "I think I'm being followed."

The young man replied, "Excuse me, ma'am?"

She looked up, and explained, "A man in line is following me. He's an older gentleman with a white cotton shirt buttoned all the way up with suspenders on. He looks like an Amish fella."

The young man leaned over to look out at the people in line, and said, "I don't see anyone, ma'am, who looks like that." She turned to look at the people in line, and saw the man was gone.

She shook her head, and stated, "I'm sorry, but he was there. I just know it."

The young man looked at her now, and asked, "Are you okay, ma'am?"

"Yes, I'm fine, just these two boxes please."

I was in my study working that evening while Malden was in his usual place in the great room. Gretchen was sitting at the kitchen island thinking about what had happened that afternoon. She could still see that man's angry face while he stared at her. She was trying to figure out what he wanted from her, and was convinced the man she saw had looked at her.

She was in a deep trance, couldn't stop seeing that man's face when she felt a tap on her shoulder, gasped loudly, turned around, and saw me. With a concerned look, I said, "Whoa there, it's just me, Gretchen. Are you all right, honey?"

She turned quickly, saw Malden standing at the kitchen entrance, and said, "Oh, my God, Travis, you startled me," while she held her chest with her hand. She looked at Malden, knew she had startled him as well, and said, "It's okay Malden, honey, you can go back to reading your book." He stared at her for a moment, like he was making sure she was all right before he turned to walk away.

I said, "Geez, honey, you almost gave me a heart attack."

"I'm sorry, Travis, I guess I'm tired."

Later that evening Gretchen and I had retired, and said our goodnights. She laid her head on her pillow, and fell asleep almost immediately into a dream state.

She dreamt I had startled her again in the kitchen when I asked her, "Why don't you get yourself a glass of wine, and let's take a load off out on the patio?"

"Sounds like a great idea, Travis." She poured herself a glass of wine, met me on the patio, and sat down.

I looked at her, and asked, "You sure you're okay, honey?"

"Yes, I'm fine, Travis."

I blurted out, "Crap! I totally forgot to do what you asked me, Gretchen." I got up, shook my head, and headed back into the kitchen. She watched me rush past the island, and turned left toward the great room as I left the room. She got up curious to find out what I was doing, entered the kitchen, and closed the slider behind her.

She got halfway through the kitchen, and heard some noise coming from the great room. The noise got louder as she continued to walk. She turned out of the kitchen, down the hall to the great room, but for some unknown reason, she was standing on the side of a bridge with lots of traffic moving left to right going really fast.

She looked up, and saw me with Malden staring at her from the other side of the bridge. She shouted out over the noise of the traffic in front of her, "What are you doing, Travis?"

I shouted back, "I'm sorry, Gretchen, it just got away from me!"

She shouted again, "What are you talking about, Travis?"

I turned slowly to Malden next to me, and said, "All right, Malden, I want you to jump off this bridge."

Her face was in a panic now after she heard that, and talked out loud to herself, "No, Travis, please." She paced back and forth trying to find space between the traffic to cross the bridge, but there were too many cars and trucks zipping by in front of her.

She continued to pace trying to cross while cars and trucks were honking at her now. She heard me shout, "Watch out for the traffic, Gretchen!" She stopped pacing, and stared in shock when she saw Malden on the top railing of the bridge staring back at her.

I looked over the railing, turned to her, and shouted, "Wow, honey, we're up really high." She stared in horror as I turned to him, and said, "Don't make her wait, son."

Gretchen's world stopped for a moment while she talked to herself, "No, Travis, please," then shouted out loudly, "Don't you do it, Malden!" She was frantically trying to cross the bridge to get to the other side, but couldn't, and heard only the horns from the cars and trucks as she tried. She waited now for several semis to pass in front of her.

As they passed, she could only see me standing there, staring at her from across the bridge. She couldn't see Malden anywhere. Her eyes were wide open in shock as she held her hands up to her face, tears running down her cheeks, and whispered, "Please, God, no, not Malden."

I shouted out now, "You were right, Gretchen. He did exactly what I told him."

She screamed after she heard that, "Travis nooooooooooooo!"

Gretchen woke up, still in a dream state, sitting up in bed breathing heavily, wiping the tears from her face while she tried to calm down. After a few moments, she had composed herself when she looked around the room, and was confused at where she was. She called out my name, "Travis," but there was no response.

She looked down, saw a thin quilt covering her legs, pulled it away from her body, and got up from the bed. She wondered for a moment, still confused, and asked aloud, "Where am I?" She looked around the small room, saw just four walls, and no windows. She glanced down by her side, and saw an old wooden table next to the bed with an antique oil lamp, with a Bible lying next to it. She reached out to touch the Bible, ran her fingers across the leather cover, looked up, and could see into another room past the doorway.

She walked out of the small room, and noticed there was no door built into the frame. She was in a larger room now, and saw an old wooden table with three wooden chairs directly in front of her. She walked farther into the room, and saw an old-fashioned fireplace beyond the wooden table and chairs. There was a large cast iron pot hanging from a metal arm next to it. She noticed several cast iron pots and pans that hung on the fireplace by metal hooks protruding from the stone face.

She glanced around the room, but saw only one window next to an old wooden door with leather-like hinges supporting it, and almost nothing else. The window was covered with a thin white material that looked like it was made of silk, supported by some wooden pegs allowing the daylight into the room. She called out my name again, "Travis," but still no response.

She slowly walked to the old wooden door, opened it, and walked outside. She could see what appeared to be a bunch of these old shack-like homes up and down both sides of the dirt road she was standing on. She looked past her nightgown at her bare feet, standing in the dirt when she heard someone shout out, "WATCH OUT, ma'am," and turned to see two large horses coming at her.

She stepped aside in the nick of time, and watched the horses pass by her drawing an old wooden wagon. She watched the young man who called out to her, staring back as it continued on down the road.

She looked around, and saw people, mostly mothers with their children holding hands walking on both sides of the dirt road wearing dresses and bonnets like something from an old Amish movie.

She walked out farther into the street, and saw a young woman down the road walking away holding a young man's hand. As she looked more closely she could see it was Malden. She shouted out, "Malden," and walked toward them to try and catch up. She noticed a group of men hastily approaching the young woman, and Malden walking on the dirt road. She could see the men's faces that were angry, and determined.

She quickened her pace, and watched while the bigger man in front approached the young woman. He shoved Malden to the ground, still holding the young woman's hand. Gretchen shouted, "NO! Malden." She rushed to get to him, watched in horror when she saw the large man raise an open fist, and strike the young woman in the face. She was startled by the violent impact, and the sound of the young woman being struck. She stopped dead in her tracks, covered her face with both hands after she witnessed that, and watched the young woman fall straight to the ground.

Malden screamed, "MOTHER," while he got up from the ground to get to her. The larger man grabbed him, and violently shoved him back to the ground.

Gretchen shouted again, "NO!" and watched while the large man stepped closer to the young woman on the ground. Gretchen could see the blood on her face, and the woman still dazed from the violent hit she sustained.

The large man was holding a closed fist out to her looking down with an angry voice, almost spitting at the young woman while he spoke, "We found him, he's dead." Gretchen looked down now, saw Malden on the ground trying to reach out to the young woman, and heard him say, "Mother." The large man still standing over the woman said just as angry now, "You're a witch! You'll pay for this!"

Gretchen heard soft voices all around her now from the mothers and children whispering, "She's a witch, burn the witch. The witch's spawn must also die," over and over again. She looked all around while she listened to the voices, and looked back at Malden, still on the ground as he turned to look at her.

She stared at him while tears ran down her face, speaking out, "No, please, Malden." Malden was still calling for his mother as the tears rolled down his cheeks while he continued to stare back at Gretchen.

She was frozen by the sight of seeing Malden cry, and spoke softly, "Please, Malden, don't cry, honey, it will be okay." She looked at the group of men still standing over the young woman beaten down on the road when one of the men looked up and over at her now with an angry look. She stared back at the older man, and remembered. She whispered aloud, "Oh, God, please no," recognizing the man who had been stalking her.

Her eyes were wide open in shock when the man now separated himself from the group, and started to walk toward her on the dirt road. She shook her head, and said, "No, please, God, don't let this be happening." The older man was almost running toward her now. She was frozen with fear as the angry man was upon her. She covered her entire face, and screamed, "Noooooooooooo, Travis!"

Gretchen woke up abruptly, sitting on her bed, hands still covering her face, and her breathing labored over the dream she just had. She looked over at me asleep next to her, wiped the tears from her face, and looked over to see Malden standing in the bedroom doorway. She slid out of bed quietly, so she wouldn't wake me, walked over to Malden, knelt, and whispered, "You okay, Malden?"

He stared back at her, and responded, "Yes, ma'am." She pulled him toward her, and hugged the young man for a brief moment then stood. She wiped her face again, and looked over at me, still sleeping.

She turned to him while he stared back at her still, and whispered, "Come on, Malden, let's get you back to bed."

The following days Gretchen often thought about the dream she had, but didn't want to burden me with that, and tried to carry on normally. She had tried her best to understand what her dream meant, but couldn't for the life of her understand any of it. She eventually put that aside in the back of her mind, had no more bad dreams, and wasn't bothered by any more thoughts, or premonitions of people watching her. She was back to doing what she did best now, enjoying the Christmas holiday season with her family.

CHAPTER 14

I woke that morning feeling a little different, I recalled, sitting up in bed. Perhaps a little anxiety since it was Christmas Eve, but not quite sure. I shrugged off the feeling, so I could enjoy the Christmas spirit all around me. I remembered how great the house looked with all its charm and decorations. Gretchen certainly got into the Christmas spirit, and decorated everything so perfectly.

I made up my mind that today would be the day I enjoyed the holiday, and put aside work for a change, or at least some of it since I still had responsibilities to attend to at the store. I remembered past Christmas', and felt like they had come and gone without a moment to enjoy them. Well, I thought, today will be different.

I pictured Malden, trying to imagine his reaction when he wakes up on Christmas morning to a boatload of gifts wrapped under the tree. I know Gretchen's heart was in the right place, and felt guilty now for telling her all the presents she bought for him was a little over the top. After all, it is Christmas.

I smiled, staring at my wife sleeping next to me, and knew how lucky I'd been to have met a woman like her. I could go on and on about all the positive qualities she's brought to our marriage. The endless love and support she provided, and how awesome a mother and protector of the family, just to mention a few.

I recalled how fortunate I was to have met her parents, and got to know them long before they passed away. They're the main reason my wife is who she is today. I miss her mom and dad as much as she does, I imagine. It was cool when the kids were younger, and we all got together with them from time to time.

Her dad was in the military when he was younger, so I attributed his call of duty type of personality to that. Her mom was a sweetheart, but a firm mom with rules when the children were growing up. I can honestly say if asked, providing a one-word answer to the question, what best describes the love between Travis and Gretchen? My answer would be, "Miracle."

I started to think about my own parents who occasionally call, and miss their voices, but get so busy at times I forget that while life goes on. I'm glad my mom and dad are onboard with Malden, and hope to introduce them to him soon. Maybe a trip to Florida after the holidays is in order. I am glad they both live a full life, and keep pretty busy doing their own thing in retirement.

I leaned over, looked at the clock, then to Gretchen, who's still sleeping, and said to myself, you know what? I'm sleeping in this morning. I, Travis Scott, have worked tirelessly all year long, and deserve some extra time. So by God, that is what I'm going to do. I leaned back down on my pillow, and fell right back to sleep.

It wasn't long before I was awoken by the smell of breakfast sausages cooking, and the sweet aroma of coffee brewing. I leaned over to look at the clock and saw it was 8:30. I had to refocus my eyes to believe it was several hours from the time I first woke. I said to myself, holy crap, 8:30. I never sleep in this late.

I said to myself nice going, Travis, you made up your mind to sleep in because you deserved it, but slept the whole damn morning away. "Crap, crap, crap," I silently spoke while I got up, and went to the bathroom. After finishing my business, I leaned over the sink, and looked in the mirror while that uneasy feeling came over me again. "What the hell, Travis," I said to myself, trying to set the feeling aside.

I went downstairs, walked into the kitchen where Gretchen was busy making breakfast, and the first words I heard after I kissed her was, "Morning, sleepy head."

I responded, "I know, I know."

She stated, "Well, you need to hurry up, eat your breakfast, and shower soon, Travis. I have a lot of things to do before we can sit down this evening, and enjoy our Christmas Eve with Malden."

I asked, "Where is Malden? Is he here?"

"Marshall swung by around 8:00 to pick him up, and bring him to the store." I recalled Malden was technically on Christmas school break this week, and it was okay for him to spend more time at the store, which he freely accepted.

I looked at the wonderful breakfast she cooked in front of me, and said, "I'll try to wrap this up, and take a shower, so I can get to the store."

"What time do you think you'll be home this evening, Travis?"

I answered, "We're closing the store at five p.m., so I imagine somewhere around six. It depends on how many late shoppers are around getting last minute presents for Christmas. Not to worry, there's no place I'd rather be than here on Christmas Eve. I'll play the Grinch role if I have to."

She announced, "Okay, I'm done, and need to get going. Remember, Travis, five p.m. close the store, so we can spend quality time with Malden tonight. I want us all to sit down, watch "A Christmas Story," and order Chinese food. I'm so excited."

I responded, "Yes, ma'am."

She looked at me, smiled, and said, "You sound like Malden now."

I chuckled, "Ha, Ha, funny girl."

I finished the quickest shower and shave I believe I've ever taken. I reminded myself again as I was leaving the house that today was all about enjoying the holiday, and remembering all the good things we're blessed with. It can be so hard to focus on the holiday, and the true meaning of Christmas with the associated glitz, TV commercials, and all the presents. I mean, honestly, isn't Christmas supposed to mean something more?

I know we live in a me generation, mostly due to the incredible technological advances we enjoy now with computers, CD players, and everything in between. I guess that's the price we've paid for making it to 1995. Well, I'm not buying it. I'll remember today it's the people around me I care about, love, and those who love me. Not because I'm a wrapped present with some stupid toy inside, but the person whom everyone looks to for enjoyment, support, and just want to be with. That's what I want for Christmas, a nice day with my family, colleagues, and friends. So be it.

I blurted out, "Wow," turning into the parking lot of the main store, and seeing all the cars, and foot traffic of people coming and going into the store. Pretty cool sight. It looked like one of those massive hornet nests with one side of the entrance as busy as the other. Not to say our customers are hornets, just saying what came to mind when I pulled in.

It took a bit to get to my parking space on the side of the building though. I decided today I'll walk out to the front entrance, and enter the building like everyone else. It was a fairly warm day for this time of year, particularly on December 24th. I got my briefcase out of the back seat, and started my ascent into the parking lot area toward the front entrance.

It was nice to see all the people that looked happy, and excited it was Christmas Eve. I didn't want to spoil my earlier thoughts of what I wanted Christmas to be about, so I dismissed the idea they were all here to buy gifts for the holiday. I kept that to myself since after all, I am responsible for the outcome of sales for the store. I certainly wouldn't last long, promoting a no buying Christmas gift policy.

I approached the main entrance, and said, "Good morning, Claire."

She responded with a smile, "Well, hello, Mr. Scott. How are you, and Merry Christmas?"

"Thank you, Claire, and a Merry Christmas to you, and your family! How are things this morning?"

Claire is one of our seasonal store greeters, and I have to say, I've never met a sweeter person. She is a person you'd wish was your grandmother, with an incredible smile, and positive personality. I can't tell you how many suggestions I've received this past year recommending her, for employee of the century. It's remarkable how friendly she is, and how she makes our customers feel welcome when they walk into the store.

She responded, "Well, Mr. Scott, I have to say this is one of the busiest Christmas Eves I've seen in a long time. She added, "Much busier than last year."

I agreed, "Yes, I can see that, Claire. It is nice, isn't it? Well, enjoy your day, and take a break here and there."

"I sure will, Mr. Scott, and please give my best to the Mrs."

"I will, Claire, and Merry Christmas again." I walked past the front entrance, and heard

Claire's voice fade in the distance while I walked farther into the store, still hearing the customers respond to her greetings. Now I thought, finally, a sign of what Christmas was shaping up to be.

I saw Winette by the checkout area, and proceeded over to say hello. She noticed me as I approached, "Merry Christmas, Travis!"

"Same to you, Winette," I exclaimed. "Very busy here today. You surely have your work cut out for you."

"Not to worry, Travis, we are at full staff, and all is running smoothly."

"I can see that, and wouldn't have imagined it any other way." I asked, "Have you seen Malden, or Marshall around?"

"No. I know Marshall is here since I saw him earlier this morning. Do you want me to send someone to look for them?"

"No, that's all right, Winette. I'll find them myself, but thanks for the offer. Well, have a nice day, and I'll see you at closing." I remembered something now, and announced, "Almost forgot, Winette." I reached into my briefcase to find her Christmas card among all the cards I had for my managers. "Here it is," and handed it to her, "Merry Christmas again, Winette."

She smiled, and said, "Thank you, Travis."

I turned to walk away, and called out, "Don't spend it all in one place unless it's here." I smiled while I walked away enjoying the funny comment I came up with. Okay, so no Malden, or Marshall in sight. Oh well, I'm sure they're working somewhere in the store. I'll hook up with them later, and make sure Malden has a ride back to the house.

I truly was getting into the Christmas spirit, and what better way to spend it by being somewhere you enjoy. The first item on the agenda is to see the rest of my managers to wish them a Merry Christmas, and deliver them their Christmas cards.

While I walked the short quarter mile to the entrance of my managers' offices, I reflected on what a special year this had been for me in so many ways. It's not just that the store did well financially, and the fact I received a nice bonus check due to that.

I couldn't stop thinking about how much happier I'd been since Malden came into our lives. Still, for the life of me, couldn't figure him out to this day. I know it's only been six months. It seems, so ironic, for as much love, joy, and happiness he's brought to the table, I still can't tell whether the child is happy, or sad.

I know Gretchen feels differently about him. I guess with her it's that maternal instinct that mothers are blessed with that nobody can figure out. I just don't know. I think I should feel sad because of it, yet all the while I'm happy he's in our lives. I hope someday he opens up his feelings, and expressions, so I can tell if he's actually happy, or sad. My God, I'll even let him take his best shot at me, just not in the face, if that would open the child up. Well, I guess all I can hope for is to pray he is content, has found a place he can grow, and prosper.

I arrived at the entrance to the offices, and stopped for a moment to look out over the store. I saw all the decorations my staff worked tirelessly on, and paused for a moment thinking how cool it was to be a part of all this.

I opened the door to the offices, and walked up the stairs. About halfway up in my mind, I was brought back to the days I worked with some pretty smart people that designed these supercenters. I thought for a moment, and wondered why I never suggested a damn elevator to my office. I announced, "Man, I must be getting old," as I stepped onto the landing at the top of the stairs. I didn't even get to walk to my office when Mary stepped out of hers, and said, "Your wife is on the phone, Travis."

I acknowledged, "Thanks, Mary, and Merry Christmas!"

She offered, "You can take the call in my office if you'd like."

"Okay, sounds good." I walked into her office while she handed me the phone, and mentioned she'd be right back to speak with me.

I greeted Gretchen, "Hi honey, what's up?"

She responded, "I ordered the Chinese food, so you and Malden need to stop by, and pick it up on your way home. You're on schedule, right? Closing at five?"

I affirmed, "Yes, honey, I'm on schedule and will pick up the food."

"Awesome, you're the best. Everything is all set for this evening. I spoke with the girls, wished them a Merry Christmas, and sent them your love."

"Thanks, honey. I should've been there to speak with them. After all, it is Christmas."

"That's all right, Travis, they understand how busy you are, and wished you a Merry Christmas." Both girls are usually with us during the holidays, but this year was different. One was off on a cruise with her boyfriend, and the other was spending time out of state visiting college friends. Having Malden spend the holiday with us was filling that void for Gretchen with the girls being away. It's funny how life is sometimes, and how certain people believe everything happens for a reason. Well, I may be one of those people now.

"Okay, honey, let me go, so I can finish my tour, and find out where Malden is."

She responded suspiciously, "What do you mean where Malden is, Travis?"

"I just haven't run into him yet today, honey. It is a big store, Gretchen."

"Well, it's like 3:00 in the afternoon, so watch your time, Travis."

"I will, honey, I promise. I'll look for Malden when I'm done with handing out the rest of the Christmas cards to my managers."

"All right, well, just call me if you'll be late, so I don't worry."

"Yes, dear, and love you."

"Love you too, Travis."

Mary entered her office as I finished my call with Gretchen, handed her back the phone, and again wished her a Merry Christmas. I reached into my briefcase to present her with her Christmas card, and handed it to her.

She smiled, and said, "Thank you, Travis, it's been a good year for the store."

"I know," while I added, "It was a good team effort."

She looked at me, and noticed something different. She asked, "You okay, Travis? You look a little flustered of sorts."

"I'm all right. I just woke up this morning with a pit in my stomach. You know, when you feel like something bad is going to happen. I've been trying to convince myself all day it's just holiday stress. Not to worry, I'll be fine, Mary." I walked over to her, gave her a hug, and said, "Thanks for all the hard work, and putting up with all the extra Malden work this year."

She smiled, and responded, "Look, Travis, I know I was somewhat skeptical when this young man came into everyone's lives, especially yours. I can see now why you were drawn to him in such a way. He's a terrific kid." She continued, "I'll be selfish, and say if we could clone him, I would put one of him on every shift, in every department. I mean this kid is a working machine."

I agreed, "I know, Mary," while I laughed at her assessment of him. I added, "He definitely grows on you. It's strange, Mary, every time I think of him, or being around him, I don't know whether to laugh, or cry. It's so weird. I've been on this planet for over fifty years, and have never met a person like him."

She went on to say, "Look, Travis, we still don't know a darn thing about this child outside of what he's shared with us, and that amounts to almost nothing. There's an underlying reason for that behavior, whether it's his mom dying, or some bad way he was raised. Nobody knows, Travis, no one except for Malden."

Mary added, "He's no different than any other child, and will open up when he's ready. I've seen the way he looks at you." She paused a moment when she added, "He's like a lost sheep trying to find his flock with you as his guardian angel protecting the path to wherever it is he's trying to get to. He'll come around, I'm sure, just give him a chance, and some more time."

"Thanks, Mary, you're the best."

I walked out of her office, and saw Marshall coming up the stairs. "Hey, Marshall, where've you been all day?"

He answered, "I've been here, Mr. Scott, just coming up to see Mary in HR."

"I guess I just missed seeing you around. Do you know where Malden is right now?"

"No, sir. I don't think he's even at the store."

I looked at him with a nervous blank stare, and replied, "Excuse me, what do you mean, he's not here? You picked him up from my house this morning. My wife told me you did. So, why would he not be here with you?" My voice was at a stern pitch, slightly shouting, while I spoke with him now.

"I'm sorry, Mr. Scott, I did pick Malden up this morning, brought him here, but he said he needed to do something, and left the store. I'm sorry, but I haven't seen him since this morning." Mary heard the slight shouting, and came out of her office.

She nervously asked, "Travis, what's the matter? Why are you shouting?"

I looked at her, and responded, "Not now, Mary," and quickly turned my attention back to Marshall. "Marshall, what did Malden say this morning after you dropped him off?"

"I don't know, sir, he just mentioned he was dropping off a gift, and said that thing he mentions from time to time."

My voice was louder now, clearly shouting at him while I continued, and said, "Marshall, what gift, and what thing are you talking about?" I leaned toward him with even more concern growing in my voice.

Mary interrupted, "Travis, please, what's the problem?" while she grew nervous about the whole situation.

I shouted back, "Not now, I said, Mary!" and extended my arm toward her like I was trying to point the words I had just said to her.

Marshall nervously continued, "He dropped off a wrapped present in your office, sir before he took off this morning."

I shouted again, "Damn it, Marshall, what else did Malden say?"

"He said that thing, um, he would say occasionally. Oh, I know, it was, *LIKE A*

WITCH'S BREW. I'm sure that was it. I never understood some of the things he said, Mr. Scott. I'm sorry, sir, I'm going out right now to look for him."

As he turned, I grabbed his arm, stopped him from leaving, and announced, "It's all right, Marshall, you don't have to do that," in a much softer tone. I realized this was the moment in time I'd been stressing over all day. I somehow knew in my heart Malden had left, and wasn't coming back. I said to Marshall again, "It's all right."

Visions flashed through my mind from the first encounter of seeing him on the surveillance video in the parking lot. I saw all the times in between, up to last night when I walked past his room, and said goodnight before he went to bed.

I turned to see poor Mary holding her hands up to her face in disbelief of what just happened, not used to seeing that side of me, in almost a fit of rage. I walked past her, patted her on the shoulder, for reassurance the moment had passed, and no more shouting, nor angry words would be said. I walked into her office, picked up my briefcase, and walked down the corridor to my office.

I opened my office door, and saw a shoebox-size package wrapped sitting on my desk. I was still grappling with the images of young Malden flashing through my mind while I sat, and stared at the present. I was confused, and still reeling from the sick feeling in my stomach I'd felt all day.

I mustered up the nerve to move the package closer, opened the shoebox top, and looked inside. I couldn't believe what I saw as I lifted the contents out of the box. It was the book Malden cherished, *LIKE A WITCH'S BREW*. I tried to understand what that all meant, and why he would part from the one thing that was so important to him.

My mind strayed while I tried to handle the book that had seen better times. I could barely hold the book without the pages falling out from the worn and tattered spine. It looked like it had been through all the world wars. I never gave this book much thought other than it was the central focus point for Malden, who would read the darn thing every time he had a chance. I mean, if I had to guess, he'd probably read the book a hundred, or more times.

I tried to come to grips with the whole situation, and why he'd given me this as a present. I could see Gretchen in my mind, at home waiting for us to show up to spend Christmas Eve all together, and not sure what I'll tell her. I just knew she'd be devastated.

My mind switched back again to Malden, the small child I reached out to in his time of need. I wished I could have another chance to speak with him, and ask what I could've done more to help, or understand his situation. I was wrecked emotionally, questioning if I did something wrong, or was there some sign I missed I should've reacted to. All the while I kept thinking I'd miss him, and wondered if I'll ever see him again.

I looked at the book, and saw the image of him holding it, reading it endlessly. For whatever reason, I theorized this was the boy's release from dealing with the past, or some tragedy in his life, and was the coping mechanism to escape from those memories.

I stared at the book, *"LIKE A WITCH'S BREW,"* and read the book's preface.

"A tale of a time long lost and forgotten where folklore belief trump the basic laws of nature, and common sense. A time when logic is not the common sense denominator of truth, but the bias of folklore handed down from generation to generation. A time unlike no other where unexplained things are attributed to witchcraft and guilt is decided by elders swayed by the folklore."

"This is a story that takes place in a small township called Salem's Village in 1692 in a colony of Massachusetts. A young woman with her thirteen-year-old child was accused of being a witch after the mysterious death of her husband. Sally Crenshaw knows all too well this accusation will lead to her death, the capture, torture, and eventual death of her son Malden. It is the endless love for her only child to act to save his life, and releases him secretly one night into the cruel world she brought the child into."

"Sally is eventually tried and convicted of being a witch along with her son. She is sentenced to death, hung in the public village, and her body burned to ashes. The township elders form an Alliance, a group of men sworn to die in their pursuit to find, and destroy the spawn of the witch's brew. The Alliance soon discovers the young man can manipulate portals of time, and must follow the child through these passages to fulfill their mission to bring justice to the Alliance. Now the hunt is on, for the missing child named Malden."

I finished reading the preface, leaned back in my office chair, and said, "Son of a bitch." I couldn't believe what I was reading. How did I miss that? This whole thing about Malden being Malden is from a book. I was so confused after what I had just read. Was Malden trapped in some storyline in a book he's read all these years? Is that possible? I whispered, "Why would he do that?" I was interrupted now by a knock on my door. I put the book into my briefcase, turned to my office door, and said, "Come in."

It was Mary letting me know it's after five pm, and everyone was getting set to leave for the night.

I responded, "All right, Mary, I'll finish the close. Just lock the doors, and I'll alarm when I leave."

Mary, with a concerned look, asked, "Are you all right, Travis?"

"Yes, Mary, I'm fine. I just need some time alone to figure out a few things."

"Okay, Travis, call me if you need anything, and Merry Christmas."

"Thanks, Mary, you're a good friend, and Merry Christmas to you." She left me sitting in my office trying to figure out why Malden would assume a life of a character out of a book, but I couldn't understand any of it. There had to be a damn good reason for all of this, I thought. I decided to think about that more, but needed to get home to Gretchen, and try to explain to her where Malden was.

I left my office, finished the store close, and alarmed the building while I exited the employee entrance. I was conflicted, thoughts of Malden not going home with me, and not knowing where he's at, or if he was in trouble were weighing heavily on my heart.

I walked over to my car, but all the while I had stared down the access road hoping I would see him again. I opened the door, put my briefcase in the front seat, and decided I needed to go back to the place where it all started. I reflected, for a moment, and started to reach in to grab the flashlight out of the glove box, but stopped, and realized, I didn't need it. I no longer had any thoughts of fear going into the woods. I walked down the access road, and stopped at the tree line behind the store. I thought back to the last time I was here, and how vivid the memory was that seemed so long ago.

I ventured into the woods, and made my way to the place I first found him. I stared at the makeshift tent, that's now collapsed, that was once the place he slept at night. I leaned over to touch the dirty tarp that looked like it collapsed on the tree branches from the weight of it over time. I looked at some old rotting boxes of food on the ground I assumed he retrieved from the dumpsters in the back of the store. No sign of Malden though.

I chuckled, and remembered how scared I was the last time I was here. I could see him in my mind that night, so long ago, staring up at me with those innocent eyes, after he scared the crap out of me. Well, I'm glad he wasn't here, hoped wherever he was that he's all right, and prayed that would always be the case.

I wasn't sure why I needed to be there again, but maybe in the corner of my mind, I was hoping he would be. I realized that place was just a moment in time that led the young man to me. I thought this was like some cruel joke, never understanding the meaning, because the punchline was never revealed. I gathered myself, decided to leave the place I met him, for the last time, and head back home. I reached the back of the supercenter, and turned to the woods one last time before I headed back to my car.

I arrived home alone, not knowing how I'd explain where Malden was to Gretchen. I decided to park in the driveway, and use the front entrance just so I could walk past the sitting area Malden frequented almost daily to read his book. I entered the front foyer, closed the door behind me, and heard the sounds of a Christmas song, by Burl Ives Gretchen had playing over the sound system in the house. My favorite song was playing, "Christmas Can't Be Far Away."

I stood in the foyer holding my briefcase, and listened to the music. Gretchen walked out of the kitchen, into the great room wearing her Frosty the Snowman apron, and drying her hands with a towel. She looked at me, and asked, "Where's Malden?" I was frozen, and couldn't seem to find the words to say that would make this any less hard for her.

She stared back at me, saw the sadness in my eyes, could sense something was wrong while she dropped her arms to her side, and the towel she'd been holding dropped to the floor. I stared back at her, still unable to speak when the inevitable unfolded. Her eyes started to well with tears. She knew Malden was gone. I dropped my briefcase, and walked over to her, and wrapped my arms around her to comfort her while she cried uncontrollably. She looked at me while she wept, and declared, "Why, Travis, why?"

I tried to deal with the situation, and could barely contain the emotion of crying myself. I continued to hug her, whispering, "Shhh, it'll be okay."

She continued to cry on my shoulder, and tried to say, "It's Christmas, Malden has to unwrap his presents, it's not fair, Travis."

I continued to comfort my wife, and tried not to cry myself when I told her softly, "I promise you, honey, this is not over. We'll find Malden again. It's not over, sweetheart." Gretchen and I continued to hold one another as the music continued to play, both in denial, not wanting to accept Malden was no longer with us.

CHAPTER 15

I leaned against the kitchen counter while Gretchen sat at the island the following morning. I had tried to figure out if it was one, or two hours of sleep we both got last night. She was struggling to drink her cup of coffee, and could see how upset she was about Malden not waking up this Christmas morning with his family.

I thought back to last night, and the phone call I made to Detective Cody after I settled her down after hearing the heartbreaking news Malden had gone missing. I remembered the conversation word for word, and agreed to meet with Detective Cody back at the store since that was the last place anyone could remember seeing him.

I remembered how I pleaded with Gretchen to wait at the house while I took care of that, but she would have nothing to do with it. She was as anxious as any mother who had just lost a child, to be there no matter what, in the search for him.

It's difficult, for me to see sadness, or despair in my wife, especially when she cries. It breaks my heart, and is the one thing in life I try to avoid like the plaque. I recalled why Detective Cody wanted to check out the store last night, but I knew in my heart Malden wouldn't be there, and the whole thing to me was a useless exercise in futility.

Just the same, Gretchen and I drove back to the store on Christmas Eve, to meet with

Detective Cody. I revisited how I opened the store back up, turned on all the lights, and waited outside with Gretchen as she sat in the SUV while I leaned against the passenger door next to her.

I broke from thought, and looked at her sitting at the island, her eyes all puffy from crying all night, trying to come to grips with the situation. I said to myself, this is the worst Christmas ever.

I was brought back to last evening again while we waited for Detective Cody to arrive. Gretchen and I didn't speak a word while we waited. I was startled by the response of the town's police department when I heard police car after police car with sirens wailing, pulling into the store parking lot. I remembered seeing ten or more police cars that showed up. Detective Cody was leading the pack, and was the first to drive up to Gretchen and me.

I could still see the detective walking up to me while I had my arms crossed. He clearly saw the pain and suffering on our faces over Malden's disappearance. He apologized for having to meet this way while I nodded in agreement. He asked the typical detective questions, hoping something said would bring light to where Malden might be.

I answered all the questions as best I could, but knew Malden was somewhere else now, for reasons unknown to anyone. I thanked him for the large police response.

Detective Cody looked back at me, and acknowledged, "I have kids, too, Mr. Scott. I would expect nothing less." He continued to see the heartbreak and pain in my expression only a father could project when he's lost a child. I remembered Detective Cody saying, "We won't stop looking, Mr. Scott, until we--," but paused, and never completed his sentence.

I looked at him, for a moment, and said, "I know, Detective, I know."

The search turned up nothing, as I expected. Several hours passed before I could secure the store, and take Gretchen home to an empty house, now void of the young man she fell in love with. I surmised when that moment might have been, and decided, maybe the first day I brought him home.

I thanked several police officers who all projected a positive outlook on finding the young man, but Gretchen and I knew the disappearance of Malden was deeper than anyone could imagine. I realized this was as mysterious as his unknown past.

Gretchen and I got past Christmas Day, which in itself, was a miracle based on all that had happened. I was convinced that waking up the following morning was the hardest for her, not pouring young Malden a bowl of cereal for breakfast.

I was so frustrated over all that's happened, and questioned how you comfort someone whose child was missing. You can't, it's just impossible. I felt bad now when I tried to salvage Christmas in some small way, and hoped, maybe presenting Gretchen with her Christmas gifts might help take her mind off of things. That was a colossal mistake. She told me with no uncertainty that Christmas would only be celebrated when Malden returned home, period.

It was difficult to watch her on Christmas morning get the phone calls from our daughters while she tried to explain why Malden wasn't there, and fought back tears on several occasions. I realized those moments had been the hardest times I've had to go through in my entire life.

I decided to take a break from all the hardship around me. I headed into my study, walked past Malden's desk that sat in front of mine, and couldn't help but chuckle while I saw him sitting there in past thoughts. I remembered how long it took to put the darn thing together, and how he was dwarfed by the size of it when he first sat at his new desk.

I remembered having to buy him a special chair, so he could sit at the desk normally because of its size. He didn't seem to mind though since I knew he was just content to be in my study. I made my way to my desk, had a seat while I looked at my briefcase. I saw Malden's book *LIKE A WITCH'S BREW,* I'd placed in there on Christmas Eve when Mary came to see me in my office.

I shook my head, remembered reading the preface, what the story was all about, and seeing

Malden's name front and center of the tale. I took the book out of my briefcase, straightened out the pages against the spine, and decided, why not read the book? What else did I have to do right now, other than feeling like crap that my buddy wasn't here with me?

I initially struggled with the story while it seemed to have been written in a sort of English slang of the period it was written about. I recalled thinking, I know this is English, but why did people talk like that back in the day, and what's with all the random capitalized words? I thought I was reading a new sentence after every capitalized noun, for God's sake.

I read on, but often had to read a sentence or two over again to get the full meaning. As time passed, I felt like I could carry on a conversation with someone who actually grew up in the 1600's. I spent hours on end reading his book, but would occasionally take a break to find Gretchen to see how she was doing. Little had changed though which didn't surprise me in the least.

I continued reading the book Malden read constantly, and was surprised how well-formed the Alliance was in tracking down the main character Malden, in each chapter. He outwitted those Alliance thugs one at a time. I said to myself, good for you, kid. They were some sick individuals who stopped at nothing to eliminate Malden, in the name of justice for the Alliance. Chapter after chapter I read, was ready to take a break from these sick puppies, spend time with

Gretchen, and hopefully make some small difference in comforting her emotional wounds.

The next day I was ready, for my first day back to work without saying goodbye to Malden. I was sad, frustrated, and angry at myself for not seeing any clues I might have acted on to avert his disappearance.

I finished my coffee, and was set to leave, but didn't see Gretchen anywhere. I checked the main floor, and dropped my briefcase down in the kitchen to go check upstairs. I made my way up, walked by Malden's room, and saw her sitting on his bed holding something in her hand. I walked in, and asked, "You okay, honey?" She kept looking at something in her hands while I sat next to her on the bed. I could now see her holding Malden's picture ID, and noticed she'd been crying.

She said, "I miss him so much, Travis."

I answered softly, "I know you do, Gretchen," while I held my wife close trying to comfort her.

She sighed, and said, "Well, Travis, you need to get to work."

I sat there holding my wife, and responded, "I can sit here all day if I want."

She smiled, turned to me, kissed me, and said, "Don't be silly, I'll be fine," as she got up, and we both walked out of Malden's room.

***

I was back to work, and had to deal with the uncomfortable meet and greet of my life from my staff since word traveled fast around the supercenter. I decided that's all right. I probably would do the same if it were someone else on my staff that had to go through the same. I made my way to my office when I saw Marshall down one of the houseware aisles, and diverted my walk over to him. I could sense a difference in him after I said, "Good morning, Marshall."

He responded, "Morning, sir," but didn't look directly at me. I knew at that point he somehow felt responsible for Malden's disappearance.

I stared at the young man, and said, "Marshall, look at me." He stared directly at me while I shook my head, and said, "None of this is your fault. Listen carefully, and never forget what I'm about to say to you. You need to understand you're one of a select few people in this world that Malden associated with. You've been a good mentor and friend to him, and I'll never forget that now, or in the future, son. None of this is your fault, Marshall, not one bit. You understand me?"

He nodded in agreement, and said, "I hope he comes back soon, sir."

I smiled at him, and answered, "I hope so too, son."

I managed to get through the rest of the day, but was dreading the thought of leaving, knowing I wouldn't be looking for Malden to take home. I was constantly reminded of the young man in my mind, and was struggling with everything that's happened in the past week. I had left for the day, exited the side employee entrance while I stared down the access road, thinking, I hope you're all right, buddy, and really miss you.

Gretchen and I got past another dinner without Malden as little was said, and the conversation had been mundane at best. I finished the dishes, walked by her, kissed her forehead, and said, "I'll be in my study. I love you."

She smiled, and responded, "Ditto, Travis."

I was in my study, had a seat at my desk, and pulled out Malden's book, *LIKE A WITCH'S BREW*, from my briefcase. I noticed now I'd almost finished the book. I leaned back in my chair, and started to read. Several hours passed when I turned the last page, and finished reading the last paragraph, but was confused at how the book ended.

I looked more closely, saw a gap in the book's spine where pages should be, and said, "What the heck?" I put the book down on my desk, and leaned down to my briefcase to see if any of the pages had fallen out, but didn't find any. I picked up the book again to reexamine it, and confirmed the whole last chapter was missing. I repeated again, "What the heck?"

Well, it was late, I was tired, drained from the long day worrying about Malden, and decided I'd had enough of this. I got up, left my study, and turned the lights off to head upstairs to bed.

***

I was up and showered, ready to start another day when I remembered tomorrow was New Year's Day, and another holiday not spent with Malden. I shook that off, headed downstairs, and stopped in my study to get my briefcase before I head into the kitchen to have coffee with Gretchen. I walked past Malden's desk to get to my briefcase when I noticed what was on it, and said, "Crap."

I walked out of my study toward the kitchen, saw Gretchen smiling when I entered the room, heard her say, "Morning, Travis," as she cooked breakfast.

I looked at her, and responded, "Morning, Gretchen," but was a little confused over how happy she looked, which was fine, but concerning. I said now, "I couldn't help notice all the school assignments lined up on Malden's desk, honey when I got my briefcase."

She turned, smiled, and said, "That's correct."

I replied confused, "I'm sorry, Gretchen. I don't get it."

She was getting me a cup of coffee, walked over to me, handed me my cup, and said, "I'm done feeling sorry for myself, the crying, and carrying on how much I miss him." She continued, "So I decided a better way to deal with that is to think positive, be thankful for the times we had, and the times we will have when he returns."

I curiously asked, "So you're all right then?"

"Travis, I'm fine. I know in my heart he'll be back soon, and we'll be a family again." She continued to say, "If there's any truth to knowing how another person feels when you love someone, the last thing I want is for Malden to feel any pain, or suffering coming from me." She concluded, and said, "I'm sorry, but that's not going to happen, not now, or later."

I nodded in agreement, smiled at her while I held my cup, and said, "You're amazing, Gretchen."

I had left for work, was on the road to my office, thought of my wife at home, felt like half the weight of the world was off my shoulders that morning, and just smiled.

I was in my office thinking about Malden's book, why the last chapter was missing, and couldn't seem to find a logical reason for that. I wondered if anything, I should have found missing pages from all over the book based on the poor condition it was in. I realized something, and couldn't believe I didn't think of that.

I went into my briefcase, retrieved the book, and examined it some more. I searched the front, back, inside and back pages, but couldn't find what I was looking for. I paused for a moment, and decided, let's approach this in a different way. I turned my computer monitor on to launch an Internet browser to do a search, but my computer wouldn't respond. I looked at the monitor, and hit the side of it, pissed off. "Come on, you blasted piece of crap!" I was exasperated with that, got up to walk out of my office, and down the hall to see Bishop.

I knocked on his door when he looked up, and greeted me, "What's up, Boss?"

"Can you do me a favor, Bishop, and fix my damn computer before I turn it into an anchor for my boat, please."

He got up, smiled, and answered, "Sure, Boss, be happy to." He and I headed back to my office. I sat in the chair in front of my desk while he worked on my PC. I looked around, saw a different perspective from that vantage point, and said, "So this is what my office looks like sitting here."

He looked up from working on my PC, and said, "Did you say something, Boss?"

"It's nothing, Bishop. So what's the verdict? Is she a goner, or what?"

He chuckled a bit, and concluded, "No, Boss, you just have some corrupt sectors on your hard drive that need to be fixed." He continued, and said, "The utility I'm running should fix the problem."

I stared at him while he spoke, and replied, "I didn't understand a word of what you just said, Bishop."

He smiled while he looked at the book on my desk, and said, "This looks like Malden's," but hesitated when he looked at me.

"It's all right, Bishop, and yes, it's the book Malden used to read."

He apologized, "I'm sorry, Boss."

"Again, it's all right. I was going to do a search to see if I could find where that book came from, or who wrote it." He pointed to the book while he looked at me for permission to examine it. I nodded. "Have at it, Bishop."

He examined it, but couldn't find any copyright information, or any publishing marks. He stated, "That's weird, Boss," and read the title, *LIKE A WITCH'S BREW,* and said, "You'll have a tough time finding anything out about this book, Boss."

"I know. I looked for the same things you just did, Bishop." He looked at the disk utility he just ran on my PC, and checked the browser that was working now.

"It looks like you're all set, Boss. Can I do a quick search for you?"

"Sure, be my guest." He searched for the title of the book, but only similar titles came up with a variation of the Witch's Brew name.

He confirmed, "Yeah, Boss, this will be tough. Nothing comes up for the exact title, and without an author, or who printed the book, it'll be near impossible to find out anything about it."

I asked now, "Any suggestions?"

"Well, Boss, I'm a fan of this witch stuff, or I should say I used to be. The book has a witch connotation that would suggest, or at least could narrow down your search if you looked in the right place."

I enquired, "And where would that place be?"

He replied, "Salem, Massachusetts, the witch capital of America, Boss." He explained, "I used to take several trips there when I was younger when I was into that sort of thing. It's a pretty interesting city, Boss. It's quite the place to be if you're into witches, ghosts, and goblins."

"I hear what you're saying, but how is all that going to help me find out where that book came from?"

"Well, Boss, they have a lot of bookstores that cater to this stuff, like Malden's book here. I would have to say, if you're looking for someone who could tell you anything about his book, you'll find it in Salem."

I sat there analyzing everything he said, got up, and thanked him for all his help.

He left my office now while I sat back down staring at Malden's book on my desk, and decided, I'm taking a trip to Salem. I got up to leave my office, and walked down to Mary's to explain what I was about to do.

She was a little concerned about my decision to travel to Salem. She thought that was a byproduct of missing Malden so much that I'd do anything to find him, even go off on a wild goose chase to find where his book came from. Well, she was right about both. I made up my mind that evening at the store when Malden went missing, that I'd do anything to get him back. She wished me luck just the same, and said to take as many days as I needed.

I arrived home later that evening, explained to Gretchen what I wanted to do, and was so happy she was on board with all of it. Maybe it was the desperation in my voice, or my face that projected the need to find him, no matter how far-fetched the idea may be. It was just, I guess, something inside of me that wouldn't leave any stone unturned in the search for him. I wouldn't rest until this young man was home safe and sound where he belongs with his family.

The following morning I was going over the itinerary I put together, and had mapped out a bunch of bookstores in Salem, Massachusetts while Gretchen helped me pack some clothes for my trip. Just before leaving, Gretchen and I hugged one another that seemed to last forever. She was still in that positive mood when I mentioned, "Add New Year's to the list of missed holidays we'll celebrate when we find Malden." I remembered the great smile from her after I said that, and decided I'd bring that with me on my trip.

I was on my way to the airport after I booked a one-way ticket to Boston, and made a reservation at the Hawthorne Hotel in Salem. I got to the airport, boarded my flight, and was already missing my wife. I spent most of the three and a half hour flight reviewing the maps of Salem I printed out to help minimize the downtime of getting lost, but my mind confirmed to me, you'll get lost.

My plane finally landed in Boston. I walked out of the terminal to get my bag, and car rental. I could feel the chilly air all around me outside, but was thankful there wasn't a lot of snow one would expect this time of year in the northeast.

I was amazed at how I drove from Logan Airport to Salem without getting lost, significantly at least, and found my hotel. I parked the rental, grabbed my briefcase, and my suitcase to get checked in. I decided while I walked from the back parking lot of the Hawthorne Hotel, that this was a nice quaint place I picked out while I entered the main doors, and proceeded to the check-in counter.

My thoughts were confirmed when I looked around the hotel foyer, and could even see a concierge desk. I confirmed my reservation, got my room key, and walked away to make my way up to my room. I walked past the lounge entrance next to a set of elevators, peeked into the bar, looked around, and said, "This is nice." If I were a drinker, that is. I eventually settled into my room after a quick call to Gretchen to let her know I arrived safely. I looked at my watch and said, "Let's get this show on the road, Travis."

I was out and about driving through Salem, and recalled, Bishop was right about this city. I drove by some interesting places like the Salem Witch Museum, House of the Seven Gables, Witch House circa 1642, and all the specialty stores around me with witch motifs, to mention just a few. I thought to myself, this is a place Malden would not like one bit.

I stopped at the first bookstore on my list, and parked my rental to head on in. I'm amazed at all the effort put forth in the places I've seen so far that glorify all that has to do with spooky things. If you like Halloween, and all that's associated with that holiday, this is the place to be.

I walked over to the main counter to speak to the young man standing there, and introduced myself while I took Malden's book out of my briefcase. I explained I'm looking to find out if you know anything about this book, or who may have authored it, and perhaps where I could find another copy with the last chapter intact.

The young man took the book, inspected it, and responded, "Wow, this is an old book." The young man flipped through some pages, most likely looking for some identification of the maker, or author, I concluded.

I asked, "So what do you think?"

The clerk responded, "Well, Mr. Scott, this book is amazing," while he continued to inspect it. The young man added, "I've seen some old books in my day, but this one blows me away."

I curiously asked, "What do you mean?"

"Well, look at these drawings in the book," as he showed me one of them, and said, "These are woodcuts, very rare to see. Also, look at the spine of this book" while he showed me, and further explained, "These small holes along the pages in the book are missing the cord that would have held this book altogether." I concluded that explains why the damn pages want to fall out all the time. The young man continued, "I'm not surprised that the cord is missing based on how old it looks, and the condition it's in."

I enquired, "So is there any way to tell who might have written it, or who published it?"

"Yeah, I don't know," replied the young man when he said, "I'm not sure, but it's possible, I guess. I just have no idea, or what else to tell you, Mr. Scott."

I responded, "Well, thank you just the same." I retrieved the book being handed back to me, and hoped that this didn't become a common theme. I left the store in search of the next bookstore on my list.

The day progressed with the same results after I finished my tenth visit to a bookstore in Salem. I crossed it off my list, looked out my car rental, and saw how late it was getting. I looked at my watch, saw it was almost five p.m. and said, "Well, only two bookstores left," and realized, that wasn't good.

I had been challenged all day driving around Salem, and had to stop often to ask for directions. At one point I passed by my hotel twice looking for one of the bookstores on my list. I thought, add Salem, Massachusetts to the list of places next to the woods, you'll want a compass handy if you're with me.

I drove to the next bookstore on my list when I came across an area of town covered up and down the streets with bricks you'd normally see a business built out of. I decided what the heck, and navigated the narrow streets in this common-like area. I came to a stop sign, looked to my right down a small alley, and saw a place called Witch City Book Store. I looked at my list, but didn't have that one written down. I thought what the hell, turned hard right to proceed down the alley, and parked my car out front.

I walked into the bookstore, and reasoned they should have more lights on since it was dimly lit. I could barely see an older gentleman in the back of the store behind a counter staring at me. I walked farther into the store, and could smell the books all around me that looked really old. I concluded, maybe in this place, I'll have better luck finding out something about Malden's book.

As I approached the counter, I saw the older gentleman still staring at me when I greeted him. "How are you?" I reached into my briefcase, took out the book, *LIKE A WITCH'S BREW*, placed it on the counter, and left my briefcase on the floor beside me. I turned my attention to the book, and asked the older gentleman, "Could you look at this, and maybe tell me where it came from, or something about the author? I'd like to know if there are any reprints, so I can read the last chapter that's missing in this copy."

I was holding the book open to show the older man the section in the back that's missing when he responded, "There is just the one."

I looked up to the older gentleman, and questioned, "How do you know that?"

The man continued to stare at me, and then spoke, "Because I wrote it, Mr. Scott," he paused, and said, "Over 300 years ago."

I stared back at him, laughed, and responded, "Yeah, right." I continued to look at the older man across the counter showing no emotion, and blurted out, "Wait a second, how do you know my name?" I paused, waiting for a response from him, and added, "Who are you?"

The older gentleman replied, "My name is Samuel Stoltzfus, and I know everything about you, Mr. Scott."

I continued to stare back at Samuel with a mystified look when I said, "Well, Samuel," I tried to pronounce his last name, but couldn't, "Whatever your last name is. You look pretty good for someone whose 300 years old." I continued to chuckle, but still, no reaction from Samuel after I said that.

He spoke after a moment, while I continued to smile, "Why do find that so difficult to believe, Mr. Scott?"

I responded confidently, "Because it's crap, Samuel, and not possible," while I chucked some more.

Samuel, staring at me intently, now stated, "I don't understand. You once said it yourself."

"Said what, Samuel?"

He responded, "Nothing is impossible."

I thought about that, for a moment, and remembered the last time I said that was in

Mary's office the day Malden got hurt. I wondered still, who is this nutjob in front of me?

I looked up from my thought process when he said, "I know you're searching for the child, Mr. Scott."

I stopped smiling after I heard that, and got mad. I leaned over the counter, grabbed him by the suspenders with a fist full of shirt, looked straight at him, and said angrily, "How the hell do you know what I'm looking for, Samuel?" He looked down at my hands holding him, slowly looked back at me as I released my grip. I leaned back, still angry and confused who this person was in front of me.

He continued to stare at me with no emotion while I looked down onto the counter staring at Malden's book. I looked back at him, and said, "This is just a book, a fairy tale, it means nothing." He continued to stare without a response while I looked away for a moment, shook my head, and continued, "Nope, no way, Samuel, I won't let you draw me into this bullshit." I picked up Malden's book from the counter, grabbed my briefcase, turned to walk away, and stopped halfway out the bookstore.

I turned around with anger in my voice, pointed at him, and shouted, "You're a freakin' weirdo, Samuel." I paused a moment, and said, "I will find out how you know me." I continued to watch him stare with no response when I turned, walked out of the store hastily, and was so pissed off over the whole whacked out situation I had encountered.

I made my way back to my rental still angry, threw my briefcase into the car, got in, and slammed my hands onto the steering wheel. I looked at my watch, saw how late it was, shook my head, and started the engine to make my way back to the hotel.

I arrived at the Hawthorn Hotel, and parked the rental. I couldn't stop thinking about this whacked out person I just met. I couldn't figure out how he knew my name, and even more concerning, how he knew I was looking for Malden.

I got my briefcase, started to walk over to the main entrance of the hotel feeling broken, and beat down over a long day. I felt like such a disappointment to my family, and especially toward Malden. I stood in front of the elevator waiting while I stared at the lounge entrance, and said aloud, "What the hell," walked in, and had a seat at the bar.

I looked around, saw I was the only person there when the bartender came over, and asked, "What can I get for you, sir?"

I responded, "Well, I'm not much of a drinker, but based on my day, I'll take whatever you have that's strong."

The bartender chuckled, and responded, "That covers a lot of territory, sir."

I looked at him, and said, "Well, I suppose you're right. Preferably something from the whiskey family would do, I guess."

He enquired, "And how would you like that, sir?"

"In a glass preferably," I insisted.

He smiled at the response, and said, "Yes, sir, coming up," and walked away.

I sat there alone for several hours thinking about the last few weeks, and missed Malden even more after each drink I consumed. I recalled my beverage of choice was whiskey neat in a glass.

At one point the bartender asked, as close as I can remember now if I was staying at the hotel. I guessed that was my queue, I'd had enough, and responded, "Yes, I am." I paid the nice young man, and thanked him for his service. I hoped I had tipped him enough before I got up from my bar stool to make it back to the main lobby, and take the elevator to my floor.

I made it to my room while I was pretty not okay at that point, and tried to figure out what it was about drinking alcohol, outside of the spinning room effect, that people enjoyed so much. I kept chuckling over meeting Samuel, the things he said while I dialed my home number, and Gretchen answered. I blurted out, "Hi, honey. How are you doing tonight?"

Gretchen, after listening to me on the phone said, "Oh, Travis, have you been drinking?"

"A little bit, honey."

With concern now, she asked, "Travis, you didn't drive, did you?"

"No, no, honey, I was drinking downstairs in the lobby since I couldn't find Malden anywhere today."

She whispered, "Oh boy." She could only remember seeing me drunk maybe two times in the last twenty years, and knew how much I hated to drink.

I chuckled, and said, "Guess what, Gretchen? I met a person today who knew I was looking for Malden, and you know what? He said he was over 300 years old. Isn't that great?"

"Travis, you need to get to bed, call me in the morning, and sleep this off. Can you do that for me?"

"I would do anything for you, honey." I paused a moment, and said, "I wish I could bring Malden home to you right now."

"I know, Travis, but what I want is, for you to go to bed now."

I sat on the side of the bed, and whispered, "I'm just tired, Gretchen, so damn tired."

She listened to that, and surmised, no honey, you're just drunk, then restated, "So, Travis, I want you to go to sleep now, and call me in the morning?"

"All right, Gretchen, and honey, I love you very much."

"I love you, too, Travis, so hang up, and get some sleep?"

I responded the best I could remember, "Okay, honey," and hung up the phone. I was still fully dressed as I lied back on the bed staring at the ceiling, and thought about Samuel while my eyes shut slowly, still whispering, "So tired."

The following morning arrived when I woke up abruptly, looked down at myself all dressed, and could see I didn't even bother to take my coat off last night. I looked over at the clock, saw 9:15, and said, "Crap." I moved my legs off the bed, and sat upright on the mattress, holding my head, thinking, My Lord, how do people deal with this?

I worked my way through my hangover, and kept telling myself, "It'll be a cold day in hell before I have another sip of alcohol." I got ready, had finished my shower, and the call I made to Gretchen to apologize for my drunken behavior last night, succumbing to the point I was at. She gave me a pass on that, and knew this morning's pain and suffering was punishment enough for me.

I sat on the bed trying to figure out what I was going to do, and realized there were only two bookstores left on my list. I'd gotten squat from all the rest. Just the same, I couldn't get that Samuel person out of my head. I thought about that some more, but needed to get some food into me, and remembered the last time I ate was on the plane yesterday morning.

I got up, headed downstairs to the restaurant in the hotel to get brunch, and more important, several cups of coffee. I had a great meal, was feeling much better now as I left the hotel. I decided I needed to speak to that Samuel guy to find out how he knew me, and more importantly how he knows I'm looking for Malden.

    I drove through the center of town, and found my way back to that common area with the brick street pavers when I saw the entrance to the narrow street. I turned down the alley, parked out front, and entered the bookstore. I saw Samuel at the far end of the store behind the counter staring at me.

    I made my way down to him, but before I could say anything, he announced, "I've been expecting you, Mr. Scott." I looked at him, and nodded when he said, "Come with me, please." He walked into a back room behind the counter while I made my way around, and followed him into the room.

    He sat at the head of an old antique table with six chairs around it, but all of them were turned inward except for the one he sat at. I walked past him, and made my way to the other end of the table when he offered, "Have a seat, Mr. Scott."

    I replied, "No, I'm all set, Samuel."

    He stared back at me now with both arms by his side, and responded, "Then ask your questions."

    I was inspecting the room I was in, looked all around, glanced back at him when he said that, and repeated, "Questions? I have no questions, Samuel. I don't know what the hell is going on here."

"You read the book, Mr. Scott?"

"Yeah, I read the book."

He responded, "Then you know."

I was quite agitated now, shook my head, and immediately responded, "Know what, Samuel?" I paused a moment, and said, "What is it? You still expect me to believe you're 300 years old, and I suppose you want me to believe Malden is 300 years old, too, huh?" He continued to stare at me while I spoke, but didn't respond.

I paced back and forth while I continued to inspect my surroundings, and thought for a moment how I could turn the table on this with Samuel to get to the truth. I turned to stare at him, just sitting there. "All right, Samuel, I'll buy what you're selling right now." I asked, "So you wrote the book?"

He looked at me, and said, "That question has been answered."

I paced again while I spoke aloud, "You wrote the book," then turned sharply to Samuel with conviction, and shouted, "Then *you* know how it ends, Samuel, and can tell me right now where Malden is, damn it!"

Samuel, with anger in his voice, leaned forward in his seat, and shouted back, "It doesn't work that way, Mr. Scott!" I stared back at him with that look of anger on his face while he leaned back in his seat, and stated, "The final chapter isn't written. The child determines that." He paused a moment, and said, "It's being written as we speak." He continued, "You should know that, Mr. Scott."

I looked back at him, and said, "No, Samuel, I don't."

He spoke now, and pointed out, "Of all the people, Travis, in all the times this world has existed, past or present, you haven't wondered why you were the one Malden picked, the one person out of them all?" I had asked myself that question many times while I thought about what he just said. He continued to look at me, and said, "You read the book, then you should know you're the last."

I looked back over at him after hearing that, and asked, "The last what?"

He paused, stared at me, and responded, "The last of the Alliance, Mr. Scott."

After I heard those words, I responded with conviction, "No way, Samuel. No, freakin' way. I'm not one of those sick bastards in Malden's book."

He responded angrily, "Don't think so much, Travis! Look into your heart and soul, only then will you understand this."

I did a double take while I continued to pace, looked back at him, and said, "You know Samuel, you have a mean streak in you. You should get that checked."

He continued, "I can help you, Mr. Scott, but you must understand the child knows who you are, and if you read the book, you know the Alliance is strong, made up of men determined, willing to sacrifice their lives, who will stop at nothing to destroy the child. Each one more deceitful, more vicious and cunning than the one before. Malden knows this all too well, and is the reason, Travis, why he fears you."

"I will help you, but we must get to him soon, and try to convince him you're not the person he thinks you are." He paused, and confirmed, "The Alliance is dead. Something has happened to change what was supposed to be. I believe in my heart you wouldn't bring harm to this child, but you must find him soon."

"Why, Samuel?"

"Truth be told, Mr. Scott, for if the child returns where it once he came, everything you know, and have loved in your life, everything in your past, your family, your career, Travis, everything...," He paused, and said, "Will cease to exist." My face turned to a blank stare while I listened, and looked at him. He continued to speak, "You'll be a prisoner in your own world, with no past, and no future, to grow old, and die alone without a life to be remembered by."

"Unlike you, Mr. Scott, my destiny has been fulfilled. I can't go back, and am stuck here in your time, a prisoner of your world. Your destiny, Travis, is yet to be determined. Find the child! Look into your heart and soul, and you'll know where to find him. I'll do what I can for you, but you must act quickly." I finished listening to Samuel, had stopped pacing, and was troubled by all of what was said, but knew in my heart I needed to focus on finding Malden now.

CHAPTER 16

That afternoon I was determined to resolve what Samuel spoke of that would tell me how, and where to find Malden. I spent most of the afternoon driving around Salem studying what I saw, trying to imagine the place, or some clue that would tell me where he was. I was conflicted all day worrying about where he could be, and if he was okay.

With most of the day all but gone, I realized the futility of what I had set out to do. I headed back to my hotel feeling beaten down and broken, for not stepping up to the plate, without a clue, or being any closer to knowing Malden's whereabouts.

I settled back into my room at the Hawthorne Hotel, and sat on the edge of the bed to reflect on all that's happened in the last few days. I tried to figure out what Samuel knew that I couldn't understand about where Malden would be. Samuel seemed confident I knew where to find him, for some unknown reason. I said to myself, what the heck. I mean, I'm a thousand miles from home, and know nothing about where I'm at. How am I supposed to find Malden here when I can barely find my way back to my hotel?

I was drained, tried to think harder and logically as best I could. Okay, Travis, if you were here, or lived here once, where would you likely be at? I surmised everything to that point had to do with the book Malden gave me, and reasoned, all right, maybe there's a place in the book he might go to.

I took the book out of my briefcase, and thumbed through the pages of the earlier chapters to see if I could find what I was looking for. I remembered reading of a place his father used to take him and his mother too, by the shoreline to watch the British clipper ships pass by the harbor.

I found the spot in the book, and remembered it had a picture of the place I read about. I stared at the black and white picture that illustrated a house with the backdrop of a rocky point with a lighthouse in the harbor. I theorized this might be the place Malden could be at, but questioned, where the hell is it? I imagined hard, trying to figure out who could look at this picture, and tell me where it was.

I grabbed the telephone book from the nightstand, and looked to see if it had a listing for a historical society somewhere around here. They would know if I show them the picture, right? "Bingo," I said as I found one right here in Salem. I wrote down the address, left my hotel room to head over to the Salem Historical Society, and see if anyone there could help me.

I pulled up to the address on North Street in Salem, and parked while it looked like they may still be open. I was relieved, and said aloud, "Awesome, I can hopefully get some information about this today." I made my way up the stairs, and rang the doorbell. I confirmed while I looked around that I've never been anywhere quite like

Salem, where most businesses look like regular old houses. It's strange at best. A woman answered the door now, and asked, "Can I help you?"

"Yes, ma'am," I replied. "My name is Travis Scott. I was wondering if someone could look at a picture in a book I have, and see if they recognize where the place is. I believe it's a picture of someplace here in Salem, and thought who best to ask who could tell me where it's located."

The woman stared at me, and responded, "Please come in, and I'll see if I can help you." The woman said, "My name is Beth," and pointed to a large conference room table in the middle of the room. She announced, "We can sit over there, Mr. Scott."

I sat with her at the table, took the book out of my briefcase, explained to her I'm not from around here, and hoped she could tell me where the place is in the picture.

She looked at me, and announced, "I know you're not from around here, Mr. Scott." After I heard her say that, I leaned back in the chair, shook my head, and thought, aw, come on, not another one.

My patience was worn down at that point, and spouted out sternly, "You know I'm not from around here? Okay, fine, so what am I looking at here, Beth. I suppose you're going to tell me you're some 300-year-old broad from some never, never land?"

She looked at me with a shocked expression, stood, and said, "Excuse me, Mr. Scott?"

I continued my rant, and said, "All right, I'm too tired to play guessing games with you, Beth, so just tell me how you know I'm not from around here?"

Beth, still in shock, looked straight down at me, and answered, "Your accent, Mr. Scott." There was a long awkward pause while I realized my mistake, and what I just said to this poor woman.

I looked at her, and tried to apologize, "I'm so, so sorry, Beth." I could barely form sentences while I tried to mend the broken trust with this person whom I just insulted and worse yet, compared her to a 300-year-old woman, who was only trying to help me.

I again tried to apologize, "Oh, my God, I'm truly sorry. I don't expect you to understand any of this, Beth, but in my defense, the last few days here in Salem have been extremely stressful." I stood, all the while looking at her while she was still in that reactionary taken aback moment. I once again said, "I'm sorry, and will understand if you don't want to help me."

She looked at me not as upset anymore, sat back down, and stated, "Geez, I'm only fifty-two, Mr. Scott."

I sat, looked at her, and said, "Thank you, Beth."

She composed herself, and enquired, "All right, let's have a look at what you have then."

I turned to the page in Malden's book with the picture, and slid the book toward her, so she could see it. She looked at the picture, turned to me, and asked, "Where did you get this, Mr. Scott?"

She glanced back at the book, started to examine it while I tried to recapture her attention from the inspection, and answered, "It's just an old book handed down through the generations in my family, that's all. So do you recognize the place in the picture?"

She looked at me with some skepticism, for the explanation of where the book came from when she responded, "Well, Mr. Scott, the picture appears to illustrate two places in one."

"What do you mean by that? I don't understand."

"Well, the building in front is actually the House of the Seven Gables here in Salem, and the lighthouse on the rocky point in the background is a place called Castle Commons." She continued with a perplexed look on her face, and added, "I've never seen an illustrated picture of the two together."

"I'm still confused about what you're saying, Beth."

She explained, "The House of the Seven Gables was built back in the 1600's in a place called Salem's Village, but was relocated here in Salem sometime around the beginning of the eighteenth century."

I asked, "So the Castle Commons you referred to is here in Salem also?"

"Not quite," She explained further, "Salem's Village, most notably around the late 1600's, was a place famous for the witch trials that took place here in Massachusetts. Everyone has the misconception, Mr. Scott, these trials took place here in Salem, which they did not. Salem's Village at that time was actually part of another town next to Salem called Danvers now. It's odd, you have this book with a picture that shows the House of the Seven Gables in the original spot it was built."

I looked at Beth, redirected her attention, and said, "Yeah, I suppose, but can you tell me how to get to Castle Commons in Danvers?"

She looked at me like she could see the desperation on my face that concerned her while she responded to my question. "I can, Mr. Scott, but realize this. Things in life can appear unexplainable, but in reality, of the quest in pursuing the answers we search for, we sometimes find the hard truth within that reality. It's not logical." She paused, and said, "But it's often true. Take heed in your quest." She slid the book on the table back to me while she said that. She got up now, saying, "I'll draw you a map to Castle Commons," and walked away from the table.

I grabbed the book, and put it back into my briefcase. I got up to follow her, and thought about what she'd said. I wasn't all that concerned for two reasons while I mulled everything over in my mind. I knew first off, I didn't understand what the heck she just said, and second, I confirmed,

R.P. Christman

there's nothing in this world that would stop me from finding Malden, period. Beth finished the rough sketch showing the location of Castle Commons in Danvers, handed it to me, and said, "Good luck to you, Mr. Scott."

I looked at her, and responded, "Thank you. I really have to go now," as I turned to walk out of the building.

I was in my car, backed out of the parking space, and headed back to the heart of Salem to see Samuel, hoping Castle Commons was where we needed to be to find Malden. I eventually found my way back to the center of town, came across the alley I remembered, pulled down to the front of the bookstore, and parked the car.

I grabbed the piece of paper Beth gave me while I exited my vehicle, and walked toward the bookstore entrance praying, please God, this has to be where Malden is. I opened the door, walked in, noticed a young lady at the counter at the back of the store, and approached her. I stated, "I'm here to see, Samuel."

The young woman looked at me, and asked, "I'm sorry, sir, who are you looking for?"

I anxiously replied, "The older gentleman who was here earlier, Samuel."

The young woman, with confusion, looked at me, and answered, "I'm sorry, sir, no one by that name works here."

With a concerned look, I responded, "What are you talking about? I was here two days in a row, and met with him." I added, "You must be new here."

The young woman replied, shaking her head, "No, sir, I've been working here over a year, and trust me there's no one here by that name."

I raised my arm, pointed past the young woman as I startled her with that, and sternly announced, "Look, I was in that back room just this morning speaking with Samuel. I was here, for an hour talking with him."

The young woman stared at me standing a few feet farther from me, and said nothing. I looked down for a moment confused, and questioned why this was happening? I'm so close to finding Malden. I composed myself, looked at the young woman standing there frightened, and apologized, "I'm sorry I bothered you," and turned to walk out of the bookstore.

I stood by my car thinking about that, and looked all around me to verify what my mind had told me, that I'm in the right place. I thought for another moment, decided what the heck, and said aloud, "I'm doing this with, or without Samuel's help."

I got into my car with determination to get to Castle Commons as quickly as I could. I drove trying to figure out exactly what to say to Malden when I find him that would convince him who I am, is who he had always known me to be. I exited Salem driving over a bridge that connects Salem with Danvers from the sketch I looked at while I drove.

My mind wandered, wondering what this place might have looked like back in the 1600's, and saw only dirt roads void of businesses all around. I focused on my destination, and felt like this had to be where Malden was. I had mixed feelings about the reaction I may get from him seeing me while I went over everything Samuel had told me.

I turned onto the last road from the sketch Beth drew out while I drove along the coastline, and saw my destination ahead. I looked at a small sign with the name Castle Commons, and parked alongside the roadway.

I turned off my car, got out, and scanned the area. It appeared to be a public area with a bunch of park benches outside of where I parked. I guessed it was most likely, for tourists to come to, and take in the beautiful view of the ocean beyond a grassy knoll about the size of a football field.

I walked past some benches in front of me, walked out to the end of the knoll, and saw the image of the lighthouse beyond the rocky point pictured in Malden's book. I scanned the area, but saw nothing else. I heard the waves breaking on the rocky shoreline as the tide pulled them in.

I looked up to see it wouldn't be long before the sun sets, and saw blue sky with a slightly chilly wind coming off the open coastline. I closed my eyes, breathed in the ocean air, and could taste the salt from the ocean, and said, "Please, Lord, let Malden be here. Please."

I stood there, hands on my hips, lowered my head back down when I saw something in the corner of my eye. I turned to look, and saw Malden standing a short distance from me, staring back. My world stopped, for a moment as I looked at him with relief, while all the love I had for the young man traveled in waves throughout my body. I shed a tear while I continued to stare, and shouted, "Malden!"

I rushed to him, knelt to hug him, and whispered, "I missed you so much, Malden." To my surprise, he reciprocated, and hugged me back. We exchanged hugs that seemed to last forever while I had a hard time containing my joy.

I unembraced him, held his shoulders, looked into his eyes, and rambled on. "Malden, I would never, ever hurt you. I'm not the person you think I am. All I ever wanted was to protect, and make you feel safe. I promise you, Malden, as long as I live I'll love and protect you like you were my own son. You have to believe me, Malden. I don't care what the book says, or if I'm from some past world long ago. I know in my heart I could never bring harm to you. Do you understand me, Malden? Can you trust what I'm saying, and believe what I'm telling you? Please, Malden, you have to tell me you're all right with this." He looked at me with an expression of joy that confirmed no words need to be spoken.

After a moment, he spoke, and said, "He lied to you, sir."

"What do you mean, Malden? Who lied to me?"

I had an uneasy feeling about where this was going when he responded, "Samuel."

I paused for a moment while I thought about that, and stood before I said, "Son of a bitch." I kept repeating, "Crap, crap, crap," when I realized what had happened. I leaned down to him, and proclaimed, "Samuel is the last of the Alliance, isn't he, Malden? I'm not that person he told me I was."

I stood, covered my forehead with my hand, and announced, "Oh my God, Malden. We need to get you out of here. I can't believe he tricked me like that, and I led him straight to you." He looked up to me while I tried to figure out what to do to correct this, and make sure he was out of harm's way.

I looked down at him while he stared back at me, and said, "It's all right, Mr. Scott, this needs to be over." I continued to look at him when he said that, and could see in his eyes something I'd not seen before. I saw no more despair, or unhappiness, just the shiny glimmer you'd expect to see in a young boy's eyes.

I was downright pissed off at that point, and shouted, "I won't let you die, Malden!" I knelt back down, and said, "Look, son, you need to go back through that portal of time thing, or whatever it is, so we can trap Samuel here, so he can't hurt you. Can you do that, Malden?"

He looked at me, and simply said, "I can't do that, sir."

I shook my head, and announced, "Why, Malden? Why can't you do that?"

He explained, "Not everything Samuel told you was a lie." He paused briefly, and said, "If I go back, then yes, Samuel will be trapped here forever." He continued to say, "But so will you, Mr. Scott, and everything you know, or have known will be lost forever." He paused again, and said, "I can't do that, sir."

I thought for a moment, saw no way out of this, was pissed off now at myself, and especially at Samuel. "All right, Malden," I declared, "Screw this! I'm tired of all this crap anyway. Samuel wants a fight, or try and hurt you, then so be it. He'll have to go through me first." My voice was stern, and the anger in my tone was unlike any time in my life. I no sooner stopped my rant when I noticed Malden staring at something behind me.

I stood, turned sharply, and saw Samuel standing about twenty feet from us, his back to the distant lighthouse against the point of the Commons. I looked up as the sky turned gray, and storm clouds appeared out of nowhere. I moved Malden with one arm behind me while I stared at him just standing there as if he were studying us. Finally, he spoke, "You played a good game kid." He paused slightly, looked at me then announced, "Some things don't change, even after 300 years, Mr. Scott."

I responded, "Yeah, what things, Samuel?" in a pissed off tone.

He replied, "Gullible people."

I responded angrily, "Screw you, Samuel!"

He looked at me, and declared, "It's over, Mr. Scott. The circle is complete, and justice for the Alliance is all but done now, thanks to you."

I responded, "I don't think so, Samuel."

He replied angrily, "It doesn't matter what you think!" He continued, "You see, Travis, you were the one person who got Malden to do what hundreds of years, and the whole of the Alliance couldn't."

I answered back, "Yeah, what's that, Samuel?"

He paused, and said, "You got him to love you, Travis. So much love, he's willing to die now to save you and your family." He paused again for a moment, and said with an angry tone, "For that reason alone, and not because of what you think! I owe you this moment in time to say goodbye to the child."

I stared at him for a second, turned to my side, and looked down on Malden, still staring at Samuel. I called out his name in a soft voice while he looked up at me. I stared deep into the young man's eyes with the love only a father could have, for his child, and said, "I love you, Malden," paused, and said with conviction, "Don't you *ever,* forget that, son!"

I turned back to Samuel with rage in my eyes, hands clenched into fists, and shouted, "To hell with you, Samuel! You'll get to Malden over my dead body!"

I listened to him respond, "That's a shame, Mr. Scott," and briefly paused again, and said with anger in his voice, "Then so be it!"

I quickly turned to Malden, and shouted, "RUN!" I watched him run away, quickly turned back to Samuel, but he had already rushed me, and hit me with a force, so great, it knocked me back onto the ground six feet away. I was barely breathing and twisting on the ground trying to catch my breath from the impact.

I looked over, saw Samuel slowly walk toward me, and stop next to my body. I looked up, saw him reach into his pocket, and take out a dagger that looked like something from the medieval times. I was still reeling from the impact of whatever sent me flying through the air.

Samuel looked down at me now, and announced, "The final chapter is written, Mr. Scott. The witch's spawn will die now, like his mother."

I looked at him angrily, and said, "I hope you rot in hell, you sick son of a bitch." He raised his arm with the dagger, and was about to bring it down to end my life when we heard Malden scream, "Noooooooooooo!" At that same moment, a thunderous voice appeared from nowhere that startled us as we were compelled to look toward the voice.

I turned my head to see my wife standing in the distance holding Malden tight next to her body, and a startling figure of a young woman floating above them with a pissed off look in her eyes. I guessed that must be Sally's spirit floating there high above my wife, and Malden.

The woman shouted out again, "It's not over, Samuel!" in a deafening voice. My eardrums were ready to burst as I listened to her voice. Samuel stood from leaning over me, still holding the dagger in his hand, and looked up at the image floating high above.

He spoke, "Sally Crenshaw." He paused, and shouted out defiantly, "The final chapter has been written, and your son dies. Nobody can stop this now, not even you, Sally."

The voice of Sally Crenshaw responded angrily, "You will not harm my son, Samuel." I looked at my wife standing there holding Malden close to her side when I saw Malden saying something, but couldn't quite hear the words he was saying.

I stared more intently, heard Malden repeat, "*LIKE A WITCH'S BREW*," over and over. For some unknown reason at that moment I moved my hand into my pant pocket, looked down, and pulled out a dagger. Samuel looked down at me, saw the dagger in my hand, looked at his own, and saw it gone now. He slowly stared back at me on the ground.

Time froze, for a moment, while I realized in my heart what I needed to do. I turned to see Malden standing next to Gretchen all innocent, and knew he brought none of this onto himself, but it confirmed what I needed to do with no thoughts of malice.

I looked back at him now, and simply said, "*LIKE A WITCH'S BREW*, Samuel," while I lunged the dagger toward him, and buried the blade deep into his stomach. He dropped back holding the dagger driven deep inside his body, and as quickly as that happened, the spirit of Sally Crenshaw engulfed the entire body of Samuel.

The screams were deafening coming from him while the inevitable was taking place. As quickly as it all started, it was over. I removed my hands from covering my ears, scanned the area where Samuel, and the spirit of Sally Crenshaw engaged, but saw nothing. I looked up to the sky, the storm clouds were gone now, and the sky was bright.

I thought about what just happened, and turned to see Malden and Gretchen approaching me. I looked to Malden, and asked, "Is it over, Malden? Can we go home now?"

He looked at me, and said, "Yes, Travis."

He reached out to help me get to my feet when I turned to Gretchen, and asked, "How did you know we would be here?"

She looked at Malden, smiled, and said, "You can thank Malden for that." She continued, "Malden gave me his book a while back, and asked me to read it."

I started to say, "The last chapter was missing," but didn't finish my sentence, and realized she had read the book before that was removed. I looked at her, and said, "So you knew this the whole time, didn't tell me, and let me go through this hell?"

She stared at me, smiled, and responded, "I told you, you owed me big time, Travis."

I looked at Malden, and said, "And you, Malden, you gave me the book without the last chapter. I could have been killed here today. Plus, had I known what would've happened, I could have protected myself when Samuel hit me. I mean, that shit hurt like hell, son." I looked down at him while he smiled, and said, "I can get used to that, Malden." Something dawned on me now as I spoke out, "Hey, Malden, I just realized something. You called me Travis, didn't you?"

He looked up to me, and said, "Yes, sir."

I shook my head, and chuckled while we all started to walk away from Castle Commons. I announced to Malden, "I hope you like opening your Christmas gifts in January. Gretchen refused to take the Christmas tree down until we had you back in the house." He looked up at me, smiled, and didn't say a word. I smiled back, and said, "Yup, I can get used to that, Malden."

The End

Made in the USA
Middletown, DE
24 February 2018